DEATH
IN A
GHOSTLY
HUE

DEATH IN A GHOSTLY HUE

AN ART CENTER MYSTERY

SUSAN VAN KIRK

LEVEL BEST BOOKS

Praise for Death in a Ghostly Hue

"Revenge, retribution, and redemption play out in Susan Van Kirk's *Death in a Ghostly Hue*—for both the living and the dead. An excellent addition to her Art Center Mystery series."—Grace Topping, an Agatha Award finalist and a *USA Today* bestselling author of the Laura Bishop home staging cozy mystery series

"*Death in a Ghostly Hue* is the story of long-buried secrets, guilt, and the power of forgiveness. With a charming small-town setting, a fast-paced plot, and quirky characters you'd love to know, this book is a fitting conclusion to the Art Center trilogy. Highly recommended."—Connie Berry, *USA Today* bestselling author of the Kate Hamilton Mysteries and Edgar Award nominee

"*Death in a Ghostly Hue* by Susan Van Kirk brings deeper shades of understanding to the concepts of revenge and forgiveness by beautifully blending characters, events, and subtle clues. Her deft pentimento effect makes this a book to read."—Debra H. Goldstein, author of the Sarah Blair Mysteries

"Van Kirk does it again, painting a vivid picture with exquisitely vibrant language suiting her character's artist's soul. Tightly written, *Death in a Ghostly Hue* blends a contemporary mystery with a touch of paranormal that kept me turning the pages well past bedtime."—Annette Dashofy, *USA Today* bestselling author of the Zoe Chambers mystery series

Chapter One

If I'd known my Monday morning was going to resemble *Alfred Hitchcock Presents*, I'd have stayed in bed with a pillow over my head. My mother used to tell me about reruns of that television show she'd watched when I was little. The first ten minutes were, "It's a normal day in the neighborhood," and then the terror slowly crept onto the screen. Mental hospitals, delusions, murder—each episode began with the portly Hitchcock joking about a sponsor of his show, and then the humor turned to madness. Mother told me revenge was a common theme. I sighed. In my own life, I preferred forgiveness. Well, perhaps not for one event in my life.

Gazing out the front window of the art center, I stared at the public square in my hometown of Apple Grove and thought about how recently the trees had been filled with color. Now, in the gloomy Midwest winter of late January, their stark limbs and thin, obsidian arms stood out against the gray sky, daring me to believe they'd be filled with green leaves once again. This morning, the sky was a mixture of lead white and Payne's grey. I could picture myself mixing the colors in my little studio behind our family house, my fingers itching to begin a new oil painting. But for now, I was the executive director of the Adele Marsden Center for the Arts, named after my sculptor mother.

I watched a man plod through a snowbank to get to the sidewalk. I had a feeling there was something familiar about him, but he was so bundled up against the cold I couldn't see his face. It was only when he came closer to the front door that I recognized him. Martin Stewart. He was a farmer who lived a few miles west of town.

I walked toward the door as the bell rang, announcing a visitor.

"Good morning, Mr. Stewart."

He took off his cap and made sure the door closed. "Hi, Ms. Madison."

His frameless glasses were steamed up, and he took them off briefly, rubbing them against his coat. Reddish-brown hair, close-cropped, appeared around the edge of his stocking cap. He had a burly figure, short but solid, and his face had the brown spots of someone who'd made his living in the sun.

"Oh, call me Jill, please."

He nodded, removing his gloves and hat. Then he reached out to shake my hand.

"You're out on a wintry, cold day, Martin. What brings you to town?"

"It occurred to me it had been a while since I'd come to the art center, and I thought I'd bring you some additional money for my son's memorial." He unzipped his coat partway and reached into his shirt pocket. Pulling out a piece of paper, he said, "Here. The farm had a good year. I'm adding to Matthew's fund and hope it brings more kids in for classes."

I took the folded check, glanced at the amount, and smiled. "We have plenty of kids in need of a little financial help to engage in art. Plus, we always have art supplies to buy for those classes. They'll be so thankful, as are we."

"I can picture Matthew watching over their shoulders, smiling because he loved painting. Doris and I are grateful we could make something good come out of such a horrible time in our lives. Thank you."

I added my own thanks and watched as tears welled up in his eyes. He put his hat back on, lowered his head, and added gruffly, "You're welcome. There will be more. Have a good day." Head still down, he pushed out the door before I could add another word.

I heard footsteps on the wooden floor and Louise Sandoval walked toward me from the office area. Louise was tall and willowy with olive skin and brown hair. I always felt like a midget next to her, even though I was five feet six. She was my manager at the art center, and together we ran classes, exhibits, a gift shop, events, and gallery openings.

"Who was that?" Louise asked.

"Martin Stewart. He brought a sizable check in for Matthew's memorial fund."

"Our classes will be bursting at the seams." She took the check and was about to turn around when she added, "His death was quite a while ago. How long was it?"

"Let me think. Seven years, I'd guess. I was working in Chicago, and Mom mentioned it to me in a phone call. He committed suicide. Now you mention it, I remember. Drugs. He left a note they never revealed to the public. So sad."

Louise pressed her lips together and pondered the memory. "He was just a high school kid. The artwork his dad brought in was exceptional. Too bad, too bad." Glancing again at the check, she added, "Wait a minute. He didn't sign it."

I sighed. "Not surprising. He was a bit emotional." I checked my watch. "I have time over my lunch hour, so I'll stop at his farm. He won't exactly be in the fields in January."

In the quiet, I heard my phone blaring with the ringtone "Welcome to the Jungle." Andy. My crazy brother. He was the total opposite of my law-and-order, rational brother, Detective Tom. Andy owned a gift shop in town with his partner, Lance Hughes, and they played in a popular rock band throughout the area. I walked quickly back to my office.

I grabbed the phone. "Hi, Andy."

"Morning, favorite sister of mine."

"*Only* sister of yours?"

"Well, there's that."

"So, what's up?"

"Checking on the wildlife. Any new animal emergencies today?"

He was referring to the stampede last week. North of our building is a pet shop with which we share a wall. Saturday, someone walked out of the pet shop, accidentally letting out three dogs—a chihuahua, a Yorkshire terrier, and a dachshund. The canines saw their chance for freedom and took off. At the same time, Paige Lemon, one of our teachers, was coming in the art center door. The three dogs exploded in the door with Paige, chasing each other throughout the gallery, tracking snow and mud everywhere. Paige managed to grab a tall, white pedestal that was teetering and save a sculpture of a Native American man. Finally, Louise, Paige, and I corralled the three dogs, who were excited by their newfound liberation, and returned them to the pet shop. It was a bit scary for a few moments. Artwork plus dogs running amuck. Not a good mix.

"No animals in the art center today, thankfully. I'm heading over to Priscilla's Pub tonight to see Angie and Sam." Angie was my best friend, while Sam was my boyfriend.

"I was planning to go there for a beer with Lance once we're both off work. Meet you there?"

"Sure."

The bell on the front door rang. Louise would get it.

"Around six?"

"I'll be there."

We both rang off, and I got back to my to-do list.

After finishing a grant request before noon, I told Louise I was going to stop out at Martin Stewart's farm. I grabbed the unsigned check and left.

The Stewarts lived three miles west of town on a large farm with a winding dirt drive to the house. At this time of year, the fields lay fallow, their lumps of ground covered in snow. Come spring, they'd be covered in verdigris green as corn or soybeans peeked up through the tilled ground. A huge barn was yards from the house. Painted Hematite red, a darker cousin to scarlet, it had a dark green roof and dominated the other farm structures. I counted three or four smaller buildings spread throughout the open area. It was a well-kept, tidy farm. The Stewart home was a typical farmhouse, two stories and a wraparound front porch with three dogs of undetermined breed. As I pulled in, the dogs barked in a cacophony of noise, running toward my car, and I saw Martin come out of the barn next to the house to see what the uproar was about. I opened my car door just as I heard the farmer yell something at the dogs. They trotted back to the porch silently and assumed their previous resting positions. Whew!

I walked toward the barn, following him in with the check and a pen. He was working on a tractor. The odor of hay and horses immediately hit my nostrils.

"Having motor problems?" I asked.

"It's only a problem with the starter. I'm used to fixing machinery around here. Something's always breaking down. Got the parts I needed when I was in town this morning. What brings you all the way out here to my farm?"

I pulled the check and the pen out of my pocket. "Well, I'd love to put this money in the account for Matthew's memorial, but you seem to have forgotten to sign it."

A sheepish grin crossed his face. "I'm sorry. Guess I've had a lot on my mind. I don't usually do such dumb things. Here, give it to me, and I'll take care of it. You shouldn't have had to come out here to deal with this. I'm sorry. My fault." He took the check and walked over to a wooden cabinet, signing his name quickly. Then he handed me the check and pen.

"It's absolutely no problem. Is that one of Matthew's paintings?" I pointed to a bright oil painting on the wall behind him. It was a depiction of the farm with bold strokes of color from the vantage of the dirt drive.

"Uh, yes. He loved this place. Several of his paintings are of our pastures or rows of crops." His eyes left mine and looked back at the painting. "It's hard for me to believe he's really gone when I stare at his work. It's as if he's here with me." He looked thoughtfully out the huge barn entrance.

"He had amazing talent."

Stewart bent his head down momentarily, and I wasn't sure if he was saying a prayer or collecting his emotions.

"It wasn't always that way, you know."

I was puzzled. "What do you mean?"

"Matthew began drawing and painting when he was in grade school. Guess I didn't appreciate his talent or his passion until it was too late. I figured he'd stay and run the farm once he'd grown up, or maybe leave and go work in some city job like banking or business. How could he ever make a decent living painting? But he only had one straight-line ambition. Sometimes, I feel guilty that I was hard on his choice. His high school art teachers told me he had an exceptional talent for painting. It was—it was—too little, too late."

I shook my head. "You aren't wrong about the art world. I spent six years in Chicago trying to make it on my own. The arts are a tough way to make a living. It's always been my experience that my parents, their thoughts, their values, and their genes are all a part of my artwork. Painting is my ardent ambition too. Believe me, you and your wife are right there on the canvas in every stroke of his brush. You may feel him still with you, and he is on that canvas."

He smiled. "Nice of you to say. Thanks. Makes me feel better."

An awkward moment followed. I said, "Well, I need to go back to work. Thanks again, Martin. This money will be used carefully, and we're so thankful you donated it."

After I grabbed lunch to take back to the office, I settled in and sent Louise on her way for her own lunch. I had finished my salad and was getting ready to start on a membership list when I heard the bell chime on the front door. I stood up and straightened my skirt, wiping away any crumbs from the crackers I'd devoured. I headed out to see who was there. A man in a dark parka and red stocking cap had walked into the building, a paper in his hand. His skin was very pale. As he took off his cap, I saw brown hair matted down across his head. A brownish moustache and chin stubble barely brushed his chalk-white skin. By the time I'd crossed the floor and was fifteen feet from him, my heart was pounding. My lips trembled, though I was holding my breath. Gripping the corner of the nearest sculpture pedestal, l took a backward step or two.

"Hi, Jill," the familiar voice said.

I lifted my eyes to meet his blue ones. I must have been dazed because I shuddered, but my heart continued to pound, my memory returning to seven years ago. It couldn't be, but it was. Quinn Parsons was the man who had murdered my parents.

It took a moment for me to catch my breath and reach some equilibrium. "What—are you doing here?"

"Here? In this building?" he said with a smirk on his face.

"No. Here in Apple Grove. You should be in prison."

"Been there, done that." He stuffed his hat in his jacket pocket, holding out a paper in his other hand. "I'm out. Done my time. I'm back here and speaking at the church." He pointed to the paper he'd handed me. "Wednesday night."

I scanned the circular. He was…speaking at a local church. Trying to hand it back, I said, "Why would you think I or anyone I know would be interested after what you did?"

His face dropped as he pushed the paper back toward me. "Cause I'm sorry. I wanted to say that to you, your brothers, the whole community." He searched my face. "I'm in AA now, and it's important to apologize. I was stupid. I lost seven years of my life for that—"

"What? What about my parents losing ALL their lives for that? Can you bring them back? Did you think saying 'I'm sorry' would bring them back? You took everything from us. No amount of sorry will make a difference. Leave. Get out of here, and don't come back."

"But I'm going to live here again. This is home," he said, his hands held toward me in supplication.

What? I thought. To see him here in Apple Grove wherever I went? Why did he think this would work? I took a deep breath and resolved to tell him exactly what I thought of his plan. "If that's the case, stay out of my way. No one in town is going to want anything to do with you. You've killed three people with your ignorance and bad decisions. This isn't your home anymore." I walked toward him as I yelled in his face.

Quinn Parsons' eyes opened into huge pools of anger, but he turned and left me standing there in the gallery. Just before he reached the door, he turned and shouted, "You'll see. I'm a changed man, and I have every right to live where I want."

I was shaking, quivering all over with anger and rage. How dare he come back here and try to act like nothing was wrong. How dare he think an "I'm sorry" could bring back the lives he'd taken with his carelessness. We'll see, I thought. No one will be happy with this. Walking back to my office, I crumpled up the paper he gave me and thew it on the floor.

Chapter Two

Somehow, I got through the remainder of the day, but I was thankful I would be seeing some family and friends tonight. Talking to them about my shock at Quinn Parsons' appearance would help. After work, I stopped at home and ate some takeout. I still lived in the house I grew up in. Andy and Lance had vacated it when they bought their own place. I can't begin to describe all the frat boy items I cleared out of this house, including a basketball hoop in the dining room. I won't speak of the disgusting refrigerator and baked-on food in the microwave. All looked much better now that I'd sterilized the entire place.

I loved this house. It was two stories with a full attic and basement. All three of us kids had fond memories of growing up here. We created a bowling alley in the upstairs hallway with orange juice cans for pins. I had my own room because I was the only girl. Andy and Tom shared a room, and I suspected Andy sneaked into mine and picked the lock on my teenage diary. At Christmastime, our dad hung lights everywhere. So many memories.

I changed into what I called "bar clothes"—black jeans, a black turtleneck T-shirt with a fuchsia sweater over it, and boots. I grabbed my purse, coat, and car keys and headed out to my little Austin Mini for the drive across town. I was looking forward to seeing my friends. I wanted to erase the memory of Quinn Parsons walking into my space. Once again, I realized how happy I was to be back in the family nest after six years in Chicago. My brother Tom had talked me into coming home to run the art center and carry on my mother's work.

Halfway to the bar, my phone pinged with a text. It was Sam, my handsome doctor-boyfriend. Probably something had come up. He often had work emergencies at the hospital that broke into our plans. I had learned to be patient. I hit the play button on the Austin's hands-free system.

"Sorry, Jill. Last-minute accident. I've gotta stay at the ER for a while and won't make it to Priscilla's. I'll call you later."

The voice from my screen asked if I wanted to reply. "Yes." When she told me to start, I said, "I'm sorry, Sam. I'll miss you. It's okay. Kisses to you. Call later." I was disappointed, but Sam's ER hours were unpredictable.

Angie Emerson and her husband, Wiley, owned Priscilla's Pub. They named it after their pet dog, an Akita. Priscilla's even had a little pink sleep bed with white-and-rose red shag faux fur near the bar for the dog.

A pink neon sign flashed "Open" as I walked past it through the doorway.

As usual, it was a blue-collar crowd, a mix of people in their thirties and forties. They were crowded around the bar or shuffling on the dance floor. A band I'd heard before was playing country, but they couldn't shine a candle to Andy and Lance's band. I counted the usual five beers on tap behind the bar. The walls held multiple flat-screen televisions tuned to sports and framed photos of local teams. I walked over to the bar, and Wiley Emerson sauntered toward me with my favorite beer. Everything behind the bar sparkled with cleanliness and care.

Wiley was tall and handsome with a bushy moustache like my mom's favorite movie cowboy, Sam Elliott. A light, citrus aftershave scent followed him. Angie had met him shortly after high school, and it was love at first sight. As her maid of honor, I was forced to wear an ugly, pink dress with netting and ruffles. Ah, yes. We were that young and foolish. An unforgettable memory and sacrifice I made for my bestie.

"Haven't seen you here for a few weeks," he said, leaning on the polished cherrywood bar.

"Busy, busy, busy." I saw Angie at the other end of the bar serving customers. She'd catch up with me when she could.

"More like hiding, hiding, hiding. I heard who's back in town."

I put my hands to my eyes and rubbed gently. "Well, yes. Then there's that."

"I doubt you're planning a big welcome home party," Wiley said, picking up a glass and moving it into a sink behind the bar. "What do you suppose his game is? Why would that nitwit come back here?"

I shook my head, pulling the wadded-up paper from my pocket. I'd retrieved the balled-up church event announcement from the floor of my office after having a fit. I passed it to Wiley, who flattened it out as I took several swallows of my beer.

"Oh, my. He's found religion. Babbling Brook Community Church? Where the heck is that?"

Setting my bottle down, I took the paper back. "I think it's the nondenominational church down near the junction. You know, lots of shouting and clapping."

"You gonna go to the celebration? Welcome him home?"

Balling the paper back up again, I stuffed it in my pocket. "Not planning to. My forgiveness is something he'll never have, not after what he did." My hands clenched and so did my jaw. Every muscle in my body felt rigid. I was angry he'd come back here to the scene of his crime. His irresponsible drunk driving had killed our parents in a horrible head-on collision. Why would I ever even speak to him? I scanned the room. "Have you seen Andy yet tonight?"

He pointed to a table on the other side of the dance area.

"I think I have to break the return of the felon to him. He has a temper, you know, and Mom and Dad's deaths hit him hard. Well, all of us hard."

"Maybe your brother Tom can talk some sense into him. Or Lance."

I raised an eyebrow. That would be a hell-freezing-over day. I put some cash on the highly polished bar. Wiley picked it up and stuffed it back in the top of my purse.

"Your money's no good here."

"Thank you, Wiley. You are a saint. Guess I'll go find out what's up."

I took a seat across from my brother Andy and his partner Lance, and I grabbed Andy's hand for a moment.

Andy, the middle child of us three, was thirty-seven with caramel skin and brown hair. He had a moustache and a trimmed beard that was also brown.

Andy was built more like Dad, sturdy but muscular, since he lifted weights. There was that mischievous gleam in his eyes.

"Thank God you're here," said Lance. "This band is really bad. The bass can't keep time, and the guitarist isn't always on the right chords. At least we can all suffer together. I should have brought some earplugs."

Lance, Andy's partner in business and life, was very pale with a handsome face featuring chiseled cheeks. His dark eyebrows and brown eyes contrasted with a light brown moustache. He and Andy were yin and yang. Lance was quiet and thoughtful, while my brother was physical and crazy.

I laughed. "Maybe it will make you guys sound all the better." I took a few swallows of beer. "And how did your day go, big brother?"

Andy was spinning an empty beer bottle on the table between his hands. "Fabulous. I managed to sell the ugly yellow vase Lance picked out on our last buying trip—"

"Hey, wait a minute. That vase was perfect. Mrs. Chandler scooped it up in record time. Besides, I'm the buyer, you're the bookkeeper. Remember how our business plan works?" He narrowed his eyes and grabbed Andy's empty bottle. "I'll get us some fresh ones, bro."

"If you're buying, make mine one of those expensive imports," my brother called to him.

As Lance left to go over to the bar, I studied Andy. "Everything all right?"

"Oh sure," he said, smiling. "I have to rib him occasionally because he does have an eye for merchandise, but I don't want to let it go to his head. By the way, I'm happy there were no animal stampedes at your place today. I hear you're thinking about doing a radio play with the old geezers."

I was always amazed at the way my brother could go from one topic to another, like business to dogs to radio plays, in three sentences. "Andy. 'Old geezers' is not the name of their group. It's OFTA, Old Friends Talk Art. In fact, we have a meeting about it tomorrow. They'll have a wonderful time. Just think—sound effects, ghosts, lots of parts to get the whole group involved. It's going to be fabulous."

"Ghosts? Like Casper? Sound effects? I'm really good at sound effects," Andy said.

"Well, the play is about a ghost. I figure we might do a ghostly art exhibit with ghosts and spirits to match the radio play. And Chad McKenna's in charge of the sound effects. Doesn't it sound like a topic that would bring people in?"

He nodded, watching Lance as he came toward us with two more beers. Angie was talking to him as they approached our table. Good. Angie was our social butterfly. Her blond ponytail swayed from side to side when she walked. She always wore hoop earrings. Her long-sleeved sweatshirt, dark blue jeans, and white apron were already stained from work. She and I had been best friends since early grade school, and we vowed to be loyal forever. Although she was not a member of our family by blood, she sure was by life experiences. We'd been in some real entanglements together.

"Hey."

"Hey to you too. Thought this might be a good night to get us all together." I set down my beer and motioned to Angie to sit next to me. "Got a minute to talk about something or does Wiley need you back immediately?"

She smiled. "I'm all yours, kid."

"Good."

"Now, what is so important?" Andy said.

I took a few breaths, trying to make sure I'd stay calm. How to begin? I held up my beer to clink with theirs, figuring this was as good an opening as any. "Well, some news has come up recently in Apple Grove that needs our attention."

"Where's Sam?" Andy asked.

"Working, but I thought this was family news, and while I consider him family, we've only been dating six months. I think we need to talk about this among ourselves."

"What news?" asked Lance.

I paused. "It's let's-go-back-seven-years news."

Andy stared at me. I could see his face contort into a "let's-not-go-back-seven-years" expression.

"Old history." Angie grimaced. "Trying not to think about the car accident that took your parents is easier as time goes by. But each year, around

12

December 28th, I say a little prayer for your whole family, including your mom and dad. They didn't deserve that."

Lance was watching Andy, who was staring straight ahead saying nothing. "Well, as someone who moved into your family, Jill, I never felt so loved or welcomed. Your mom was the best, and her sculptures sang in peoples' hearts. What an amazing woman. Howard was as funny as they come." Lance took a deep breath. "I miss them too, and I wasn't lucky enough to spend all those early years of my life with your family. So, what about them?"

"Well," I began. "I had a visitor to the gallery today—"

"With something to do with Mom and Dad?" Andy asked. His face looked puzzled.

"Yes. In a way. It was Quinn Parsons."

"What?" Andy shoved his chair back, standing so fast it fell over. Lance rose and righted the chair. I looked around. A few people stared at him.

"Okay. Sit down again," I whispered and motioned toward him.

He did, but not before saying, "Why is he out of prison? What the hell is he doing back here? Why is that okay? You don't think it's right, do you?"

I examined Andy's blazing brown eyes and his strained face, and I kept my voice calm. "He stopped in to apologize and tell me he was back in town. He's on probation but has finished his sentence. When I said that was no business of mine and I'd thank him to stay away from my mother's art center, he told me he was sorry I felt that way." I put both hands out. "Geesh. How did he expect me to feel?"

"Like our parents' child who never wanted to see, talk to, or even think about him for one second," Andy blurted out. "I hate him. I hope he burns in hell. No apology in the world will make his despicable actions go away. Why is he back here?"

I pulled the paper out of my pocket and smoothed the crumpled edges out before laying it on the table, turning it in Andy's direction. "He gave me this flyer. He's going to be at a local church that has taken him in. My understanding is the church sees him as a repentant sinner who's come back to try to make things right. He told me he was in AA, and apologizing was one of the steps in his journey back to recovery. He's going to give this public talk at the church to whoever shows up."

Angie grabbed the paper. "OMG. Why would he come back here where he caused so much pain? Remember, half the town—at least—came to their funeral. No one was on his side in this. Your parents were so loved. That he could take their lives in one drunken moment on the highway to Edgington was unbelievable." She shook her head. "This is unreal."

Lance glanced in Andy's direction. "This isn't our business. Let him do his thing, then get out of town." His hand patted Andy's. "We have nothing to do with this. Past history. Years ago. You need to let it go." He looked straight at me. "We won't be there, Jill."

I nodded. "I feel the same way. It would open a gaping wound again. Those terrible memories. That awful night of the car accident. The doorbell rang from one of Tom's police friends in Chicago. My disbelieving call to Tom. The mad drive down here the next morning, only to realize it was true." I paused. "I'd just been home for Christmas and had such an amazing time with my parents. After the standing-room-only funeral, as years went by, I slowly accepted I'd never see them on this earth again." I fingered a couple of tears from my face. "This has nothing to do with us. I'm with Lance. We stay away from this. We've gotten on with our lives."

Andy sat quietly, staring down at the label on his beer bottle.

Angie gathered up the empty beer bottles. "We're resolved. Good decision."

"Unfortunately," I began again, "Parsons told me he's planning to stay here. 'This is home,' he said. 'I need to restart my life,' he said. 'People will forgive me once I show them I'm not that man anymore,' he said. We may have to come to some understanding to cohabit this space."

"What?" Andy stood up again, but Lance caught his chair this time. "You have to be crazy. Live in the same town with a man who murdered our parents? Well, I'm not staying away from this little get-together tomorrow. I want a front-row seat. He won't get away with this. He's going to hear exactly how I feel about his bogus plea for forgiveness. He deserves nothing. No, he deserves to be in prison for life or executed at dawn for what he did. I'd gladly pull the switch, push the poison plunger, or yell the countdown for the firing squad. Or—say, what do they do to execute killers in Illinois?"

14

Lance stood, too. "Andy. You've got to let this go."

"Let it go? Not on your life. He won't live in our town. I'll see to it." He slammed his hand on the table with a huge thunk. Then he took off, walking across the dance floor while everyone who'd heard his outburst watched him.

"Lance, go after him," I said.

Lance stood, pulling something out of his pocket. He held up a set of car keys. "I have the car keys. However, it might be better to let him walk home and cool down."

"Perhaps you're right," I said. "We can't watch Andy twenty-four, seven. How are we going to keep him from doing something stupid?"

Lance looked at me. "Tie him up in the storeroom at the gift shop until we can get Parsons to leave town?"

Chapter Three

The Adele Marsden Center for the Arts was in the heart of Apple Grove. It occupied a prime spot on the southwest quadrant of the public square. Besides the pet shop on the north side, it had an alley separating it from the insurance company on the south side. An art gallery and gift shop filled most of the first floor, with offices at the back of the building and classrooms upstairs. The ceiling held spotlights that could be arranged to give light to whatever artwork was currently in the gallery. One large front window held items from the gift shop, and the other was filled with objects relating to whatever event we had going. In this case, it was some of the paintings of ghosts that had been submitted for our radio show event. The room where the weavers guild met was a few steps down from the offices in the back. It was an 1870 building that had seen many business endeavors in its one hundred forty-seven years. Last year, we'd done a major renovation to make it safer and more usable.

On this particular day, I occupied a chair at the back of the gallery, waiting for the senior group to start. Old Friends Talk Art. We called it "Old Friends" for short. Chad McKenna, my custodian and president of the group, began the meeting by calling out over the conversations.

"It's Wednesday morning, second of the month, folks. That means time for our OFTA meeting. I'd like to introduce a guest as well as our own Victoria Kemp, who has information for us on our big, creative project, a radio play of *The Canterville Ghost* by Oscar Wilde."

Louise and I had set up twenty-five chairs, a podium, and a microphone in the gallery. Over in one corner was a table with refreshments. So far, people were milling around, talking, laughing, and drinking coffee. I knew I was going to love working with this group of seniors because they were so motivated, filled with experiences I hadn't had, and interested in learning new things.

Chad McKenna was a godsend. He'd applied for the custodian job when I was at my wit's end because I was working ten-hour days. I hired him right away. He had on his usual uniform: carpenter's jeans with a faded T-shirt, this time featuring The Band, and a red St. Louis Cardinals hat. He was sixty-seven, sported a red-and-white beard, and was a Vietnam vet. I valued his insight because he knew everyone in town and always had his ear to the latest town gossip. In his earlier, pre-retirement career, he sold cars. This meant he knew a lot of locals. Anytime I needed someone for a particular job, either he or Louise Sandoval knew exactly who to call. He was the one who'd suggested a senior group at the art center. So far, we'd enlisted about twenty seniors, who not only showed up for the meetings the second Wednesday of each month, but they also liked the center so much they volunteered to help with projects and classes. They were so enthusiastic. I sat in the back this morning, listening to Chad's words once the group was seated and quiet.

"Please welcome Professor Elsabeth Poppinger from the English Department at Apple Grove College. She's going to tell us about the context of this short story by Oscar Wilde."

The group applauded. Several leaned forward, making sure they could hear Elsabeth. I could feel the interest in the crowd. Three or four had notebooks out and pens poised to take notes. Art centers sponsor all kinds of creativity, and a radio show or local authors were all considered part of our art world.

Professor Poppinger walked up to the podium, arranging a couple of books and some notes. I'd guess she was in her mid-forties, and English literature was her specialty. Her brown hair was folded into a chignon at the nape of her neck with a couple of decorative, painted sticks holding it all in place. She wore a dark green wool suit with a black satin shell underneath. Elsabeth had that competent air about her. She was an expert who could answer any of our questions.

"Good morning. I'm honored to come give you a bit of background on the radio play you'll be doing, and I'm so thrilled to hear you've chosen Oscar Wilde's work for your first project here at the art center. This short work has been the subject of multiple films, including the 1944 American film version in which Charles Laughton, Robert Young, and Margaret O'Brien played roles in a strange adaptation involving American soldiers in the Second World War." Her eyes found me near the back. She laughingly said, "You probably don't remember those folks, Jill, but I imagine some of these seniors do." In response, the group began chirping merrily about the actors in the film. Call me too young at thirty to remember their culture. I was more into Emily Blunt, Dev Patel, and Michael B. Jordan.

Once they quieted, she continued, "Oscar Wilde wrote this tale as a short story. Since its original publication, *The Canterville Ghost* has been rewritten in other genres, such as theatrical plays and screenplays. It's the story of a ghost who's lived in Canterville Chase for three hundred years and scared most of the residents away. Taking place in the English countryside in the late nineteenth century, the humorous play begins when an American minister to England, Hiram B. Otis, moves his family into Canterville Chase, which he's recently purchased. This group includes his wife, his oldest son, Washington, young twins named Stars and Stripes, and daughter Virginia, age fifteen."

Liz Goodwin, a retired history teacher, raised her hand.

"Yes?" Elsabeth said.

"Stars and Stripes? I mean, seriously. Who would name their children Stars and Stripes?" Everyone laughed.

Elsabeth said, "Yes, you're wise to pick up on that. Hang on for a few minutes. I'll explain." She looked down at her notes, trying to find where she'd left off. "The ghost who haunts the castle is a dead English lord named Sir Simon de Canterville. He killed his wife three hundred years earlier. Some years after her death, the wife's family walled him up in the castle, and he starved to death. Talk about family loyalty! Needless to say, his ghost has been haunting the castle ever since. It can't rest."

Donna Filbert took advantage of the pause, exclaiming, "Shades of Edgar

Allan Poe and Amontillado wine." Laughter once again.

"So, true. You know your Poe," Elsabeth said. "The library window of Canterville Chase contains a prophecy. It's a riddle that says when a golden girl prays and weeps for the soul of the ghost, he will be released from his earthly domain and allowed to rest in the Garden of Death. He must be forgiven for his murderous act, and he's already suffered over three hundred years. So, finding a girl with empathy will free him of this prison and redeem him."

Victoria Kemp said, "Let me guess. The daughter, Virginia, is blond."

"Good guess." Elsabeth consulted her notes again. "Much of the humor came from Wilde satirizing Americans of the late nineteenth century. They had money to buy anything, a belief in science, and no fear. This was a time when the British peerage was looking for money to keep up their castles, and Americans could supply treasure in abundance.

"To answer your question, Donna, products and patriotism reigned. The children's names indicate the way Americans could commodify everything. According to the Otis family, the bloody stain on the floor that kept reappearing could be washed away by Pinkerton's Champion Stain Remover and Paragon Detergent. The ghost's chains could be oiled with Tammany Rising Sun Lubricator. Any problem, Americans could use 'modern' science to fix it. Even the twins gave the ghost a run for his money by making a butter slide he skidded on, putting a bucket of water over the door that soaked him when he came into the room, and throwing pillows at him. To the ghost's dismay, no one in this modern American family was afraid of him. Not even little kids."

Chad rubbed his hands together. "This sounds like it's going to be great fun. We'll be able to use lots of cool sound effects."

Elsabeth nodded. "Yes, Mr. McKenna. Lots of screams and spooky laughter. It does have a happy ending. Virginia's love and generosity break the spell. The ghost is freed." She consulted a book. "He teaches her love is more powerful than life or death, and forgiveness, in itself, is a strong emotion that changes the lives of both the giver and the receiver." She closed the book from which she'd read her last thought, gathering up her notes.

The audience clapped politely, and she moved over and took her seat in the front row.

I listened as audience members began talking about the possibilities for the play. Finally, Chad moved up to the speaker's podium, thanked Elsabeth, and announced, "We'll need lots of volunteers on this. I can see eleven actors plus backstage help to do the sound effects, lighting, and scenery changes. We'll also use makeup and costumes from Apple Grove College." He paused. "I went through the script looking for sound effects. We could make these cool sounds: cracks of thunder, rain falling on the roof, clanging chains, a demonic laugh, a doorbell, and a door knock. We'll have a bloodstain on the carpet that keeps appearing and disappearing."

Another person—I couldn't see who it was—raised a hand, asking, "So, will we have microphones?"

Chad looked at me, and I nodded.

"Yes. We'll have a raised stage in the gallery over there," he said and pointed. "I need to explain an important point. A radio play is not a play like a stage play where you walk around and have lots of scenery changes. Actors sit in chairs and walk up to the microphone as they're in a scene. They use scripts, so there's no need to memorize."

"Good!" shouted Liz Goodwin. "That's a bonus if we don't have to memorize." Several people nodded at this.

Once Chad quieted the group down again, he introduced Victoria Kemp. I knew her because she was the archivist at the *Apple Grove Ledger*. She was seventy-seven and had lived in town for seventy years. Anytime I asked her about someone, she could discuss their family back multiple generations. Who married whom, any scandal that tainted them, and where their living relatives were now. She was a storehouse of information in a brain covered by curly white hair. As short as she was, I wasn't sure we'd be able to see her behind the podium.

Victoria walked up to the speaker's podium, adjusted the microphone to fit her short stature, and consulted her notes. I really liked her. Since I'd returned to Apple Grove from my Chicago art years, she'd been able to fill me in on a lot of things I'd missed over the six years I'd been away. I knew she had a wicked sense of humor.

Now, she cleared her throat and began.

"The author of our production of *The Canterville Ghost* is the British writer, Oscar Wilde. But his whole name was Oscar Fingal O'Flahertie Wills Wilde. Born in 1854 and died in 1900. Short life. His reckless pursuit of pleasure led him down a dark path, and"—she pointed at each person in the front row, giving them a comic, nasty stare—"let it be a lesson to all of you who consider the demon rum or illegal drugs." More laughter.

"Three of his works made him famous. First, the novel *The Picture of Dorian Gray* in 1891. Also, he was known for his social comedies *Lady Windermere's Fan*, 1892, and *The Importance of Being Earnest*, 1895. He was a promoter of the Aesthetic Movement, or art for art's sake.

"Wilde was married and had two sons, but he spent much of his time in social and artistic circles. He was known for his wit and outrageousness. From his lectures in the US and Canada in 1882, he learned about Americans. Unfortunately for him, homosexuality in Britain was a criminal offense, and he was gay. The court charged him with gross indecency when a lord whose son he'd had a relationship with accused him. He spent two years in prison, 1895 to 1897, and those years destroyed his health. His death came three years later.

"Our play, *The Canterville Ghost,* is a humorous look at Americans of that time, who, as the professor said, believed science could solve any problem, even eradicating a ghost from the castle they'd bought. I think we're going to have a wonderful time with this, and it will bring lots of people into our art center for performances. Oh, and I nominate Chad to be Sir Simon. Although I know he'd never murder his wife, Sandy, I think he'd make a great three-hundred-year-old ghost."

Again, everyone clapped and laughed at Chad, who doffed his cap, bowing at the same time. "Thanks, I think, Victoria. We'll have opportunities to try out for characters in another week. As I mentioned, we'll need sound effects people, lighting people, ushers, and scenery movers. Just a little scenery."

Donna Filbert once again raised her hand.

"Yes?" Chad said.

"You haven't said who's going to direct this show."

Chad signaled me. I walked up to the front of the group. "I'm not sure yet, Donna. Chad and I have been discussing it. We have some possibilities. But more on the director later. Stay tuned for an announcement about trying out for parts or signing up to help. We'll get information out to you via email. The show will go on Friday and Saturday, February 17 and 18. And, to add some fun, I put out a Call to Artists back in November. We'll have an exhibit that will include paintings, drawings, photographs, and sculptures that will have something to do with ghosts."

At that surprise, everyone started talking at once, their enthusiasm growing. People usually hung around to talk and eat a few goodies since we always had refreshments. Chad had devised a sign-up list. It was Molly Ripple's turn today. She'd brought in various pastries, cheese, cookies, grapes, and crackers. As they milled around, Chad followed me back to my office.

"Got an idea for the director?" Chad asked.

"Yes. I'd like to ask Evan Shelly. He retired from the theater department at the college a couple of years ago."

Chad rubbed his chin. I could see he was thinking about it. "Isn't he kind of strange?"

"Oh, maybe a little odd. But we all are in some ways, right?"

"If you think he's the one, I say go for it. We'll get it figured out."

I rummaged around on my desk. "Somewhere, I have his phone number." I let out a deep breath, still looking. "Oh, why can't I have a neat, well-organized desk?" I gave up and turned to Chad. "Once I get a director, we'll have auditions. Sound good? By the way, have you seen my turquoise pen?"

He smiled. "No. I take it it's missing. I'll watch for it."

Once he left, I looked up at the photograph of my parents on the wall of my office. My Jamaican mother and Caucasian father smiled down at me. We had brought diversity to our mostly white town several decades ago. Tom, my oldest brother, was white like our dad. Andy and I both had honey-colored skin. No one blinked an eye these days, so I guess we'd worn them down. Well, I hoped Mom and Dad were keeping an eye on us, especially Andy. I hoped they had given Andy the common sense not to show up at the church meeting tomorrow night. I had no idea what he'd do, but I feared the worst.

Chapter Four

I studied my phone. "It's almost seven. Ten more minutes." I checked to make sure the sound on my phone was turned off.

"What can he possibly say that's going to make a difference?" Angie said. "You sure you want to hear this? We can still leave and go drink ourselves silly at my bar. It would be a better use of our time." She was sitting beside me about ten pews back from the front row at the Babbling Brook Community Church on Wednesday night. Angie and I had been known to put down a bottle—or two or three—of wine on occasion.

I turned to Angie. "Why, oh why did I convince myself to come here and listen to his drivel?"

"I think it's like watching a train wreck. You can't look away. I just want to hear him confess."

"He never did, you know. But he did it. Tom was the first cop on the scene."

Tom slid in beside Angie. "Did I hear my name mentioned?"

"Hi, Tom. Keeping an eye on Andy if he shows up, or gathering information?" I asked.

"Well, Parsons never did say much about the accident. I thought he might at least answer some questions we've had over the years. He put his six years in. I can't deny it, although it doesn't seem like punishment when you consider we lost Mom and Dad, not to mention one of Parsons' friends dying too. But that's the sentence for reckless homicide. The judge tacked on a year for the DUI."

I let the words slide in and out of my ears. Tom's belief in the law had obviously helped him make peace with this awful tragedy in our family. I'm not sure I'd heard him mention it in at least the past two or three years.

I inspected the church. I'd never been here before. It was a bigger sanctuary than I'd expected, with a slightly raised stage at the front. Walnut was the wood of choice throughout the church, contrasting beautifully with the electric blue shade of the carpet. Band instruments sat toward the right end of the stage, and a lectern for the minister was in the center and slightly elevated.

To the left was an organ, its pipes rising to heaven and a cathedral ceiling. A huge screen dominated the wall behind the band instruments. Three aisles ran parallel to each other from the back to the front. It looked like an area to the far right was for a choir, with chairs set up on three risers, which were also covered with the restful blue carpet. I couldn't complain about whoever designed the color palette. I reached over and thumbed through the papers stuck into a shelf on the back of the pew in front of me, along with a Bible and hymnal. Some little kid had scribbled on the papers and contribution envelopes with crayons. One of the scribbles was a naughty word, misspelled. Giggling, I remembered doing that myself in the long, long ago. Of course, I'd never misspell it.

Angie and Tom sat quietly, waiting to see what would happen next. I turned around in my seat and scanned the audience. Ned Fisher, Dominic Aubrey, and Chief Wilcox were in various parts of the room in full police uniform. Were they expecting trouble? I turned a bit farther and saw Jeeter Crockett, the deputy sheriff, at the back. His real name was Otis, but everyone called him Jeeter. I could see why. Really, "Otis?" Why name a baby Otis? I think Andy told me the word "jeeter" used to be a slang term for a joint. I have no clue if that fit him.

Paul Darnell and his wife, Buffy, were seated in a middle pew about halfway back. Paul was a banker and used to be a friend of Quinn Parsons. He was on my art center board and did an excellent job. Next to Buffy were Sharon and Finnegan O'Brien. He sat in the aisle in a wheelchair. He'd been gravely injured in the accident that killed our parents. Paralyzed. At least he was living. I'd take my parents alive, even if impaired. Branson Green, the third occupant of Quinn's car, died at the scene. Sharon O'Brien had a seriously angry look on her face. She had no love for Quinn Parsons since he'd put her husband in a wheelchair. I knew they barely scraped along, and Finnegan must have huge medical bills.

I scanned the seats behind me. Martin Stewart was here, too. His son had been quite a bit younger than Quinn Parsons. Maybe, like the rest of the town, Martin was curious. Victoria Kemp was a row behind him. She had an iPad out, so I figured she was taking notes for a newspaper article. Even though she worked in the archives, she also did reporting when they needed her. Fortunately, the horrible editor who used to run the *Ledger* left town after she was almost murdered. A long story, and one I'd like to forget.

A few rows behind Stewart sat Tigger Hastings. He lived next door to me all by himself. I'd guess he was in his mid-twenties, walked a Heinz-57-but-mostly-chihuahua dog named Wingate, and got a lot of package deliveries from technology companies. What he did with all that was a mystery to me. He'd hinted at expertise with computers, and my own guess—from his carefully worded description—was that he might have some talent hacking databases. Maybe someday I'd get up my nerve to ask him about his job description. But he'd been friendly on the occasions we'd spoken. Even in a small town, I was curious about the lives of people who lived around me. But this guy was a recluse, which led to my curiosity. I was surprised to see him here.

I swiveled back around. "I don't suppose you can arrest him for something, can you, Tom?"

He chuckled. "He hasn't done anything yet."

"I heard he's staying at Paul and Buffy Darnell's cabin at the lake," said Angie. "I know they were good friends once upon a time, but does Paul have to be so forgiving?"

Tom leaned over and spoke to both of us. "I hear rumblings around town this church has taken Parsons in, and the good people of the congregation are helping him. I think the Darnells go to this church. I could be wrong. Anyway, better to have Quinn removed to the lake, away from the temptation of someone wishing to take a potshot at him."

"I can think of legions of people who wouldn't mind permanently disposing of him," I said. "Plenty of people he's hurt."

"True," said Angie, "but there's nothing like a sinner looking for redemption to stoke up a crowd in a church."

The constant sound of conversations throughout the room began to die down as two men strolled down the middle aisle from the back. A short man I didn't know was walking beside Quinn Parsons, who at least looked decent in a navy suit. Parsons carried a Bible in one hand. Maybe the other man was the church's minister. They reached the lectern at the front, and the taller man checked the microphone. Once he was satisfied it was on, he began.

"Good evening. My name is Pastor Ellis Frump."

Angie tried hard not to sputter at his name and leaned toward me, her hand over her mouth, her shoulders jiggling up and down, and I could tell she might burst out loud into laughter at any moment, so I shook my head and put my hand over my mouth in case it was catching.

"We welcome you all to our sanctuary, a place of contemplation and peace. Tonight, Brother Quinn Parsons has asked to use this time to address you about his past. I know, as he does, that his choices in the past have hurt many people, some of you in this building tonight. If so, I pray his words will bring you peace and understanding."

At his phrase I thought, peace and understanding? Seriously? Quinn Parsons will never give me those qualities, not ever.

"Mr. Quinn Parsons has been counseling with me, and I believe he is truly remorseful for his past transgressions." At that, the older man stepped aside and motioned Parsons to the microphone.

Quinn reached for the mic to pull it up slightly, and it let out a screech. His brown hair was neatly groomed, his blue eyes stared straight ahead, and he set the Bible down on the lectern and unfolded a few pages of paper. He paused, and you could have heard a pin drop in the entire sanctuary. In that pause, Sharon O'Brien—she always was a loudmouth—yelled, "Go back to prison. You don't deserve any peace or understanding."

Though I despised Parsons, I could imagine his anxiety, not knowing the crowd's reaction. Sharon had made her opinion clear.

"Well," he began, pausing for what seemed like a whole minute. "First, I thank you for coming. I wasn't quite sure what to expect. I'm grateful to be able to speak and explain some of the changes in my heart and mind since the accident I caused here seven years ago. December 28, 2010. It's a date I can never forget."

"Believe me, neither can my family," I whispered to Angie.

As if he'd heard me, Quinn glanced in our direction. "I'm thankful some of the Madison family are here also. And the Green parents, whose son, Branson, was also"—and here he paused—"in my car. A better friend I could never have had." He stumbled a little on the last few words. He scanned the other side of the audience, and I assumed Branson Green's parents were sitting there.

It was so quiet, everyone focusing on Quinn Parsons. The thing was, the entire town remembered that night. It was almost like the adage, "Where were you when you heard the news about…the Madisons?" It had become part of the town's history, and I've heard newcomers are told about it in hushed tones. Anger welled up in my chest. Not exactly what I wanted my family to be remembered for.

"I want to express my sorrow and regret for my actions that night. I've learned a lot about myself over those six years in…in pri-prison," he stuttered. "I joined Alcoholics Anonymous and am now a recovering alcoholic. Those folks at Ballyyard Prison were kind and generous with their time to someone who had caused so much pain. I owned up to my struggles and my bad decisions. Keeping the pain inside me cost me dearly. I learned when you hold on to pain, you pay a terrible price for it. If you embrace forgiveness, it gives you a chance to find peace or hope." He opened the Bible in front of him and read, "Psalms, Chapter 130, Verses 3 and 4 say, 'If thou, O Lord, should mark iniquities, Lord, who could stand? But there is forgiveness with thee.'

"The thing is," he said, faltering a bit on the last word, "the thing is there are many details of that…event that people don't know. It wasn't only me. Other people were involved, people who didn't come forward at the time. I plan to see those individuals and talk about their roles that night, as well as their part in some illegal activities in Apple Grove."

My mind focused on Parsons, but out of the corner of my eye, I saw the heavy back door of the sanctuary open quietly, and my brother Andy slid through the gap, closing it behind him. He stood there against the wall, staring at Quinn Parsons. I nudged Angie to tap on Tom's shoulder, but Tom had already seen our brother. He turned back around and glanced at me with the worried look we both shared about Andy showing up. Forgiveness was not in his vocabulary...or mine. But I was far less likely to do something stupid. Not so Andy.

If Quinn saw Andy slide in, I didn't see any indication. He consulted his notes and went on. "That night, December 28, 2010, I selfishly drank too much and drove back with friends in my car. It was stupid of me and reckless. Wrong on so many levels. Because of my selfishness, I killed three people from this community and put one of my friends in a wheelchair. I pray God will forgive me and those I hurt will at least focus on finding peace. I can't ask the resentment or anger they feel to go away. I can't ask them to forget or excuse my behavior.

"But one thing I did discover in prison. One of the doctors there hypnotized me to help me quit smoking. And during the procedure, I remembered the brakes on my car didn't work that night. I stepped on them over and over, and nothing happened." He paused. "That wasn't the only thing I remembered under hypnosis." He looked over at one area of the audience. "You know who you are, and so do I. While you have my forgiveness, you need to pay a price for your part in the past."

At those words, people in the audience gasped and began whispering in quiet tones.

I looked back across at the O'Briens and Greens. They were whispering to their spouses and covering their mouths. If facial expressions could kill, Quinn Parsons was in deep trouble. Buffy Darnell grabbed Paul's arm while Finnegan O'Brien took the brake off his wheelchair, turned, and veered up the aisle toward an exit. Sharon O'Brien called to him and hastily followed him out the back exit. Mr. and Mrs. Green looked extremely uncomfortable but stayed seated.

About this moment, Andy came barreling down the center aisle shouting, "That's like you, Parsons, to blame something else for your reckless, self-centered behavior. It'll be a freezing day you-know-where before anyone forgives your rashness and your murder of three innocent people. My parents—who my family will never see again—are gone because of you. They were decent, loved, well-respected members of this community, something you'll never be!"

And now Andy was at the front, climbing the steps to the stage, and I watched as he lurched toward Parsons, who stepped back as Andy raised his fist, hitting Quinn on the chin and knocking him to the floor. I think everyone was in shock. Not so my other brother. Tom jumped from his seat, pushed his way past several people to the aisle, and raced up to the stage about the same time as Jeeter, Dominic, and Ned.

I watched as Andy grabbed Parsons and hit him again, yelling, "You don't deserve anyone's forgiveness! You decimated my family because of your stupidity and recklessness. You don't deserve to live!" Tom, who had made it to the stage by then, grabbed Andy's arms and pulled him back. Ned and Dominic took Andy from Tom, pushed him off the stage and down the side aisle, out of the building. It was chaotic. Some people stood, while others sat in their seats unable to believe what they'd seen. Tears stung my eyes as I thought about the pain my brother was in. Angie inspected me, wiping away my tears.

"Now what?" I asked. I shook my head. "Andy has such a temper. Now he'll be in real trouble."

"Perhaps Quinn won't press charges. He seems to want everyone's forgiveness."

"It may not be so simple." I looked around. Andy had broken the mood, and people were rising and leaving the church. On the stage, the minister put his arm under Quinn's shoulder, helping him stand. Parsons was rubbing his chin where Andy'd hit him.

Angie gazed toward the back as people left, and she turned to me. "Well, I'll say one thing. Andy sure knows how to bring an end to a memorable night and clear a room." She pointed. "I'll bet those folks in the front row with their phones out will have great footage for the ten o'clock news."

"Tom's going to be so mad at him."

"I remember what that feels like, Tom's being mad. Yikes. I wouldn't want to go there. You remember when he was so angry because we'd solved a murder case for him?"

"Ah, yes. We do bring out the best in Tom."

"Victoria's here, so the headlines in the paper tomorrow should also be memorable."

"I hate to think. I hope Mom and Dad can't see this."

Angie stood to leave. "I don't know, Jill. I think they might be proud of their kid."

Chapter Five

I'd had a sleepless night, waking from dreams and nightmares, falling asleep only to wake again. I wasn't real peppy this Thursday morning. I was studying a set of earrings in the art center gift shop. They might be perfect for Angie. The front window exhibited scarves, jewelry, pottery, books, and other unique items in our shop. Behind the window display several platforms on the main floor held artwork and sculptures available for shoppers. I loved the scarves woven by our guild. Several of them in blues, reds, and russet browns hung in my closet at home. I was examining a set of classy silver hoop earrings when the bell on the front door jangled. My wonderful boyfriend, Sam Finch, came walking in the door. His scent preceded him—cloves and sandalwood. Yum. Forevermore I would connect that scent to his handsome face.

"On my way to the hospital. Figured I'd stop in to test your memory about what I look like."

I turned around and checked him out. A black leather jacket topped by one of our weaver's scarves—in blue—brought out the color of his Cerulean blue eyes. He walked toward me with the nonchalance of a confident doctor on his way to morning rounds.

I smiled and gave him a big hug, planting a rapturous kiss on his lips. "Thank you, Sam. I'm sorry you couldn't make it to Priscilla's the other night. Seems to be the story of our lives."

He nodded, sighed, and put his hands on my shoulders. "I know. It's cold and flu season. We've had some bad accidents lately because of the snow. But I always think about you, despite my inattentiveness."

His hands came down and took both of mine. I was in love with this gorgeous man. However, I was not in love with his schedule. Seemed like he was on call a lot.

"Speaking of accidents," Sam said, "I heard Andy had a big run-in last night. Is he okay?"

"Well, I'm not sure. An accident, it wasn't. I think Tom went over to Andy and Lance's house to try to talk some sense into him after the brouhaha at the church. Fortunately, Quinn refused to press charges."

"That was kind of him."

"More like guilt."

"Well, no one showed up at the ER, or I'd know about it."

"I doubt Andy hit him hard enough to break anything. Probably just some bruises." I shook my head. "That temper of his is going to get him into trouble. I don't blame him, of course. I'd like to punch the guy in the mouth, too. He totally changed our lives in one careless moment. What I wouldn't give to have my parents back again. I should have taught Andy to punch harder."

Sam tilted his head slightly, his expression feigning shock. "Really? I thought I was in love with a woman who professed goodness and peace."

"Usually. But Quinn Parsons coming back to town has changed the entire picture. I can't imagine he thinks he can stay here with all the pain he caused so many people. The Greens, the O'Briens, and us. A fraternity of walking wounded. Guess we'll see. I don't know what to do about Andy. Maybe Tom will have some ideas."

He pulled me into his arms, the smell of leather, sandalwood, and cloves enveloping me in a warm cocoon. "Whatever I can do to help, just let me know. I'm on your side...always." Another deep, lovely kiss.

I brushed a stray strand of blond hair back from his forehead. Then I pulled back and examined his face. "I know. Thank you."

Checking his watch, Sam said, "Gotta go. Tomorrow night. Let's go out to dinner. I'm not on call for a change."

"Perfect." I smiled. "It'll give me something to look forward to. Thank you, Sam."

He turned as he was almost to the door. "For what?"

"For not telling me you should have nothing to do with my crazy family."

He grabbed the door. "Aw, I love your crazy family." Then, a sweet smile and he was gone.

Louise came in around nine. We discussed the tasks we had to do for the day while sitting in my office, making lists as usual.

"Louise, have you picked up my pen?"

"What pen?"

"You know…the turquoise one my dad gave me. I swear I left it right here on my desk, but it's been gone for several days."

Louise laughed. "How can you find anything on that desk? Checked the floor? It might have rolled off between the stack of files, the papers at all different angles, and the precarious stack of mail you didn't open yesterday."

I gave her a rueful nod. "No one has ever accused me of having an organized office."

"So true."

Chad showed up midmorning, humming an old Animal's song, "We Gotta Get Out of This Place," as he walked in the door. Jill could hear him back in her office. He stuck his head in the door. "Did you have an interesting night?"

I swiveled my desk chair around and rubbed my eyes. "You heard too?"

"Of course. I always know what's going on in town. Guess Quinn Parsons got some of what he deserved. Is Andy okay?"

"Lance called earlier. He told me Andy was swearing at his hangover and bruised knuckles this morning, and he left him in bed to sleep it off."

Chad came in and moved some things from the loveseat, as always. He handed me a newspaper. The front page of the *Apple Grove Ledger* had a photograph of Quinn lying on the stage of the church. Andy was standing over him. The headline was "Decisive Knockout Wins Church Brawl." I glanced at Victoria Kemp's story. At least she tended to be fair without falling back on dramatic innuendo. She wasn't like the last editor. It was a straightforward news story with Parsons' and Andy's names, plus the basics of the situation. It mentioned Andy was Detective Tom Madison's brother. Tom wasn't going to be happy about that.

"Well, it could have been worse, I suppose. At least Victoria has some integrity. What are people saying?" I gave the newspaper back to Chad.

"Far as I can tell, it's fifty-fifty. Half the town wish they'd been Andy and popped him, and the other half think Andy's a bully who should spend a few days in jail."

"Great! I can hear Lance now, considering the business they'll lose."

"There is that. So, to change the subject, how is the radio play doing? Any new thoughts?"

I pulled some papers off the leaning stack on my desk. "Evan Shelly said yes, he'll direct. The dates are solid—a show on Friday, February 17, and Saturday, February 18. I put the call to artists for the exhibit out weeks ago as soon as we decided on the radio play. I've already seen forty pieces of artwork with ghosts on the online page for entries. By the end of this week, we should have them all. Then I'll cut them back to thirty pieces. Artists can decide to sell their artwork and price them. It won't be like an exhibit where we have a juror judge them. The exhibit will provide ambience on the nights of the play. Win/win."

"Sounds perfect. Molly Ripple is excited to try out for the part of Virginia, the daughter of the Otis family. Of course, Virginia is sixteen, and Molly is eighty-two. Bit of a stretch. Are you thinking of bringing in kids to play Stars and Stripes?"

"Good question. I thought I might ask Evan Shelly about using kids. He's scheduling auditions. I'll email everyone and get the word out on social media."

"Great!" Chad checked his watch. "Oops, I need to pick up the grandkids. They're having a short day because of some kind of teacher meeting. See ya tonight."

It was a good distraction to have this radio play to concentrate on. I began humming Chad's Animal's tune as I searched for my grant file. Ah! Found it! I pulled a stapled set of directions out of a pile. I could hear Louise humming the same song as she walked down the hallway past my office door on her way to the gift shop and gallery. Thanks, Chad, for the earworm.

I'd settled into the grant information when I heard the front doorbell chime. Louise would take care of it. She was already out in the gallery. Vaguely, in the back of my mind, I heard footsteps. This was not good for my concentration.

"Jill?" my brother Tom's voice came from my doorway. I turned around in my chair. He was standing there, pulling off a scarf and unzipping his coat. I got up and helped him. Oh. This meant more than a simple check-on-my-sister visit.

"Hi. Why the gloomy face? What's up?" I motioned to the loveseat inside my office. He came in, closing the door. Oh, no. Closing the door always meant I was in trouble. The last time he did that, workers had discovered a corpse in the basement of the art center. I scanned his face. It hadn't changed. Bad news.

He pulled off his coat and sat. This was even worse. What had I done now?

"I smell pizza," he said.

"Louise brought in her lunch and heated it in the microwave a few minutes ago. It's already eleven-thirty. Surely your day hasn't been this bad already?" I asked.

He paused. "Well, it has. I was called out at seven a.m."

"Oh." I stood up, and my mind raced. "It isn't Andy, is it? Is he all right?"

"Yes, Andy is okay. But I was called out this morning to Paul Darnell's cottage at the lake."

"Isn't that where Quinn Parsons is staying?"

"Was."

"Was? What do you mean?"

"He's dead."

I gasped. "What? How?" I fell back into my desk chair.

"A good question. Darnell found him this morning and called 9-1-1. Parsons was at the bottom of a set of stairs that goes down to the beach. Cement at the bottom. Looks like a broken neck. It might have been an accident, but the deputy thinks it was helped along."

"Oh, this isn't good."

"You're telling me." Tom stared at my computer screen for a moment, lost in thought. "Unfortunately, since Andy made such a show at the church last night, he may end up being a suspect. This means I can't investigate because I'm his brother."

"Surely, there are plenty of people who hated Quinn Parsons. Even me. What will they do?" I bit my lower lip, thinking about my stupid brother Andy. Why couldn't he control his temper?

"Well, they've moved the case to the sheriff's office."

"Good. Sheriff Detweiller will be fair. He's always struck me as a good man." I felt better because he knew Andy and liked him.

"If only that were the case. Detweiller fell down his basement stairs, breaking his pelvis about four weeks ago. He's out on a medical leave of absence. They're shorthanded at the sheriff's office. Jim Beals runs the office, so he isn't an investigator. They have three deputies, but one oversees a canine unit, one is a patrol deputy in the county. The third is Jeeter Crockett."

"Oh, no." I put my hand on my forehead. "I know where you're headed."

"Unfortunately."

Jeeter Crocket was an arrogant, self-important, rotten person. Those were his better qualities. His uniform was always immaculate, his pants creased just so, and his black hair groomed perfectly with lots of product. His aviator glasses were always on his face or hanging from his neckline. Rumor had it he'd slept with half the women in the county, some married, some not. When Andy was in high school, Jeeter bullied him because he always picked on guys who were younger, smaller. That was my brother Andy. Tom had often confronted Jeeter, since they were in high school at the same time. But he couldn't always be around. Once Tom graduated, Andy sometimes came home with bruises he covered up so Mom and Dad wouldn't see them. This was not good. Jeeter was always involved in bullying kids.

"Isn't there something you can do about it, Tom? Can't you talk to Chief Wilcox?"

"I doubt it. There's nothing to stop Jeeter from planting evidence. He's in charge. I can't go near it. I went to the crime scene this morning, but the chief came out, too. Once he saw who the victim or potential victim was, he sent me packing, saying he'd have to go outside the department. Jeeter and I have a history, too. When I made detective, and he didn't, he switched from the local police to the sheriff's department. I don't think he's all that happy there, but he hasn't forgotten I got the job he wanted. Fortunately, our paths rarely cross, but now this. Word is all over town about Andy at the church last night. Unfortunately, Jeeter is the next in line at the sheriff's department. It makes sense to send it out of our local police office and move it to the county."

"I imagine you had a small head start. Did you see anything suspicious at the scene?"

"Tire tracks. Two different sets. But I didn't get much further because Chief Wilcox pulled me out fast. I'm sidelined. Can't go near it."

I thought about that for a moment or two. "Hmm. You can't go near it, but no one said Angie and I couldn't."

He stood quickly. "No. You and Angie need to leave this alone. Jeeter isn't a pleasant person to cross. You must stay away. I mean it, Jill."

For the first time in a long time, I decided the better part of valor was to keep my mouth shut. Hard to believe—even for me—but true.

Pulling his coat on and grabbing his scarf, Tom said goodbye.

I stared at the photo of my family on the wall. Mom and Dad, Tom, Andy, and me. I loved my brothers so much. Andy looked so young, so vulnerable. He was. He might have been a freshman in high school when they took this photo. I stared at his face. So filled with joy. He was the comedian in most of his classes, and his only sport was track, where he was on a relay team. He had lots of friends in high school because he was so funny, but it hadn't kept him from having detractors, too. One of them was Jeeter Crockett, king of the auto mechanics class at the high school, now deputy sheriff of Lincoln County.

I didn't care what Tom said. If Andy ended up in this mess, I would have to help him. I couldn't feed him to the wolves and wouldn't let Jeeter continue to bully him. They didn't have any evidence against him, and it might have been totally an accident. Andy could never have done this. But somewhere deep inside me, I knew Quinn Parsons had plenty of people he'd hurt. It wasn't only us Madisons. If he'd been murdered, there were far more suspects than my brother, who wouldn't hurt a fly. Well, I take that back. He did give Parsons a surprisingly good right hook. Regardless, I knew who Jeeter would go after.

And the first person who would help me prove his innocence was Angie. She'd jump off a cliff for my family. Without looking.

Chapter Six

L ater in the day, I was on my computer in my office studying the ghostly artwork. I'd eventually have to narrow the entries. Many were astounding, telling me they'd be such a perfect addition to the art exhibit accompanying our radio show. I checked my calendar. There was still plenty of time for people to get artwork in.

My phone beeped with a text message. Sorting through the minutiae on my desk, I found my cell. Now, I wished I hadn't. Ivan F. Truelove III was back from his vacation to the Northeast. Oh, joy. He was a CPA and president of my art center board. He spent his days making my life miserable by texting me about my shortcomings and what I *should* be doing. Ivan F. Truelove was a thorn in my side. What was his problem now?

> Why is there a bill for carpentry work in the basement of the art center? I don't remember approving this experience. I don't remember the board approving this experience.
> Ivan F. Truelove III, CPA

Sadly, Ivan could not figure out autocorrect, so he was still sending me strange messages with misspelled words. "Experience" must have been "expenditure." I was getting rather good at translating his screw-ups. I'd love to autocorrect him, but he'd turn into some other weird creature I'd have to deal with. I suppose I should text him back on this one. So, I explained the board had approved the expenditure while he was in the hospital. He had been laid up from falling down the old basement stairs at the art center, which had no handrail at the time. The bill for the new handrail was just coming through. I tapped the "send" button, then set my phone back on the desk.

"Jill."

I came out of my reverie to see Louise standing in my doorway. Louise had worked with me as the art center manager since we opened. She was tall and willowy, a single mom, always figuring she'd meet her true love on a dating site. Louise always wore earth-toned clothing that complemented her olive skin and brunette hair.

"Yes. I'm here. Awake. What's going on, Louise?"

"I'm getting the bills put together for the next board meeting. What line in the budget should I use for the radio play scripts? We ordered twenty of them."

She handed me the spreadsheet for the budget, and I quickly located the right line. I gave it back, saying, "So, how did your date go last night? The one with the dentist?"

"Absolutely terrible. He wanted to examine my molars. I declined. Why do these people sound and look like movie stars online? You're so excited...until they show up. They're nothing like movie stars, and their small talk is drivel."

"How long have you been at this now?"

"At what?" Louise said.

"This online dating."

She sat on my loveseat. I watched her counting silently. "Six years? No, seven."

"And in all this time, how many 'possibles' have you had?"

"Well, maybe one."

I thought for a moment. "What was wrong with that one?"

"He was looking for a woman to throw knives at in his carnival act."

"So, you turned him down?" I asked dryly.

"Yes. I asked him what happened to his last assistant, but he wouldn't answer me."

"Probably a good choice. Maybe it's time to put away the dating sites and hope for a miracle."

Louise nodded. "I'd been thinking that myself. But you never know who's around the corner." And with that she left to go to her office.

"Yes," I whispered to myself. "Could be a circus act with sharp knives." Louise was forever hopeful.

Tom had called me earlier to say Andy was being questioned at the sheriff's office by Jeeter. When I asked him about a lawyer, he said not to worry. He'd never let Andy go into a criminal interview without a lawyer. That would be like feeding a small lamb to a hungry pack of wolves. There's no telling what he might say. Tom had hired Josephine (Josie) Brinkley from Edgington to sit in on the interview. It was last minute, but she owed him a few favors since their paths had crossed many times—pleasantly—in the justice system. Nevertheless, I paced around the gallery—my office was so small I'd run into the walls—and my mind kept inventing worst-case scenarios.

I waited to hear news all afternoon, but nothing. Finally, Tom called and said we'd have a family meeting tonight at his house at seven. But no. He switched it to my house since Emily and Jim, their teenage kids, would be home. No need to have them hear about their uncle. Actually, I was sure they'd heard about it at school already. This was serious. We hadn't had a family meeting over some kind of disaster since long before I'd moved back to Apple Grove. I wondered what Andy had said in his interview.

After knowing about Andy's high school experience with Jeeter and Tom's history with the deputy, I had a real reason to worry. Anxiety welled up in my chest thinking about Andy. When the clock said five, I packed my things to take off for home. I figured I'd get some dinner and try to relax before I had to host the family. Sam was working at the ER tonight, so he begged me to fill him in when I had a chance to call him.

I'd sent Louise home a half-hour ago, and now I locked the front door, turning off the lights. The last door to lock was the one on the alley we shared with an insurance company. As I turned the key and set the alarm, I grimly thought about my family. I wished my parents were still here. But, then again, none of this trouble for Andy would have happened if they were still alive.

"I'm telling you, I was home with Lance all evening last night. Well, after the fiasco at the church," Andy said. He glanced at Lance, crossing his arms across his chest.

I wasn't quite sure he was telling the truth. Andy's face had always been an open roadmap.

We were all sitting around the dining room table at our parents' house, which was now my house, grilling Andy about what they might have on him. Tom's wife, Mary, joined Tom, Lance, and me. I'd opened a couple bottles of wine, one red, one white. So far, everyone had retained their tempers. Even Andy.

I'd turned on the dining room light over the table, so it was a soft glow. On the table, I'd set out several bowls of peanuts and cashews. No one had touched them. The wine, yes. The food, no. We were all too wound up to eat anything, worrying about what Andy might have said this afternoon.

Tom took over the discussion, trying to assess where Jeeter was headed.

"I know there were tire tracks, two sets, in the driveway. We'd had a thaw the day before. When the slush froze again, the night of Parsons' death, the tire tracks were set in ice. Did they check your car?"

Andy took a few swallows of wine, nodding. "Yes. They checked it when they questioned me at the police station." But he lowered his eyes, not looking at us.

"Did they check inside your car?"

"No. There's nothing in my car that would interest them."

"Did they have a search warrant for your car?" Tom asked.

He nodded. "By then, the lawyer you got me arrived. Thanks, bro."

Mary answered, "Thank your sister, Andy. She took care of paying for a retainer."

"Oh. Okay. Thank you, Jill."

I tried to smile hopefully.

Lance chimed in. "They won't have a problem with motive. The entire town heard babbling boy here threaten him and sock him in the jaw." He gave Andy a stony look.

Andy put his hands in front of his face, then dropped them. "Yeah. Stupid,

I know. I'd had a bit too much to drink before I went over there. I wasn't going to go. I wasn't. But the more I thought about it, the madder I got. Who was he to come back here and act like he'd done nothing wrong? Like we're going to forgive him or let his life go right on."

"Exactly what gets you in trouble. Saying things like that." Tom scowled. "They have a motive, but no means or opportunity. You were at home all evening." He glanced back and forth from Lance to Andy.

I thought a guilty look darted between them, and I imagined Tom saw it too.

"Andy. You were home, right?" Mary asked.

"Well, maybe not all evening." He glanced at Lance, refusing to look at the rest of us.

I could not believe it. He'd already lied to the police. OMG. My brother. When would he ever learn? "Andy. You lied to the police?"

"Well, just a little tiny lie." He studied the floor.

Tom slapped his forehead, taking a deep breath. After he let it out, he said, "Andy. They'll know you lied. Your face says it all. All the more reason for them to think you're hiding things. To a cop, lies usually equal secrets or guilt or both." He took another deep breath. No one said anything. Total silence.

"That's not the worst, Tom," said Lance quietly.

"What do you mean?" Tom asked.

Lance turned to my brother. "You'd better tell him, Andy."

Andy stared at Lance, his face uncertain. "I—I—I—"

"Well, spit it out," said Tom.

"Andy went to Darnell's cottage at the lake last night," Lance quickly said, and gave Andy a dark look.

The expression on Tom's face tightened. "You're kidding. Tell me that's not true."

He shook his head. "I wish it weren't. I don't know what I was thinking. I was so, so stupid." He put his face in his hands.

"Don't tell me you left fingerprints in the house and tire tracks in the driveway," Tom said. "I can't believe this."

Andy hesitated, glancing up. "Well, maybe."

"Did you touch anything?"

"Of course." His voice exploded. "How can you walk into a house without touching anything?"

Mary asked quietly, bringing the anger level down, "Did the deputies take your fingerprints?"

"No."

"Not yet," said Tom. "Is there anything else you lied about or didn't tell us?"

Andy thought for a moment.

I held my breath.

"No. That's it."

"Did you see Quinn Parsons and get into another altercation with him?"

"Well, yes and no." He once again lowered his head, studying his hands in his lap.

By now I was so ticked at him for being so stupid I could have throttled him. "What do you mean, 'yes and no'?"

When he said nothing, Lance explained. "He means 'yes, he saw him,' and 'no, there was no altercation.'"

Tom stared at Andy. "Well, thank God for that. At least you kept your temper. What did he say? What did you say?"

My brother pursed his lips, trying hard not to answer Tom. We all waited. Finally, he managed to blurt the words out. "I saw him at the bottom of the deck stairs, lying there, dead. So, no. I guess there wasn't any altercation."

Tom gave him a look of disbelief. "Let me get this straight. You're saying you didn't push Quinn Parsons down the stairs at Paul Darnell's lake house?"

"Correct," he said, finally looking straight into Tom's eyes. "He was already dead when I got there."

"And you didn't call 9-1-1?" asked Mary.

"Are you kidding? I was so scared I took off out of there like a bat out of hell. I'd already threatened him earlier that evening. Why would I call the police?"

Tom raised an eyebrow, shaking his head. Resignation in his voice registered with all of us. "Why indeed?"

Chapter Seven

"Hard day?" I asked Sam on Friday evening as we waited for our dinner. We were seated at a table covered with a crisp, white linen tablecloth near a window that overlooked a snowy path into a small, wooded area right in town. Everyone in the area was familiar with "the Inn." It had been owned by three generations of the Bybee family. Diners came from other towns to eat here for special occasions. Candles delivered romantic lighting that made me appear at my best. Finally, time alone with Sam. I loved to see him in a suit and tie—black suit, turquoise shirt, matching tie in black with a thin turquoise stripe. He really knew how to dress for success!

We discussed the tilapia, passed on steaks, and finally ordered a lovely red wine, pasta, and salads. Four other tables in the room were filled with customers, and we were seated away from most of them, so we had some privacy. I reached over and placed my hand over his.

"It was a hard day, actually. We had a couple of emergencies, which meant I was called down to the ER to help."

I shook my head slowly. "I don't know how you do that. If someone fell down the stairs at the art center, I'd not have a clue. We have a first aid kit, but it would hardly be applicable for a disaster. I'm not so good in an emergency."

He smiled, squeezing my hand. "You never know. You might be stronger than you think."

The waitress showed up with our salads as I removed my hand from Sam's.

"Here you are. A garden salad with raspberry vinaigrette for you. For you, sir, a Caesar salad." She placed the plates in front of us, adding a small basket of homemade breads. "Will there be anything else?"

"This is great," Sam said, eyeing his salad. "Thank you."

"Enjoy."

"I can tell Andy's on your mind," Sam said, opening his linen napkin and placing it on his lap. "Has Tom said anything else?"

I stirred my salad around, mixing the dressing. "That's the problem. With Tom out of the picture, we have no idea what's happening. Angie had a thought, of course."

"I'm afraid to ask."

I chuckled. "If he gets arrested, she thinks we should tunnel under the jail to rescue him."

"Does she have a plan for how to do that? Especially blasting through the cement floor?"

"I'm not sure she's planned so far ahead. She sees the overall picture—the details, not so much. That's always my department."

"Great."

"It's good to keep some cash around for bail bond money. I probably should have mentioned it to you when we started dating."

"Not sure the thought would have occurred to me. Do you need bail money often?"

I swallowed a bite of salad. "Maybe once in a blue moon. I must say Tom has occasionally helped us out of scrapes, but mostly, he reads us the riot act."

He smiled. "Maybe I should do a background check. Hopefully, no felonies."

"No. No felonies. Let's just say Angie and I had a great time growing up here."

I chuckled. We ate our salads in silence for several minutes. Then Sam set his fork down, chose a wheat roll, and asked, "So what are Tom and Mary up to tonight?"

"Basketball game out of town. Jim's playing well right now. They go to every game they can when Tom isn't working, but I usually go only to the home games. Maybe we could go to one if we can find a time when you aren't on call."

"Great idea. I'm all for it. Get a schedule for me. We'll figure it out."

I felt the step tracker on my wrist vibrate. "Sorry, my phone's ringing. Let me check. I can let it go to voicemail."

"Go ahead and answer it," Sam said as he dug into his salad again.

I pulled my purse from the floor, grabbed my cell, and checked to see who was calling. Lance. Normally, I wouldn't bother to answer while on a date with Sam, but with Andy in the soup lately, maybe I should. "Excuse me a minute," I said. I strode out of the dining area and into the front foyer.

"Lance?"

"Hi, Jill. Do you have any idea where Tom is?"

"Yes. At an away basketball game for Jim."

"Oh, great."

"What's the matter? Anything I can do to help?"

"I'm not sure. The police are here at our house. They have a search warrant."

"Call the lawyer. Josie Brinkley. We'll be right there."

"I will."

I tapped the end button, walking quickly back into the dining room. The waitress had brought our entrees. "Sorry, Sam. We must go. Andy's in trouble." I'm sure he could see the anxiety on my face.

"No problem." He glanced around and waved for our waitress. "Let me get the bill. We'll box the dinners."

We drove across town to Lance and Andy's house, the aroma of tomato sauce wafting through the car. Despite my concern, I could hear my stomach growling. When we turned the corner near Andy and Lance's, it was like a major crime going down. At least four sheriff's department cars sat at odd angles, totally blocking the street in front of the house. Red and blue flashing lights lit up the houses in the neighborhood. A county car sat in the driveway with its lights blinking. As I checked out the other houses, I saw people in the windows wondering what was going on. I noticed one or two come out on their porches to watch. Great. Next, they'll be filming a video for news at ten. The deputies could at least have turned off the flashing lights. They were acting like a major crime syndicate leader lived here.

We had to park halfway down the block. The snow-cleared sidewalks enabled us to safely march up the driveway. I didn't bother to knock on the door. I looked at Sam, and we went in. As we walked into the foyer, we saw Lance first. A couple of sheriff's patrol officers were searching through drawers or closets. We must have beaten the lawyer here.

Lance wandered over. "Oh, thank God you're here. I called the lawyer."

"Where's Andy?"

"He's upstairs keeping an eye on the search. I've no idea what they're searching for." He glanced around, a worried look on his face.

A knock at the door. Josephine Brinkley had arrived. She was tall, slender, and had blond hair that was pulled back and held by barrettes. She wore mint green sweatpants and a matching sweatshirt. She obviously had been relaxing at home when this emergency hit. Thank God she was able to come quickly.

"Hi, Jill."

I walked over to her and introduced Sam. "We just got here, Josie. Andy's upstairs."

"All right. Let me manage this." She moved to one of the officers, asking who was in charge.

"Jeeter. Uh, Deputy Sheriff Crockett. He's searching right now."

"Thank you." She climbed the stairs, Lance, Sam, and me right behind her like an avenging offensive line. Andy was in the hallway. I almost cried when I saw the relief on his face as he recognized us.

"I didn't know what to do, Ms. Brinkley."

"It's fine, Andy. Take a few deep breaths, then tell me where Crockett is."

"In there." Andy pointed at Lance's room. She left with the air of a woman on a mission.

We stayed in the hall but could hear murmuring voices from the bedroom. Sam and I stared at each other, and he grabbed one of my hands for reassurance. After several minutes, Josie came back out.

"Andy, they do have a valid warrant."

Andy held out a paper. "Yeah. Right here."

"They're looking for clothes and also your car," Josie said.

"My car? Why? Why look at my clothes?"

"Did they ask you what you were wearing the night Quinn Parsons died?"

Andy regarded each of us. "Well, yes. I had a long-sleeved red sweater on with one of those gray puffer jackets over it. The weather wasn't terribly cold, so I threw those on."

"Were those the clothes they found?"

"Yeah. The deputy asked me to identify them. He bagged them and continued to search. Oh, they took my laptop. Can you do something about that since I need it for work?"

"Let me see the warrant again."

Andy passed the search warrant to the lawyer.

"Ah!" she said. "Just as I thought." She moved into the room and spoke with Jeeter Crockett. It was loud enough to hear from the hallway. I sneaked around the doorway, moving slightly into the room so I could watch.

"Jeeter. This warrant limits you to items of clothing or the car in the garage. It says nothing about technology. We need Andy's laptop back."

"Why? I figure he might have threatened Parsons on it."

Josie shook her head. "Doesn't matter. You can only search and seize items mentioned in the warrant. You know the drill. The laptop—I want it back."

Jeeter rubbed his jaw a moment. I could see by the expression on his face he didn't want to give Andy's computer back. Resignation dawned on him. He looked our lawyer squarely in the eyes. "Okay. Clint's taken it out to the van. You can catch him there. Tell him I said he was to give it to you." He glared at Andy, who had sidled in next to me. "Pretty Boy here will be in enough trouble without it."

"I'll thank you to address my client as 'Andy' or 'Mr. Madison.' None of your ignorant babbling that shows your stupidity."

That was our lawyer! I turned to Sam, who was watching Andy make a face at Jeeter.

Andy winked at us behind Josie's back, smiled, and pointed to her, whispering, "I couldn't get away with it, but my lawyer can. 'My' lawyer.

Tom knows how to pick 'em."

The lawyer stared at Jeeter again. "Since you're at a standstill doing nothing, Jeeter, I'd say you're done here. You've turned things upside down, but with what results?"

Jeeter noticed Clint Anderson, who'd returned from the police van in the driveway, walking in quietly. Clint was about my height and carried his belt with all the gadgets and a gun on it with authority. He was glued to Jeeter. His snarl and scowl said he was in the get-Andy-in-jail camp. Every time Jeeter said anything, he nodded and acted like Jeeter knew everything. Jeeter saw Clint arrive and figured he'd put on a show. "Think you're pretty high and mighty, Ms. Brinkley." He put a lot of emphasis on "Ms." as though it were an epithet. "Yeah. We're done."

"Just so you know, your client here"—he pointed to Andy—"is a cold-blooded killer, and he's going to get what's coming to him."

Josie stood there smiling at him, and he scowled. "Good. I'd hate to stay here much longer making sure you don't add anything to the evidence in this house."

Now Jeeter's face turned carmine red. He'd had too much. "Out of here," he said to the other cops. "All of you. Clear out. We're done in the house. We'll check the Madison car in the garage, and then we'll see who's smiling last." Turning to Andy, he pointed his index finger and said, "Next time I see you, I'll bring my handcuffs." He walked out, Clint Anderson following behind him like a puppy who hung on his every command. Could Clint be carrying out Jeeter's underhanded ideas to make Andy look guilty? I had no doubt.

I could hear him stomping down the stairs. He'd already left wet, muddy footprints on the way up. Oh, well. I was so thankful we'd called Josephine Brinkley. I wouldn't put it past Jeeter to plant evidence either. We all went down to the living room. The lawyer asked Sam to go out to the garage and make sure they supervised his search there.

"What are they searching for?" asked Andy.

Josie sat in a wingchair, pulling out her phone. "Tom said something about tire tracks at the Darnell house at the lake. That would be my guess. But why they want your jacket and clothes, I have not a clue. Even if you were at the crime scene, you didn't leave them there." Lance walked in with a laptop. "I'm sure this is yours, right?"

"Yeah," Andy said.

"I wouldn't put it past Jeeter to have downloaded whatever's on it, but he wouldn't know how. Could be one of the deputies did, though." Josie sighed. "Even if he found something incriminating, he couldn't use it in court because he didn't get it with a search warrant."

Sam said, "They're done in the garage. They took an impression of your tires. I saw them check the inside of the car, but I didn't see them take anything."

"Did you see anyone put something *in* the car?" I asked Sam.

He shook his head. "No, but I couldn't be everywhere."

"All right," Josie said. "I'm going to call Tom, fill him in on the night's evidence party, and keep him apprised in general. I don't trust Jeeter Crockett, but we're stuck with him. Don't say anything to the sheriff's department, either of you. Call me if something like this happens again."

"Does this mean I'm charged with the crime?" Andy asked.

"No. But if they show up and want to take you to the county jail, call me immediately."

Lance shuffled to the chair where our lawyer was sitting. "We can't thank you enough, Ms. Brinkley. Andy didn't do this. There's no way he could kill anyone."

Josie nodded. "I appreciate your sentiments. I hope if this goes to court, we have other people like you on the jury. In the meantime, we play a waiting game. Just go about your lives and hope they don't return."

"Actually," I said, "I think Andy's fingerprints are already in the system."

Josie paled. "Why? Please tell me he doesn't have any felonies."

Andy looked sheepish. "A little fraternity party that got out of hand."

I smiled. "I believe the photo in the college newspaper showed Andy with a lampshade over his head."

"And it will live forever on the internet," Andy said, a look of pride on his face.

I watched Josie sigh with relief.

Everyone cleared out, and I gave Andy and Lance big hugs. "Keep your chins up, you two. Andy didn't do this. You don't have anything to be afraid of."

Once Sam and I had settled back in his car, I grabbed some tissues out of my purse. Wiping tears from my eyes, I tried to pull myself together.

Sam leaned over and held me. "It's going to be all right. Andy didn't do this. They can't prove he did. You have to be strong. It'll turn out fine."

"I wish I felt that positive. But Jeeter Crockett is such a horrible person. He'd do anything to pin this on my brother."

"He doesn't have any evidence, Jill."

"I keep telling myself that, but with Jeeter, nothing is for sure."

Sam started the car. "He's innocent, and I have faith in his lawyer. She has Crockett's number, so she won't let your brother go to jail when he's innocent. Right now, they're just checking out the crime. If they thought Andy did it, they'd have arrested him by now."

As we pulled out of Andy and Lance's driveway and headed back toward my house, I tried to believe Sam's words. But I knew Jeeter Crockett and remembered innocent people filled prisons. So many had been investigated by various innocence projects. How could my brother's freedom be dependent on one nasty person like Jeeter Crockett? I didn't have a good feeling about any of this. Poor Andy. And though I loved my blond and handsome doctor, I still wished Tom were here. He was the expert on crime.

Chapter Eight

On Saturday morning, Louise and I were in my office examining the possible entries for the ghostly artwork exhibit, which would be a backdrop for our radio show. My office was not much more than a glorified closet. I had room for a desk, a chair, and a loveseat, all crowded into a tiny space. A set of file cabinets was squeezed in next to my desk, and I had to be sure to push in the drawers after use, or I'd fall over them getting up from my desk.

"Oh, look at that one," Louise said. She was pointing to a painting where a blue phosphorescent ghost stood out against a background of dark trees under a full moon. "So cool. Perfect for the exhibit."

I clicked to another entry. This one featured fog with a dark figure imposed in the middle of the white cloud. I clicked again. Flying sheets through dark forests. Clicked again. An old house with a face peering out the window. "Lots of ghosts, Louise. It'll be hard to cut these down to thirty."

"Keep clicking," she responded.

I clicked again. We saw an upper hallway of a ramshackle, derelict house with a ghostly figure superimposed against the wall. Several had cemeteries and full moons. I tapped on the return button, moving back to a photograph that had been entered. It had a double exposure of a ghostly figure. "Do you think this is an actual photograph of a ghost?" I asked.

"Beats me. Is there any information about the context?"

I scrolled down to check. "No. Only the name of the photographer, the size, and a few more details. But it doesn't say where it was taken."

"How many entries do we have?"

"Forty-five," I said. "The deadline is next Friday, so we're good to go. A few more will probably come in this coming week." I clicked to escape the page.

"Great. I'm going to go check the post office box for mail. Then I'll come back and inventory the gift shop."

"Not worried. I'll still be here when you return." I paused. "Louise, do you believe in ghosts?"

She thought for a moment. "Well, I don't personally. But my Aunt Lydia was shocked by what she claimed was a sixteenth-century knight in armor in her kitchen pantry."

I gasped. "What happened?"

"She offered him a cup of tea since she believed tea cured everything. But she was never the same and died a week later."

"How awful!"

"Some relatives didn't believe so. They thought she might have joined him, and they rode off together into the sunset."

Louise had some very peculiar relatives.

She left my office. I could hear her humming as she gathered her coat and boots. The bell rang on the door as she left. My phone on the desk pinged with a text.

Ms. Madison. Why r we buying 20 scripts of this play? We could easily photocopy from one. Much less expensive.
Ivan F. Truelove III, CPA

"Because, Ivan, it's illegal." I typed back. "Copyright law."

I walked out to the gallery and took a break. As I stared out the front windows, I could see some light snow falling, coating the slushy mess already on the ground. The first snowfall was always beautiful, gently falling through the pewter-gray skies and covering everything in a layer of white. But we were now at the end of January, and I was tired of the added effort it took to bundle up, blow the snow out of my driveway, clean off the car windows, or warm my little Austin Mini. As I stared out the window, I saw Tom's unmarked car circling the square. He was headed toward the police station.

I heard Andy's ringtone blare from my office. Strange. He hadn't texted or talked to me much lately. I marched back through the gallery, found it on my desk, and punched in "accept."

"Hi, Andy."

"Not Andy, it's Lance with his phone."

"Ah. What's up? Aren't you at work? And why are you on my brother's phone?"

"One answer at a time," he said. "Yes, I'm at work. I grabbed his phone because it was the closest one to pick up. The police are here."

"What?"

"Jeeter and two deputies. They just came in and are talking to Andy."

"Why?"

"I'm not sure. Hang on."

I heard the clunk as he set the phone down, then muffled voices. Whatever was going on? More muffled voices. Andy's voice yelling at someone. Background noise as Lance must have picked up the phone again.

"Jill?"

"Yes, still here."

"I think they're arresting him." I could hear his breathing through the phone, fast and labored. "Get ahold of your brother and call Josephine Brinkley. I'm heading to the sheriff's office with them. I'll take my car. Can't let him be there alone. Got it?"

"Yes," I said, punching off. So much for Sam's theory they would have arrested him before now. I hit Tom's speed dial number. Once I got Tom on my phone, we spoke quickly. I hung up, immediately dialing our lawyer. Luckily, she wasn't in court.

"Josie," I said as her secretary put me through to her, and she answered. "Lance called. Jeeter Crockett has arrested my brother. Can you head over to the sheriff's office?"

"Yes, I'm on my way."

There was nothing for me to do except wait. Louise was gone, which meant I was holding down the art center. Besides, I didn't know what I could do to help Andy. Tom and Josie were his best hopes. I remembered our conversation in which he admitted going over to Paul Darnell's cabin at the lake, leaving his fingerprints, and finding Quinn Parsons dead. Only a little lie to the police. I shook my head. Motive, means, opportunity. Add Jeeter, who didn't like Andy to begin with, and I knew my brother was in big trouble. I couldn't let him go to jail for a murder he didn't commit. It seemed like so much was out of my control. Even though he didn't kill Quinn Parsons, I was afraid his life was now in the hands of a deputy sheriff I didn't trust and a judge or jury I couldn't name or predict. Why, oh why, did he have to lose his temper and threaten Quinn in front of so many people?

I looked at my clock. Two minutes since I'd last checked it. Sit, I told myself. Think about who else might have a motive for this murder. My brother, of course, was the most obvious because he'd announced it to the world. Why, Andy? Why did you have to do something so stupid?

Who else? Sharon O'Brien had been awfully angry at that church meeting. Why wouldn't she be? The O'Briens were already married when the accident paralyzed him. And who was driving? Parsons. Finn couldn't have done it since he would have had to get out there with his wheelchair. That was impossible. I didn't know Branson Green's parents. Might they still be smoldering from losing their son? And there was Paul Darnell. How did he fit into all this?

Which left our family, the Madisons, who had lost both their parents due to Parsons' recklessness. I could take myself off the list. Tom, Lance, or Mary couldn't have killed Quinn. We weren't exactly the murdering kind. Not a lengthy list. If Angie and I were to help prove Andy's innocence, we'd have to do some snooping around to find out what else Parsons had done to make people angry. But first, it would make sense to check out Sharon O'Brien and the Greens. They certainly had motive and opportunity. Anyone could have pushed Quinn down the stairs. It wouldn't take much strength.

Where are you, Louise? I glanced at my phone and thought about calling her, but she'd be back soon. She'd only gone to the post office. Besides, what good could I do at the sheriff's office? Lance was there, maybe Tom, definitely our stalwart lawyer.

My phone played the *Law & Order* theme. Tom. I grabbed it quickly.

"Tom? What's going on?"

I heard a pause. Then, a long breath.

"Andy's been arrested. Jeeter put him in a cell, and I imagine there'll be a hearing about bail on Monday or Tuesday."

"What? Next week?"

"Yes. Now, Jill, please don't get your hopes up. This is a murder case. It's not likely he'll get bail."

I could feel tears welling in my eyes. Get yourself together, Jill. Sniffling, I said, "Does this mean he'll have to stay in jail all weekend?" I could picture my poor brother, alone in a cell, with nothing but a thin blanket and filthy mattress to sleep on. Obviously, I'd been watching too many crime shows.

"Yes. But he's safe there. I'll talk with Ms. Brinkley and see what we can do. Nothing for now. I can't be involved."

I thought for a moment. "So...you can't be, but what about Angie and me?"

"What about Angie and you?"

"There's no reason we can't research and snoop around. Surely, there are other people who had a reason to kill Quinn Parsons. He wasn't exactly a model citizen. You were in school with him. You'd remember some of the people he hung around with and what they did. Maybe there's a motive from way back when. Whoever it was could have been waiting for him to get out of prison. I think you, Lance, Angie, and I could put our heads together."

"I can't be involved in this, Jill."

"But who says you can't give us advice? Advice isn't like you're doing an investigation yourself. Right?"

I could hear him sigh on the other end of the phone. "I suppose not, but I don't want you and Angie getting into any trouble where you might get hurt. Quinn Parsons is dead. Someone means business."

"We'll be careful."

"I think I've heard that before. Let me think about it. Don't do anything rash in the meantime, got it?"

"Yes, Tom." I ended the call and considered how awful it would be for Andy to be in jail all weekend. If Andy were convicted of Quinn Parsons' murder, I might never see him again except through a glass window using a telephone. There must be a way to prove his innocence, but how?

Chapter Nine

The court scheduled Andy's hearing for Monday morning at nine o'clock. I'm not sure I slept all weekend. This morning, I felt groggy, as if I were moving and thinking in slow motion despite two cups of dark roast coffee. When I stared at myself in the bathroom mirror, I looked like a raccoon with dark circles around my eyes. Sam had picked me up and he looked as tired as I felt. His hours were long, but he was obviously worried about Andy's fate, too.

Tom, Mary, and Lance appeared as haggard as we did. As we sat on hard benches at the Lincoln County Courthouse in Apple Grove, I realized the last and only time I'd been in this courthouse was when Quinn Parsons was sentenced. But this day would be different. I gazed around the room, which was packed with people from both Edgington and Apple Grove. Conversations were vying with each other for volume. It was fairly loud as we waited for the court proceedings to begin. People were laughing. How could they have funny conversations when my brother was facing a murder charge? I looked at Sam's serious face and smiled as he reached over and took my hand. Once again, I thought about how supportive he was.

The courthouse had been built in the late 1800s. A wooden barrier separated the seats in the audience from the well of the court with a small swinging door to allow witnesses access. On the walls were photographs of judges from bygone days, their robes and glasses revealing the passage of time and change in styles. I only knew one of them. Judge Ron Spivey. He'd been my friend, mentor, and treasurer of my art center board, but he'd been murdered last year. What a terrible time. I wished he were here now to give me his gentle and always-helpful advice. He left me a pile of money in his will and the directorship of his insanely valuable art collection. What a joy it had been to lend out valuable paintings to share with other galleries. I still missed him and studied the portrait of his face.

I stared up at the judge's bench. It was a grim reminder that one person would be deciding my brother's fate if a jury convicted him. A shudder went through me, causing Tom to glance at me, worried. Lance was on my other side, his foot bobbing up and down in a jittery motion. I patted his hand, hoping to instill some of Sam's confidence.

Since Tom knew the courthouse, we sat behind the defense table so Andy would be in front of us. But with the wooden barrier a formidable presence, I wouldn't be able to reach out and touch him for assurance. My brother was in the hands of people I didn't know. The state of Illinois oversaw his fate in the form of a prosecutor I'd never seen before. It all seemed so unfair. I knew Andy was innocent, but the possibility he might be found guilty made my breathing flutter faster and my anxiety deepen. I could hear my heart beat a fast staccato in my brain, a sure sign my anxiety was out of control.

To calm myself, I shifted in my seat, checking out the rest of the courtroom. A few seats were still empty at the back. Angie slid into one of them, making eye contact with me. She waved a little wave, and her hand morphed into a thumbs-up. I smiled and gave her a thumbs-up, too, but my brain wasn't quite that confident. Sam turned also and, seeing Angie, gave her a smile. I watched Angie turn toward Martin Stewart and his wife sitting next to her and begin talking.

As I turned around, a rustling in front of us announced the arrival of the lawyers. Josephine came through a door behind the judge's bench with a man I didn't recognize. He must be the prosecutor. He was in his forties with premature balding. I noticed he walked with a limp. He and our lawyer were talking quietly and then separated to each take their own seats as we all awaited the judge and my brother.

No longer in a sweatshirt and sweatpants, Josie was dressed professionally in an indigo blue suit with a scarf around her neck in different shades of blue. She had that no-nonsense, capable air about her. Too bad she wasn't a criminal attorney. Today, she was helping Andy with his plea and his argument for bail.

I turned again and gave an encouraging smile to Angie in the back of the courtroom. Now, I saw no empty seats. In fact, a few people were standing against the back wall. It reminded me of Quinn Parsons' sentencing. My parents were loved by so many people in our small town. They all came out to hear his sentence. People crowded the hall outside the courtroom, and there was another large group in the street out front. When the judge read the sentence, a huge roar went up in the courtroom and out in the hallway. I remember first feeling the elation that he would pay for what he had done to our parents. But, as years went by, their absence still left a hollow spot in my heart. Nothing they did to Quinn Parsons would ever bring my parents back. I swallowed at my memory and turned back to the front of the courtroom. Justice was sure a strange concept.

A door opened at the far side of the room. I watched my brother come through it, followed by two deputies, Jeeter and Clint Anderson. Jeeter was smiling like he'd won the Irish Sweepstakes. Shock. That was my first reaction. Andy was in handcuffs, an orange jumpsuit, and his feet were shackled so he could only shuffle along. Now I was angry. Why did they think this was necessary? This humiliation when he was innocent? I turned to Lance and saw tears in his eyes. He was trying to wipe them away with an inconspicuous move of his fingers. Sam squeezed my hand, trying to keep calm but give me some confidence. Like Lance's, my eyes were wet, too, and I turned back to Andy.

He looked terrible. His hair was unkempt, dark circles surrounded his eyes, and I thought he'd lost weight, if it were possible in forty-eight hours. He shuffled slowly, his head down as if he didn't want to meet anyone's eyes. This wasn't my brother Andy, the crazy one who always made us laugh amid the worst moments of our lives. Andy, who I'd loved when I was a toddler and whose trusty hand I'd held wherever we went as little kids. I grabbed a tissue from my purse and tried to get hold of myself. I glanced at Tom, who was stoically watching our brother. Mary, too, had a tissue out mopping her face. Dear God, I was thankful our parents weren't here to see this. Lance reached over, took my hand, and gave it a hard squeeze. Somehow, this reassured me. I managed to take a deep breath and hold myself together.

Andy sat next to Josie without a glance in our direction. I saw her lean over to whisper something in his ear.

"All rise," the court clerk called out.

We stood as a woman in a black robe came into view behind the judge's bench. You couldn't tell much about her size in that robe, and even her height was hard to figure when she was so far above us. Her hair was black with several attractive silver streaks, and her eyes had that look of someone who would keep everything on track. The Honorable Delia Cummings called the court into session. Her voice had a strong, no-nonsense tone, and she settled in, looking down at all of us. I tried to figure out if her face held any kindness, but she had assumed a neutral expression.

"My, this is a full room for a Monday morning court session," she said. "Be aware, I tolerate no outbursts or talking in my courtroom if you are visitors. Now, council for the defense ready?"

"Yes, Your Honor," Josie said, rising and motioning Andy to stand also.

"Prosecution? Mr. Deery?"

"Yes, Your Honor." The prosecutor rose.

"Mr. Mitchum, please read the charges."

The court clerk rose and read the murder charge. The judge regarded Andy. "How do you plead, Mr. Madison?"

Andy mumbled something quietly while the judge gazed intently at him.

"My client pleads not guilty, Your Honor," Josie said.

"All right, then. I will set the trial date for three months ahead. May 1, 2017. Mr. Deery, have you considered your position on bail for the defendant?"

"Yes, Your Honor. The State believes no bail should be set. This was a heinous, premeditated murder, and the motive of the defendant was clearly announced for much of the community to hear. We believe Andrew Madison is a threat to the community. We would prefer he be remanded to jail awaiting trial."

"Defense, Ms. Brinkley?"

"Your Honor. Andrew Madison has not been proven guilty of this crime, which he vehemently denies perpetrating. He is an upstanding citizen, business owner, and family member who has no record of criminal activity. He does not possess a passport. He isn't a flight risk. We would, therefore, ask for a reasonable bail."

Judge Cummings shuffled papers, looking down at her desk. I held my breath.

"Despite your well-considered argument, Ms. Brinkley, I am inclined to keep Mr. Madison incarcerated awaiting trial. This was a heinous crime, and with a business, Mr. Madison has funds at his disposal. Therefore, I'm denying bail. The case will begin May 1, nine a.m., with time in between to file any motions the attorneys would like the court to consider."

She pounded a gavel, everyone stood, and it was over quickly. My brother would be in jail for the next three months. I shook my head. Unbelievable. How would he ever manage to get through three months? I watched him turn, and he glanced over at us for a moment. I saw resignation. This was after only forty-eight hours. What would three months do to him? Andy was a very physical person, always moving, always active. How would he manage in a small cell where he couldn't do any of that? That's the realization I saw on his face. I tried to smile, but it was impossible. How unfair, how unreal. His fate was totally out of his hands.

Tom leaned over the railing and said, "Don't worry, Andy. Josie has recommended a great criminal lawyer. We'll get you through this. We know you're innocent."

Andy didn't say anything. Just shook his head. The deputies moved him off toward the door he'd entered a few minutes earlier when this all began.

We filed out, following the crowd. In a corner of the hallway, the Madison family, plus Angie, Lance, and Sam, moved into a circle. My phone vibrated with a text. I'd turned the sound off and now turned it back on. Noticing it was Ivan Truelove, I deleted it. "Too busy now, Ivan," I whispered. "Trying to save my brother. As in more important than your pettiness."

Tom cleared his throat. "Josie recommended a criminal attorney in Edgington. I'll call today and retain him."

I nodded. "We need to get ourselves organized. Lance, Angie, and I will work on the details of the other possible killers since we know Andy is innocent. Mary, you are the one who sustains us all with your amazing recipes. If you can take food into the jail for Andy, it will keep his spirits up—along with his weight."

Mary nodded. "Consider it done."

"Tom, you have the contacts and can provide the information. Go back and check the details of our parents' accident. See who else might be in the mix as the killer. Angie, Lance, and I will research Parsons—his trial and his earlier life. Somewhere, there has to be a clue as to who might have done this. Sam, we'll come up with a job for you too. Just let me put my mind to it."

Tom was staring at me. "This makes sense, Jill. I can't leave any imprint on this, however."

"No problem," Angie answered. "Jill and I are pros at this, and Lance and Sam will be with us this time. Besides, you're checking on the accident, not Quinn's murder."

Sam said thoughtfully, "Perhaps they're one and the same."

"This time?" said Mary, just noticing those two words in Angie's statement.

"Well, I—" I sputtered. "Uh, you know. Angie and I have helped Tom solve a few crimes in the past. We're a pretty good team."

Mary smiled. "Don't let him worry about your safety. He worries on normal days."

"I have a call into the criminal attorney. I should hear from him today. Mary and I have talked it over." Tom took her hand and they both smiled at each other. "We can remortgage our house to pay the lawyer. We must have a top-notch defense for Andy."

"If I can help with the finances, just let me know," said Sam.

"Tom, you two are not going to do that," I said. "Judge Spivey left me plenty of money in his will. I hardly spend it. I know he'd approve of us using some of it to help Andy. He loved our family. You find the lawyer and leave the finances to me."

Tom bit his lip, looked at Mary and slowly nodded. "Okay."

I looked at each of them, knowing they'd do anything to help Andy. "Now

66

that we know what we're up against, we can figure out what to do next. The Madison family, plus Angie, Lance, and Sam, are a formidable team. We'll sort this out and find the real killer."

Chapter Ten

After the courthouse hearing, I walked back to the art center through the snowy paths while Sam went off on some mission. I noticed a teenager wiping the inside of the window at Turnberry's Hardware Store. Signs were up on the door for a mid-winter sale. Next door, Jinx Aubrey, whose brother was a policeman with Tom, waved at me from behind the checkout counter at Miller's Bookstore. I waved back. Dr. Chandler's office was next to the bookstore. Mary was his receptionist, so I figured he'd managed without her this morning. Apple Grove was a town of small businesses, and owners were empathetic when employees needed to deal with life problems, but I doubted very many, like Mary, needed to be in court to see their brother-in-law indicted for murder.

Louise had opened and was waiting for me. I explained what happened and sighed.

"We know Andy didn't do this," Louise said. "Anything I can do to help?"

I shook my head. "It's a matter of time. Three months seems like such a long time for him to be in jail. It's possible I might have to ask you to watch the center occasionally while I'm gone, figuring this out, but that's all I can think of right now. You are such a help, Louise."

"You know, my second cousin, Louie, ended up in jail for shoplifting."

"Seriously? Jail for shoplifting?"

"Yeah. It was a 98-inch flat screen."

"How could he do that? Wasn't it ridiculously heavy?"

"No one ever accused him of brains. Once he got out of the hospital—it fell over on him—they arrested him."

"At least he was guilty."

"Oh, yeah. Guilty as sin. Not like your brother." She turned to leave. "Like I said, I'm at your disposal. Right now, I'm going in to write some checks for you to sign. It's been pretty quiet this morning."

Normally, I would have asked her about her latest date from whatever dating website she was on this week, but somehow, I couldn't bring myself to ask. It was too mundane after the story of her cousin. How many people could Louise be related to?

I'd already decided I'd spend some time on the ghost artwork this morning. I'd eliminated several pieces and chosen others. While I was checking out a new entry, a pencil rolled off my desk, falling to the floor. I stared at it. We hadn't had any trains come through, no earthquakes, and nothing to cause it to hit the floor. I studied it. Was I losing my mind? Leaning over, I picked it up, laying it on the desk again. Getting back to my computer, I heard the hum of my phone. A text. I turned my phone over.

Ms. Madison. Do you have a full cast for your radio show? I could make a few suggestions. Or help with backstage work.
Ivan F. Truelove III, CPA

Ivan in our radio show? Now that would put a damper on rehearsals. I texted him back, explaining we were doing fine and had a full cast. Strange. He never volunteered to help with anything. I turned back to my computer, only to hear the pencil on my desk rolling. I stared at it, watching it roll off the desk again and onto the floor. Maybe my desk wasn't perfectly flat? But no, nothing had fallen from it before. This was weird. I leaned over, picked it up, and put it in a different spot. That should take care of it.

"Anytime You Need a Friend" played on my phone. Angie calling.

"Hey, Jill."

"Hey. I had a thought. I think we should start checking out Parsons' earlier life. High school, friends, drinking habits, rumors he was a drug dealer. You know, the usual stuff."

"Absolutely."

"We can start with the newspaper following Mom and Dad's accident. I remember sitting in the courthouse for the trial, but details about Parsons' life are not on the tip of my tongue. We might start there. We know some of his friends from when Andy was in high school. Of course, they might have good reasons to kill Parsons, but even talking to them might give us some ideas. You know, Darnells and O'Briens. It would be a start. Andy might have some ideas too, so when Lance and I see him, I'll ask him about possible suspects. Whatever we can find out could be important. Tom is great at synthesizing information, so if we find it, he can sort through it. I'll go to the courthouse and get a transcript of the Parsons' trial."

"Sounds good to me. Some of those guys from high school hang around at the bar on occasion. I might be able to pluck some information outta them."

"'Pluck?' When did you decide to 'pluck' information out of people?"

A pause. "Oh, I thought it sounded like a good way to express myself."

Was this Angie I was talking to? My best friend for twenty-five years?

"I'm trying to improve my speaking."

"Why? Since when?"

"Since I realized I spend most of my time around the bar, where patrons are not exactly Einsteins. When I hear them talk, I figure I need to be a cut above."

"'Patrons?' All right, pluck it is. Let's start with plucking. I'll stop in after I get the transcript." I was about to end the conversation when I remembered a question for Angie. "What are people saying around town about the murder?"

"Lots of different things, some bad, some good. Stop and think, Jill." Angie paused. "You know how people are. Lots of gossip, lots of social media, lots of talk, talk, talk. They were one hundred percent in your camp when your parents died. A raft of them figure Parsons had it coming, and Andy was within his rights to do the dirty deed."

"Wow." I stared at my desk as the pencil rolled across it again and dropped to the floor. I was not imagining it. "Angie, I think I have a ghost in the Lowry building."

"It's gonna have to wait until we deal with Andy. Put it on hold."

How do you put a ghost on hold? I asked myself.

After I hung up, I scrolled through my messages. There was a whole string between Andy and me, often funny, usually sarcastic. He was always playing practical jokes, cheering me up, or being generally silly. Now, I wish I could hear his ringtone, "Welcome to the Jungle." I scrolled through Lance's most recent messages. They'd hired the lawyer for Andy. He was collaborating with Lance to put together a defense. Lance said he was enthusiastic and confident, so there was that to hang my hopes on.

My phone popped with a news alert. I grabbed it and checked out the most recent story. The headline said it all. "Deputy Crockett Calls Press Conference." That was Jeeter. Why would he do this? Suddenly, I knew. To put more pressure on the prosecutor. He didn't play fair. I shouldn't expect him to. After what he'd put Andy through in high school, he simply didn't forget or forgive. This would make Tom livid. Jeeter had scheduled it for one o'clock tomorrow. We wouldn't have to do any "plucking" of information from Jeeter. We were going to have to stay one step ahead of his strategy, but I wasn't sure how we could do that.

The first thing I'd do is get the transcript. Then, Angie and I could do some snooping at the bar. Someone must know something valuable about Parsons in high school. Angie and I would do some "plucking."

Chapter Eleven

Thelma Davis, her large bulk sitting in regal majesty at the main desk of the court clerk's office, greeted me when I showed up to request a transcript of Quinn Parsons' trial. She was the mother of one of my high school friends, and I was well aware no one oversaw the Lincoln County Courthouse's files but Thelma. Grown men feared her. Neat piles of folders sat on her desk, anchored by a dish of chocolates. Fortunately for me, her daughter and I had remained friends after high school. Thelma liked me.

"Well, Jill Madison, as I live and breathe. I haven't seen you, darlin', in a long time. I guess you've been keeping yourself at that art center. I hear remarkable stories about it. Your mama and pappa would be proud."

I walked from the doorway to the counter as she rose from her chair and moved forward to greet me. "You're looking great, kiddo, and I hear you have a handsome doctor in your life."

I think I must have blushed. "Hi, Thelma. It's so good to see you. And yes, I am seeing Sam Finch, one of the ER doctors at the hospital."

"He's the blond dish my daughter's mentioned, stars in her eyes. She had to take my grandson to the ER to get a splinter out of his foot. Dr. Finch is on her 'Mr. Wonderful' list as far as she's concerned. Well, what can I do for you this fine Monday morning?"

"I'm here to get a copy of the Quinn Parsons' transcript. His trial, you know."

"Ah." She paused. "This have something to do with your poor brother in jail?"

"Not exactly. The accident that killed my parents seven years ago was on my mind, and I thought maybe I should refresh my memory of the trial. Not sure if it could help Andy, but who knows? It doesn't hurt to remind myself what happened then."

"I'm really sorry about Andy." She shook her head and tut-tutted. "I don't know anyone in town who believes he could do such a terrible thing. Maybe there's a serial killer on the loose."

I smiled. "I kinda doubt that, Thelma. I think you're safe. Also, I appreciate your kind comments about Andy. Our family is devastated by this injustice. Anyway, can you run off a transcript for me? I'll pay whatever it costs."

"Three-fifty will take you the whole way. Hang on, and I'll go look for it in my computer. Seven years ago, you say? Hardly seems like so long ago. Let's see what I can find, sweetheart. Monday afternoons are pretty quiet here."

I watched as she plodded over to her desk and pulled up a window on her computer. It didn't take her long.

"Ah, here it is. Hang on, and I'll have it for you in a jiffy. Printer's out in the supply room." She waddled out through a door on the far end of the room.

I could vaguely hear the printer start to copy the pages out in the other room. The door opening behind me was much louder. I turned to look at the new customer and saw it was Jeeter. What luck.

"Well, Jill Madison. Strange running into you here. Got court business?" he said, removing a toothpick from his sneering mouth.

"Nothing to worry yourself about, Jeeter."

He walked over to the counter, and I could feel his breath on my neck. Just a bit too close in my personal space. I moved back several steps, hoping Thelma would show up soon. Jetter was an expert at using his body to intimidate people. "Just what're you doing here?"

"As I said, Jeeter, none of your business."

"Well, Thelma's kinda slow these days." He moved a couple steps toward me. "You know, sticking your nose in the business of the sheriff's department isn't a safe thing to do."

"Are you threatening me?"

About that time Thelma came out of the supply room with a pile of papers in her arms. "Jeeter, are you harassing this young lady? I won't have that."

His face clouded at the word. "Harassing? That's a strong word. Now, Thelma, you know me."

"Exactly. That's why I asked you. Jill is a personal friend of mine, and I'd hate to think you're giving her mean words or threatening her."

"Well, that depends," he said.

"On what?" Thelma and I both said at the same time.

"She sticking her nose in my business? The sheriff's office business? The murder investigation of Quinn Parsons?"

Thelma slid the papers into a folder and came up to the counter, handing the folder to me. "That'll be three-fifty," she said. "And as for you, Jeeter Crockett, I'll have you know them papers have nothing to do with Quinn Parsons' murder."

Crockett was watching me as Thelma gave me a wink. He gave me one long look and turned to go. "You see that you stay out of your usual nosey investigating," he said. "I remember what trouble you got into with that body found in the art center basement. You'd be wise to stay out of your brother's poor decisions. Before long, you won't be seeing him much except behind glass."

"My only concern, Deputy Sheriff Crockett, is to make sure you don't plant any evidence that wasn't at the crime scene to begin with."

Jeeter pointed at me. "You watch your mouth, girl," he said and walked out the door.

Thelma looked at me. "Why someone like that is in law enforcement I don't know. And to think he plans to run for the sheriff's position when the sheriff retires." She shook her head. "No good can come of that."

"Thanks, Thelma, for the papers and for the kind words. I'm in total agreement with you on Jeeter Crockett. Unfortunately, he has my brother's life in his hands right now, and our whole family is uncomfortable with that turn of events." I slid three one-dollar bills and two quarters across the counter to her.

"You just watch your back, Jill. He's a hard man to cross."

As soon as I got in my car, I opened the folder and scanned the information. The transcript wasn't terribly long. I looked through the various witnesses, which included Darnell, O'Brien, and a couple other people I vaguely remembered. Parsons' testimony was apologetic. He didn't remember a lot, since he'd been drinking and was hurt in the accident. But he did talk about his regret and apologized over and over for the damage he'd done. "Damage?" Like killing our totally innocent parents and one of his friends and putting another in a wheelchair for life? My anger grew stronger as I read through his testimony. Why? Why do irresponsible people like this get to kill totally kind and generous people like my parents in a moment of stupidity?

I closed the folder, took several long breaths, and tried to regain my composure. Next stop, Priscilla's to see what Angie and I could find out about Parsons in high school.

Although it was afternoon, quite a few patrons were hugging the bar at Priscilla's when I walked in. Angie came over and motioned me to a booth across the room. I followed her, sliding into the booth.

"What's up?" she asked.

"Picked up the transcript of Parsons' trial. Wasn't much to see except his apologies for all the damage he'd done."

She nodded. "At least you have it back in your mind. Maybe something will click from it."

I sighed. "Any of those guys over there from Parsons' time in high school? I thought we might 'pluck some information' from them." I chuckled.

"Now, don't you make fun of my hard work to better myself."

"Sorry. Just had to mention it. I've forgotten it, totally."

She squinted her eyes to identify the bar patrons. "Looks like Len Walker and Fred Sanders. They might have been about Parsons' age. Probably in their late thirties, I'd think."

"Let's go for it," I said.

We walked back over to the bar, both of us moving behind the counter. Len Walker, a scowl on his face, was hunched over a beer from the tap. I recognized him because Andy had spoken of him occasionally back in the day. He played football at the high school, offensive tackle. He was known for his quick temper, if I remembered correctly.

"Len," Angie said. "Suppose we could have a few moments of your time?"

He was staring up at a game on the screen behind us, but he broke off to look at Angie. "Sure, Ang. Anything to help you."

"This is my friend, Jill Madison."

"Yeah. Think I've seen you around. Tom and Andy's sister."

"So true. We were wondering, Mr. Walker, if you remembered a guy from high school named Parsons. Quinn."

"Why'd you want to know about Quinn?"

My breath stirred because it was obvious he knew Parsons. Actually, after his murder, I was sure everyone in town knew of him.

Angie plowed right in. "One of the seniors at Jill's art center is going to write a piece for the newspaper about him, and we told her we'd try to procure some information from people who knew him."

"'Procure?' What's that? Sounds illegal."

"She means we're looking for quotes about Quinn Parsons from people who knew him. We'll give her the information." I pulled my cell from my purse, holding it out. "Mind if we record you?"

He looked at my phone, then looked at Angie. "I suppose it don't hurt. He can't do nothing to me now. Yeah, I knew Quinn Parsons back in the day. It's tough to talk about him without using words that ain't fit for a lady's ears."

"You found him an abomination?" Angie said.

Len looked at her strangely. "If you mean did I like him, no. He wasn't a guy you'd like. Always out for himself, looking to make a buck, never keeping his word, a darn liar. That's the way I'd describe him."

"Did you ever hear anything about him selling drugs?" I asked.

He took another swallow of his beer. "Well, I hate to speak ill of the dead, but yeah. Everyone knew if you needed anything, Quinn could supply it. Now, mind you, I wasn't never a customer. But some guys I knew was regulars, and I'd say he had quite a business going."

Angie closed her pocket dictionary. "Len, do you have any idea who the purveyor of the drugs was?"

He looked at her like she was speaking Latin.

"She means, do you know who furnished the drugs?" I translated.

"Oh." He thought for a moment. "No. Like I said, I never used his business. Sorry, I ain't much help."

"That's okay," Angie said. "You've helped a lot, Len. At least we know from someone who knew him in high school that he was exactly what we expected. Thanks."

"My pleasure, Angie."

He went back to his beer as we walked to the end of the bar to reorganize our approach.

"Angie," I whispered, "I don't think bettering your English with these guys is going to work. Save it for when you're in more intellectual company."

"Oh. All right. I guess that didn't suggest itself to me."

I rolled my eyes. "Let's check out Fred Sanders. Maybe he knows something."

We casually sauntered down to the other end of the bar. Fred was also nursing a beer, watching the news on the Fox News channel. He was thin, balding, and looked like he needed some nutritious food instead of beer.

"Hi, Fred," Angie began.

"Angie," he answered, "where've you been all my life? Oh, yeah. I forgot. You and Wiley. Well, that's okay. What's up?" He smiled.

"This is my friend, Jill Madison."

He put his hand out and shook mine. "Andy and Tom's sister. Sorry to hear about your brother's problems."

"Thanks," I said. "We're hoping to help him with what information we can find in talking with people. It occurred to Angie and me that you were about the same age as Quinn Parsons. Did you know him in high school?"

He nodded. "Oh, yeah. He had a nickname: the druggist."

"Really?" Angie said. "Why was that?"

"You can about guess. He supplied most of the county with drugs."

I put my phone out and said, "Mind if I record your recollections?"

"No problem. What can he do to me now? If I can help Andy Madison, I'm glad to talk."

"Thank you, Fred," I said. "Do you know what kind of drugs he sold?"

He thought about it for a moment. "Well, I know he sold weed. But he sold other stuff too, because I remember one of the guys on the basketball team went to the ER with an overdose. He never talked, and Parsons never got arrested. I had the feeling it wasn't just Quinn. Other people were backing him, and they weren't people to mess with."

Angie spoke up. "Any names? Remember who else was working with him?"

He shook his head. "Naw. I didn't do that stuff, so I was never around him much. Wouldn't have wanted to be anyway. He was no good. Didn't surprise me someone knocked him off." He glanced at me. "Oh, I don't mean your brother, Jill."

"No offense taken," I said.

"Anything else you can remember about him?"

Before he answered, a voice I recognized said, "These ladies bothering you, Fred?"

I hadn't noticed Jeeter Crockett come in because I'd been concentrating on Fred Sanders. "Jeeter, get lost. This isn't your business."

He looked at me, his habitual toothpick rolling around in his mouth. "It is if you're running around town stirring up trouble over your brother's trial."

Fred turned on his barstool and looked at Jeeter. "These ladies were asking me who I favor in the Sunday night football game this weekend."

Jeeter looked at him for a long minute. Then he said, "Football, my foot."

Wiley strolled over from the other end of the bar. "Anything we can do for you, Officer?"

Jeeter looked at each of us, then said, "Naw. All's good. Just try to keep your wife and Jill here in line. I'm tired of them running around investigating my business."

Wiley said, "Last I heard it's a free country. And keeping my wife in line isn't something I ever do. That's why she's still my wife."

Angie looked at him and smiled.

78

Jeeter, defeated, turned and left the bar.

"He is, well, something I don't say in front of ladies," Fred said.

"Wow. That's the second time we've heard that today," Angie said.

I looked at the door closing behind Jeeter. "I can't figure out how he always knows where I am. He turns up all the time. Like he's following me."

"Might be just a coincidence," Wiley said.

"With Jeeter Crockett, I don't believe in coincidence," I answered.

Chapter Twelve

L ance and I were escorted to the visitors' room at the county jail on Tuesday morning at ten. It was a large room with neon lights in the ceiling, several of them dark. Five or six round tables sat forlornly waiting for visitors. We were the only ones. The walls were painted an ugly gray, occasionally a bit of paint peeling off here or there. Signs with various rules cluttered the wall near the door where we'd come in. We weren't to touch the prisoners or hand them anything. We'd been searched before we were allowed to come into this room. It was a sad, toneless place. Any cheerfulness that might have been here had been sucked out of the room by an understanding of its purpose. I smelled the lovely combination of staleness and sweat.

I glanced at Lance after we sat in plastic chairs at one of the tables, and his face looked as miserable as I felt.

"Lance. We must be upbeat, confident. We can't let Andy see how worried we are."

"Agreed," he said and sat up straighter. "I'll try."

The door opened. Deputy Eddie Brant, a friend of Tom's, came through with my brother. Our whole family had known Eddie for years. A little older than Andy, he'd been with the county sheriff's office since college. I knew he was married with a set of twin boys. Andy had handcuffs on but no leg shackles. The saffron orange jumpsuit didn't go with his complexion, the artist in me thought. I caught myself and smiled.

"I didn't expect visitors," he said. He sat as Brant connected Andy's handcuffs to a ring on the table and turned to leave.

"You have thirty minutes," Eddie said, checking his watch. "And no touching the prisoner. Sorry, it's a rule."

"Thanks, Eddie," said Andy.

Brant left, and we were all alone. But the presence of cameras in two corners of the room reminded me to keep my distance. I wanted to hug my brother, but I knew I couldn't.

"How are they treating you?" Lance asked.

He thought for a moment. "Okay. I have my own cell. They check on me every so often, but time passes like a century. Way too slow with nothing to do. No cell phone. No laptop. No guitar. Driving me crazy."

I reached for something to say. "Are they—are they feeding you well?" I asked.

"Nothing to write home about, but it's okay."

"We can ask at the desk if Mary could bring you some of her great home cooking. We need to keep your strength up."

Lance looked at Andy and almost reached out to touch his hand. "The business is fine. You don't need to worry."

My brother gave us both a curious look. "You mean people in town want to buy gift items from the store of a murderer?"

"Oh, Andy. No one thinks of you like that," I said.

He turned his eyes to me. "A bit hard to believe."

"Tom is searching for evidence to exonerate you," Lance said. "You know he's really good at his job. He'll find out what's going on. But he has to stay below Jeeter's radar."

He took a deep breath. "I wish I'd never gone to Parsons' church meeting. Getting drunk to begin with wasn't exactly the smartest idea either."

I swallowed. "You didn't know he was going to be murdered. How could you have?"

"I know. But I keep going over that night in my head. Over and over. I remember driving over to Darnell's house on the lake. I pounded on the door, but no one came. When I tried the handle, it wasn't locked. I pushed and the door moved open slowly. All the lights were on. I called out to Parsons, but no one answered. It was kinda eerie."

81

"Did you hear anything? Did you notice any objects left out or anything unusual?" I asked.

He shook his head. "No one there. Total quiet."

"Hmm," Lance said. "Why did you go out to the back stairs?"

"I tiptoed through the house and found no one. I opened the door from the kitchen onto the deck, which was totally dark. I turned on a light switch near the doorway and looked around as the deck lit up. That's when I saw this bundle of clothing at the bottom of the stairs. I called out again. Nothing. After I wobbled down the stairs and sidled alongside the body, I realized it was Parsons."

"Did you see if he was still breathing?" I asked.

"Yeah. I think so. But his eyes were wide open. I figured he was gone."

"You didn't think to call 9-9-1?" asked Lance.

He slowly shook his head. "I was sure they'd think I did it. I moved around the side of the house, up a flight of stairs, and left."

"Well, that would account for your fingerprints and your tire tracks," I said.

"Makes sense, but why did they want my clothes from that night?"

Lance steepled his hands, his elbows on the table. "I have not a clue. Maybe Tom can find out."

"I keep thinking and thinking. I keep wondering if I could figure out something I missed, a clue that would point to the killer, but no matter how hard I go back through it, nothing comes to mind." He sighed. "Whenever I try to sleep, my brain won't stop streaming that video with Parsons at the bottom of the stairs."

I looked at Andy and Lance, swallowed, and pulled myself together. "Here's what I think. We know you didn't do this. There must be someone else out there with a motive to kill Quinn Parsons. He was only back a week or so, plenty of time for someone he'd hurt to decide to kill him. They only needed the opportunity. Pushing him down a flight of stairs sure eliminates a murder weapon. But who?"

Andy put both his hands out as far as the handcuffs would let him. "I keep thinking about that too. It must be someone from his past. He wasn't here long enough to give anyone else a reason to give him a fatal shove. It could have been an event that happened before Mom and Dad's accident. We're seven years out. How am I supposed to remember who it might be?"

"It might have been something from high school. You weren't here in college, so your path and Quinn's wouldn't have crossed during that time. Try putting your mind on the past as far as high school. Think about what might have happened back then," said Lance.

"Oh, man. That was a while ago. I don't know. I wasn't really in his social group, so to speak, in high school."

Lance brightened. "Who was?"

He thought for a moment. "Mostly the guys in that car accident plus Darnell. He hung with him, O'Brien, and Green. I kinda felt sorry for Parsons because I had this feeling he didn't have much of a home life, but I was never around any of those guys much."

"Obviously, Green is out of the picture. I don't see his parents going to the house and shoving Parsons down a flight of stairs. But you never know," I said. "If they were as angry as we were, maybe one of them paid Parsons a visit that night."

The door opened. "Time's up," said Deputy Brant. "Sorry, guys. You'll have to go."

For a brief moment, I saw fear in Andy's eyes.

Lance and I stared at my brother. The urge to touch his hand or hug him was excruciating, but the deputy was standing there watching, and I didn't want to do anything that might make them decide we couldn't come back to see Andy.

He sighed deeply. "It's okay. I'm fine. You don't have to worry about me. I can manage this."

I put two fingers to my lips, kissed them, and pointed them toward my brother, battling my emotions not to cry. My lip quivered, and I bit it.

As we all stood, Deputy Brant took Andy's arm and shepherded him out the door.

We walked to Lance's car. I remembered one of Andy's experiences in high school and told Lance. Andy was in an auto mechanics class that was a mix of all ages. Lots of upperclassmen. Jeeter was in the class. Andy said something stupid, going for the laugh, and Jeeter pushed him up against the wall with a crowbar in his hand. The teacher looked over about that time, sorted it out, and sent Jeeter to the office. The next week, Tom's car had four punctured tires. Since Andy rode to school with him, we figured it was Jeeter Crockett. Of course, there was no evidence.

"How did someone like that become a deputy sheriff?" Lance asked.

"Your guess is as good as mine. I think the job gave him the opportunity to keep bullying people."

I stole a look at Lance. We both had lost, unhappy expressions on our faces.

"We just have to work harder," Lance said, trying to show a confidence I was sure he didn't feel.

Tuesday seemed like an endless day. After lunch, I saw Angie among the crowd shuffling into the high school gym, and it wasn't hard to meet her and take a seat about halfway up the bleachers. What a crowd for our small town. That might explain why they were holding this in the high school gym. Large venues were not abundant in Apple Grove. The elementary schools and junior high had been built within the last twenty years, but our high school had a 1910 cornerstone. Made of solid brick, it rose two stories anchored by a basement level. Every time I walked in, I remembered some of the stunts Angie and I had pulled. We were lucky our faces weren't on "wanted" posters in the front hallway.

"Hey."

Angie yawned, a result of working well into last night. "Hey back. I can't believe all these people can turn out in the middle of a Tuesday afternoon. Doesn't anyone work anymore?"

I plopped down beside her. "School's going on, so a lot of them don't have kids to watch. Some work from home. From what I remember, news conferences are for journalists. But Jeeter must have something up his sleeve to open this to the public. You know, it occurred to me on the way over that Sheriff Detweiller announced he was going to retire this coming June. His accident—falling downstairs—was the last straw. Guess who might run for his job?"

I stared at her incredulously. "You're kidding."

"Putting a so-called 'murderer' in prison for life might be what he's planning to get him that position."

"Speak of the devil."

Jeeter and two of the deputies meandered in through an inner door that opened out to a school hallway. He had the principal with him. Jeeter was dressed like a detective now—creased dark slacks, a brown sports coat and taupe tie, and a bulge where a shoulder holster was strapped under his coat. Still, I thought he had a smarmy look on his face. Clint Anderson was one of the deputies, and he watched Jeeter's every move. They walked to the microphone as the principal tested it, showing Jeeter the button to turn it on.

Several screeches ensued. Then, "Good morning, good citizens of Apple Grove." A murmuring answer went through the crowd. I looked around us. Maybe a hundred-plus people, enough to spread the word, unfortunately.

Jeeter leaned into the microphone, holding up a "quiet down" hand to the crowd as they began to settle in. "Good morning, fellow citizens. Today, I bring you good news. Our streets and homes are safe from a killer due to the hard work of my department."

"*His* department?" Angie whispered.

"Shh."

"A short while ago one of our lost citizens, Quinn Parsons, came home to Apple Grove seeking forgiveness for a terrible mistake he'd made in his past. He was a regretful person, looking for his hometown to forgive him. Having conquered alcohol, he'd taken some college classes, found his God, and was simply seeking a quiet life. He was born and raised right here in Apple Grove, attending this school we're currently meeting in. Parsons had changed, and he was looking to settle down."

I almost expected the crowd to call out, "Praise the Lord." Jeeter was laying it on thick.

The deputy's head shook dismissively. He smirked, flicking an invisible thread from the arm of his immaculate sports coat. The pause was just enough to give people time to think. I glanced around. A few people nodded their heads in approval. This was not good.

"What did he get, right here in his hometown, a place that should have been a refuge? He got Andy Madison, who, it seems, didn't believe in forgiveness."

The last phrase came out with a coating of sarcasm. He paused again to give people time to think. I had to hand it to him. The audience was with him. Their expressions and the silence said they were eating it up.

"We have tons of evidence, most of which we're saving for his trial. But I can tell you this: he blasted his motive in front of an entire congregation over at the church down the road. He was angry; he was looking for revenge." He shook his head again, a dismissive nod. "His fingerprints are all over the murder scene. The tire tracks from his car are right in front of the house where he parked that night. No doubt. We have our man."

Angie turned to me and whispered. "Can he do that? Actually talk about evidence before the trial even begins?"

I let out a hard breath. "Who's going to stop him?"

"But what about finding a jury? Lots of these people might be on the jury."

"I don't know. That's the point. He's preaching to the jury pool, trying Andy in the media. As for other evidence, Tom would know about it, but he's out of the loop."

"My fellow citizens, due to the diligent work of your sheriff's department, you can sleep comfortably tonight, knowing we are on the job, providing security. All right. Do you have any questions I can answer?"

Angie whispered, "That sounded more like a campaign speech."

"I know."

A woman three bleachers from the front row asked, "Anita Thompkins. Did you consider anyone else as a possible suspect?"

"Yes, Ms. Thompkins, we did at the beginning of our investigation. Sadly, for this killer, we had him cold. Open-and-shut case. Of course, the lawyers and such will fiddle around for months making sure Madison's so-called 'rights' are not disturbed. But I personally oversaw this investigation. I can guarantee you we have our man."

Another person, Mr. Sells, the pharmacist, stood. "Did Madison try to run or take off?"

Now Jeeter patted his dark hair and turned to his deputies for a moment, chuckling. Then, turning around, he said, "No. He was sure he'd covered his tracks. He had no idea who he was dealing with."

"But if he didn't try to run, I'd think he had nothing to hide," Mr. Sells replied.

Jeeter attempted an unfamiliar smile that spoke of patience. "We'll see how that goes once his trial starts."

"What is the penalty for what he's done?" called out Nell Swanson, a woman who worked in the office of the newspaper. "I know Andy, along with his family. I'm not quite sure I can believe all this."

Ah, the voice of reason. Thank you, Nell Swanson.

Jeeter leaned into the microphone. "Well, in Illinois, sadly, we don't have the death penalty. However, we're talking life in prison here."

Several people in the audience gasped. A silence fell over the room. Lots of muttering and hushed conversations could be heard among the crowd. I felt a knife stab my heart. Life in prison. Not for my brother. He wouldn't survive that.

The principal took over the microphone. "Well, that's it for now, folks. Thank you for coming."

"At least there was some blowback from people who know and believe in Andy," Angie whispered.

I nodded as I watched people leave. They began to stand and climb down the bleachers. A few men moved toward the deputies and some shook Jeeter's hand. Angie and I just sat there, stunned. The words 'life in prison' kept circling around my brain.

"Well, not everyone," I said grimly. Jeeter had used the brief meeting to whet peoples' appetites. As I climbed down the bleachers, I knew Jeeter had the momentum. This story would be discussed in every coffee shop, across the back fences, and around the dinner tables. Andy was the topic of speculation, and plenty of conspiracy theories would be out there since people all had their own ideas.

Late in the afternoon, I waited for Sam at Angela's Ice Cream, one of our favorite places for a break from work. Sam and I came here for ice cream two or three times a month. When I thought about the way we'd met, I was shocked that this romance ever happened. The first time he'd laid eyes on me at the ER, I was covered in sweat and vomit. A murderer had kidnapped me, tried to kill me, and had the audacity to make me miss my first exhibit at my art center job. Now that really made me mad! I'd worked so hard on that exhibit, only to miss it. By the time I'd rescued myself and my brother Andy had taken me to the ER, I looked like someone who'd been through a tornado and smelled like the city dump. I can't believe Sam and I connected a few months later. So sweet of him. He showed up at the art studio in the backyard of my house, and I was hooked.

I checked the window to see if Sam was coming, but no. He was late. That wasn't unusual with his job.

If I were Sam, between our first ugly meeting and my brother in jail, I'd run as far away from me as possible. But not Sam. Nothing perturbed him. We'd dated for six months. Lately, I'd thought about mentioning the possibility of moving in with me. But I hadn't mentioned it. How amazing it would be to wake up in the morning with him by my side. Actually, six months didn't seem like very long. I could hear my mother's voice on that one. She used to have a rule when I lived in Chicago that she wouldn't even meet any boyfriend until we'd dated six months. That would be now with Sam, and I think she and my dad would have approved. Ah, there he is.

The door opened with a tinkling bell and Dr. Sam saw me, a look of joy on his face. How could I have any doubts? Sam was always so put together, even after working a long shift at the hospital. His smile brightened my afternoon, especially when I considered the morning I'd had. Soon, I was eating Blubbering Blueberry ice cream, while Sam was munching on Lemon Crunch. He reasoned the nuts made it healthy. How could you be sad while eating ice cream?

"You look lovely today," he said. "I like that shade of blue on you."

"Well, thank you. Blue is my favorite color. Has been since I was little."

He crunched on more nuts.

"What are the nuts in that ice cream?"

He examined the cone. "I think they're pecans. In little pieces."

"Ah." I took a bite of my cone, savoring the sugary sweetness. We'd already talked on the phone about the press conference. Sam tried to cheer me up. The door of the shop opened, a bell chiming, and who should stroll in but Jeeter Crockett with Clint tagging along behind him.

Jeeter nodded to me. I ignored him. I didn't want to talk to him. What a horrible person. Sam and I silently crunched on our cones looking in each other's eyes while Jeeter and Clint were busy ordering ice cream. After they paid, Jeeter turned around and was about to go out the door. Instead, he walked over toward our table, Clint a few paces behind him.

"Nice day. Good to see you're getting ice cream rather than playing amateur detective."

Sam stood, but before he could say anything I answered, "It's a free country, Jeeter. I can do whatever I want. My brother's innocent, and the truth will come out."

"The truth? Ha! In that case, you can look forward to prison visits."

"I'll be keeping an eye on you. And checking in on my brother," I answered. He chuckled in a snide kind of way.

"Oh, and making sure you don't invent evidence," I called out.

At that comment, he moved toward me, but Sam sidestepped between us. Clint strode up to Sam in case Jeeter needed a backup. Jeeter stared at Sam, decided he didn't want to carry it further, then turned and went out the door. Just like bullies. If it were little me they were after, they'd bring it on. But Sam was closer to their size and in great shape.

"He's an arrogant guy," observed Sam. "I gather he's the one in charge of the investigation."

"Yes. He wants everyone to know it. Sometimes I think he's following me. I don't know how." I shivered and looked around. "He's always a few steps ahead or behind me."

"Well, they're gone, and that Anderson appears to be his acolyte, so let's talk about a happier topic," said Sam, wadding up his napkin.

"The rehearsals have begun for *The Canterville Ghost*. Evan Shelly's running the show, but I hope he has patience. I've watched a couple of rehearsals. These are amateur performers, but their enthusiasm makes up for their lack of experience."

"I'd guess once they get some rehearsing under their belts, they'll relax and have a good time."

"Absolutely," I said. "However, I notice they have a bit of trouble figuring out when to use the sound effects. A door closes, and five sentences later you hear it." I laughed at the memory. "Speaking of ghosts, I think I may have one in the art center."

Sam's expression was worth a million bucks. He stared at me, realized I wasn't joking, and smiled. "You don't believe in that silly stuff, do you?"

"Not usually, but I can't explain the crazy things happening in my office lately. Angie says ghosts can move objects."

"Angie?"

"Yes, she's read a lot about it on the internet."

"Does she understand the internet has a lot of misinformation?"

"Not sure. She thinks we should download a ghost-hunting app to see if these weird things are truly showing the presence of a ghost. I think it would make more sense to find out about the history of the building. If a ghost is haunting it, there must be some gruesome or sad event in its history. Why would it be hanging around the old Lowry building?"

He smiled. "Sorry. As a man of science, I don't believe in ghosts."

"I'm not sure I do either, but I can't explain the sudden chill that comes over me for no reason, or objects randomly falling off my desk. It's as if someone or something is trying to get my attention."

"You've been worrying too much about Andy. I can understand why."

I thought about that for a moment. Seriously, that's all he's got? The hysterical woman theory. But I shushed that point in my head. "You could be right. I feel like I'm under a lot of pressure at the art center with the radio show and the art exhibit coming soon. I've neglected the judge's artwork a bit lately, you know, the collection of paintings I'm now responsible for loaning out to other galleries. All this horrifying news about Andy has pushed me over the edge a bit. I've been anxious, and my sleep has been off."

Sam stood, a signal to head back to the art center. "You'll get it straightened out. I know you will. Once the radio play's over, you can relax. I talked with Lance yesterday. He seems confident this new lawyer is a real go-getter. He thinks if anyone can get Andy off, he can."

"Tom says the same. I think he knows the guy. Well, Lance and I are going to see Andy at the jail. I'm hoping to cheer him up."

He looked at his watch. "I've gotta get back. I'll call you tonight?"

"Absolutely."

He reached out, pulled me into his arms, and I felt all shivery. I turned my face up to his and we kissed, long and sweet.

On the way out the door, my phone pinged with a text. Ivan. Not at all a cheerful note to end on.

> Any chance you need a volunteer to ruin lines? I have some extra time.
> Ivan F. Truelove III, CPA

I think that's "run" not "ruin," but, come to think of it, you probably could ruin lines, Ivan.

Chapter 13

Priscilla's Pub was rocking by the time I got off work on Tuesday. I put in some extra hours after Louise left since I'd been at the jail, the news conference, and the ice cream shop most of the day. Louise was so helpful to cover for me. I had stopped for some food at my house and a change of clothes. Tom was meeting us here to talk about what he'd found out.

I walked in, blinking my eyes to accommodate the change from dark to light. Strangely, I saw Paul Darnell over in a corner drinking by himself. I hadn't seen him here in ages. Stopping at the bar, I checked in with Wiley. As always, he brought me my favorite beer of the moment, Bent River Uncommon Stout.

"Hey, Wiley. How's it going?"

Wiley leaned over and looked down the bar at the corner where Darnell was sitting. "Well, Paul's been around more than usual drowning his sorrows. Don't know what's up with him. Anyway, other than that unusual occurrence, it's been pretty busy. But it is a Tuesday."

"Thanks for the info. And the beer." I hoisted it in the air, leaning the neck of the bottle toward him.

"The gang's all here, well, except Andy. I think they're cooking up a plot. They appear to be talking serious business. Angie's there too. Don't worry. I have bail money." He winked at me.

"Okay. See you later." I wandered over to the far side of the dance floor to add myself to a full table. Lance, Angie, Tom, and Sam. They were in serious conversation, but it stopped as I sat. "Oh, don't stop talking on account of me."

"I was describing our trip to the jail. Filling Tom and Sam in on what Andy said." Lance picked up his beer and took a long swig.

Tom took over the conversation. "I told Sam, since he wasn't here back in 2010, about the accident. Sam examined the autopsy report. He didn't know Mom and Dad, so I thought it would be easier for him to do it."

"Just looked for any irregularities," Sam said. "I can't pretend to know what you all are going through, but I'd say you have your work cut out for you. I studied the autopsy reports and checked Green's too. Nothing seemed out of the ordinary, but it was obvious the impact of Parsons' car was critical. If he told the truth about the brakes, it would explain the impact. If it helps, I'm not sure any medical treatment could have saved them. I'm sorry."

"Thank you, my love." He was sitting so close I could catch the light sandalwood scent of his aftershave.

Angie piped up. "I can't sit here all night. Wiley will be after me to get back to work. What did you find, Tom?"

Tom took out a small leather-bound notebook he used in his detective work. He glanced around the table. "I didn't do the interviews, you know, and since it's been seven years I figured it might be good to refresh my memory. I'm trying not to cause anyone pain, but here goes. The date was Tuesday, December 28, 2010, and Mom and Dad were in their 2009 Chevy Blazer driving to see a movie in Edgington."

"Yeah, I remember," I said. "They wanted to see *The King's Speech*."

"Correct," said Tom. "Driving toward them were Quinn Parsons, Finnegan O'Brien, and Branson Green. They'd been to the Eagle's Nest in Edgington, played poker, and drunk a few brews. Quinn had been drinking, but he was only slightly over the legal limit. He was driving his 1998 Chevy Camaro with Finnegan O'Brien and Branson Green in the back. No one had seat belts on."

Sam looked at each of us. "Anyone think that's kinda strange?"

"What?" Angie said.

Sam spread his hands out. "That two guys were in the back. No one's riding shotgun."

"Good point," said Tom. "It helps to have new eyes and ears. I don't know. Maybe there was some explanation at the time? Good question, Sam."

Tom turned back to his notebook and jotted down a few words. "Anyway, after rounding the curve at Restful Home Cemetery, Quinn Parsons lost control of his car. He was traveling at the speed limit. The road was dry. Didn't have any explanation as to what happened. Of course, between the alcohol and injuries, neither Quinn nor O'Brien remembered much about the accident."

Angie looked puzzled. "Except Quinn said at the church meeting the brakes didn't work. Could that be true?"

Lance stirred. "Andy said he'd lie about anything to try to take the blame off himself."

Tom said, "It's worth pursuing. I could ask O'Brien, but I'm not sure he remembers a thing from that night. Anyway, Parsons' car rolled multiple times in a field to the east. All three were thrown out of the car. Branson Green died at the scene. O'Brien hit a tree and ended up in a wheelchair. Parsons had a broken left arm and three cracked ribs. Mom and Dad's car...Mom and Dad's car," he repeated, his voice breaking slightly, "rolled over on the opposite side of the road, hitting a tree."

Sam interrupted. "Would it have made any difference if help had arrived sooner? How soon did help arrive?"

I explained. "A car driving from Edgington was on the scene almost immediately and called 9-1-1."

Tom turned a page over. "The new people got out and tried to help as they waited for the police and ambulances. They reported loud, heavy metal music still coming from Parsons' car. But it was too late for Mom, Dad, and Branson Green."

I lowered my head.

"And Sam," I said, "our Andy didn't help the situation one bit. He told Tom he wanted to see our parents, but Lance and Mary convinced him not to. He took off anyway in his car, driving out of town, trying to make some sense of the senseless."

Lance set his now-empty beer bottle on the table. "He told me he drove toward the accident scene but was stopped and turned back. Finally, around three in the morning, he came home. He was a mess. The next day, he went to the house you live in now, Jill, and roamed through all the rooms remembering his parents. The more he thought about it, the angrier he got."

"And," I said to Sam, "he went to the hospital to try to see Parsons. When he found his room, he saw a policeman outside. He forced his way in, shouting threats at Quinn. The police managed to subdue him and take him to the police department where Tom calmed him down."

"Only between us," Tom said, "he told me he would hate Quinn until the day he died, and if he had a chance to kill him, he would. Of course, that was years ago. I'd hoped he would soften his anger over time. I don't believe for a minute he shoved Parsons down those stairs. He wouldn't do that. But this history sure doesn't help his case."

Sam shook his head. "Wow. I knew about your parents' accident, but none of the circumstances. Andy took it really hard...not that all of you didn't."

"True," I said. "But over time, Tom and I have kinda come to terms with it."

Tom closed his notebook. "The day of the inquest was a gorgeous, crisp winter day with the sky almost blue. We were all there to hear what the coroner had to say. When the formalities were over, the police arrested Parsons. Andy marched over and punched him. I had to pull him away. Again. Strangely, Quinn said he figured he had it coming. They took Andy out in handcuffs, along with Quinn. Another display when the whole town was in attendance. I thought my brother's temper would mellow in time, but obviously, it hasn't."

Tom grabbed the empty beer bottles. "I'll drop these off with Wiley. I have an idea of someone I can question about what we've just said. The weirdness about the guys in the back seat and the car brakes. Parsons had a cellmate in prison. I'll find out who he was and see if I can quietly slip in and talk to him. A lot of times the police gain useful information from cellmates. When you're in prison with time on your hands, talking is a luxury. But I'll have to keep it on the down-low so Jeeter doesn't hear about it."

The group broke up, Sam kissed me goodbye, and I stayed a while to talk to Angie.

"I think I'm losing my mind, Angie."

"Why?"

"I can't talk to Sam about this again. He thinks I'm mentally in a funk because of this worry about Andy. Maybe he's right. I keep having these weird things happen at the art center. The temperature drops about twenty degrees. I check the thermostat, and it's right where it was."

"Any more objects moving?"

"Not lately. I think you should order that book about ghosts we were talking about."

"Already did, my friend. Arriving soon."

"You know me so well."

On my drive home, I thought about my dreams the last few nights. They were weird dreams, but my parents were always in them. All this talk and Andy's situation brought up so many emotions. They were causing me to dream a lot. Could be Sam was right. I was imagining those crazy things at the art center. My parents were sure on my mind, as was my brother. I remembered the day of their funeral. A line snaked out of the funeral home for the visitation, and the funeral was packed to the rafters. It was an unseasonably warm day for December, as if God himself had welcomed my parents into heaven and was letting their children know all would be right with the world...eventually. I wished my parents were here to give me some advice about Andy. Mostly, I missed them.

Chapter Fourteen

I flipped the month on the calendar in my office at the art center. February. Time was rushing by. The radio show would happen in a little over two weeks. Yikes. As I sat, I heard Chad out in the gallery running lines with Oliver Winston, another member of the senior group. The main gallery was very echoey due to the high ceiling. Chad was playing Sir Simon de Canterville while Oliver was Hiram B. Otis, the American minister to Great Britain. Oliver was saying they would have to take away the ghost's chains if Sir Simon wouldn't agree to use Rising Sun Lubricator on them.

I had decided I'd go to the newspaper office tomorrow morning and check on the history of the Lowry building. I knew it had sat empty for a couple of decades before we created the art center. But I knew nothing about its early history or why someone had built it in the first place. I was fairly sure Victoria Kemp could fill me in.

I pulled out the list of artworks I'd decided to use for the exhibit. As I examined the list, I could tell we had quite a variety. Thirty. They should start rolling in this next week. People would ship them, or, if local, bring them in. We'd install them around the gallery so a ghostly ambience would surround the audience for the radio show. They had let me know if they wanted a price attached so people could buy them. Some would be on loan with no price and not for sale.

Chad and two friends had already built a "stage" by creating a platform about a foot off the floor. We could take it apart and use it for other productions. Donna Filbert and Liz Goodwin were working on a backdrop to represent the castle interior. It was almost done. I hummed a bit as I considered how well the production was coming along. This group of seniors was all in on this project. Chad was a gem. I don't know what I did before he showed up to become my custodian. He'd grown up here, served in the war in Vietnam, sold used cars when he returned, and knew everyone in town. That last item had saved me on many occasions. Chad was devoted to his wife, Sandy, and his grandkids.

I closed the folder when I heard the sound of thunder coming from the gallery. What the heck, I thought. I walked out the door, just as Louise came out of her office too. In the gallery we saw Chad with a two-by-four-foot sheet of high-impact styrene plastic. He laughed as he grabbed it with both hands and used a punching motion to make it ripple. It really sounded like thunder.

"Where did you get the idea to use that?" I asked.

"Found it on the internet. I had to do some research. Listen to this. It's even better." He strolled over to a table and picked up a popcorn can, the metal kind people pack popcorn in to give to friends for Christmas. Opening the lid, he showed each of us what was in it. I could smell popcorn from the tin's previous use.

"What is all this stuff?" Louise asked.

"A broken ceramic coffee mug, a crushed Pabst Blue Ribbon can, a handful of pennies, several Phillips screws, a piece of wood, and a half-cup of pea-sized gravel. It's called a crash box. Now watch, or I should say, listen." Chad grabbed gray duct tape, using it to tape the lid of the popcorn can shut around the seam. Then, he handed the tin to Oliver.

"Okay, ready, Oliver?"

"Sure," Oliver said, focusing on the popcorn tin.

Oliver used both hands to shake the crash box and roll it around, followed by Chad shaking the thunder sheet in a loud rumble.

"Wow, that is so cool," Louise said.

"I'll teach two of the guys to do the sound effects. I have a couple in mind. We have some effects on a tape recording too—clock chimes, a doorbell, and a door knock. Sandy, my wife, helped me record those. They sound very authentic. Here's a second recording with groans and shrieks. Oh, we have rain on this tape. It's the sound of bacon frying. We made the recording last weekend when we were making breakfast for the grandkids."

Winston added, "I have several chains for my car tires that I use when I drive up to Wisconsin to see my grandkids in the winter. We'll be able to shake those for the ghost's chains."

"I'm impressed. This is going to be so much fun. When you have the next rehearsal tonight, you'll have to show the whole cast how cool these sounds are."

Louise headed back to her office, and I needed to make a couple of phone calls. I'd call Angie later in the morning or after lunch, since she tended to sleep in after working late at the bar. I had just started to pick up the phone when I heard the most horrible demonic shriek. It made me jump, and I just saved my phone from crashing onto the desk. Wow. It sounded so terrifying. I pushed my chair back and walked out to the gallery to congratulate the guys.

They were both standing there, mouths open, staring at each other.

"What a terrifying shriek," I said. "Did you record that too?"

"No," said Chad, after waiting a moment. "Did you make that shriek, Jill?"

I looked at him skeptically. "No, I was about to make a phone call, and I almost dropped my phone."

"We—we didn't either," said Oliver, ashen-faced, and I strode over, took his arm, and helped him sit.

I stared at them. "What do you mean?"

Chad put his hands on his hips. "He means we didn't make that laugh."

"Well, I didn't," I said.

"Then, who did?" Louise said, walking across the gallery floor to us.

I looked at Chad. "Oh, come on. 'Fess up. One of you did it."

They turned to each other, shaking their heads.

"No," said Chad. "We didn't."

"Someone else is in the building," I said to Louise. "Has anyone come in? Could anybody be upstairs?"

Chad marched over to the stairway. "I'll go check. It wasn't a great practical joke, however, if someone thinks it's funny." He trooped up the stairs, muttering under his breath.

I looked at Winston, whose face still seemed ashen. "You okay?"

"Yes," he said and nodded. "But I swear we didn't do it. It sounded like it came from the classroom in the back where the weavers meet."

Louise turned. "I'll go back there and check, Jill."

After a few tense moments, I heard footsteps on the stairway. Chad was back.

"No one up there. I checked all the closets. Nada."

About that time, Louise came back and said the same thing.

"Hmm. Group hysterics?" I tapped my mouth with my finger. "Makes no sense. But we all heard it." I took a deep breath. "Well, okay. I guess I will get back to work. But let me know if you hear or see anything else suspicious."

The rest of the morning passed without incident. I called Angie, and when I told her about the demonic laugh, she gasped.

"I knew it. There's a ghost in the art center."

"I doubt it. Maybe there's some other explanation."

"Such as?"

"Well, I don't know. A blower on the furnace going on?"

Silence at Angie's end of the phone. "I'm expecting the book I ordered to show up tomorrow with the UPS guy. And I changed my mind and also ordered a Ouija board. Once I have them, we'll figure out who's haunting the building."

"You haven't forgotten the great Ouija board disaster from ninety-six when my mother outlawed us from ever doing that again?"

"Yes. But your mom isn't here anymore. I think we're a little older and wiser now, and I'm all for taking chances."

"I'm going to check that tomorrow. Once we combine the building history and your book and Ouija board, we should have some answers, especially if my art center is haunted."

Angie chuckled. "Do you believe in ghosts?"

I thought for a moment. "I don't know. But since I work here occasionally at night, I think I should know who—or what—is in the building. It's never happened before. Why would it be spooked now?"

"Beats me."

"Back to work for me, girl."

After I talked with Angie, Lance called. Man, my phone was busy this morning.

"Ordinarily I wouldn't bother you with this," Lance told me, "but I'm so upset I didn't know who else to talk with."

"Oh, my. Are you okay?"

"No. I mean, yes, I'm okay, but I'm really angry, and this is a disaster."

I sat back in my chair. "Lance, I'm listening. Start from the top."

He paused a moment before speaking. "Well, I was working at the gift shop and this customer came in—Maude Fairley."

"Yes, I know Maude."

"All right. She looked around the shop checking out several vases. I let her walk around for a while and waited for her to ask a question."

"Lance, where are you headed with this?"

"I'm getting there. Bear with me."

I heard him swallow.

"Anyway, she came over to the register with a cut-glass Waterford Lismore vase, one of my favorite patterns. After I wrapped it and she paid me, she seemed to want to say a little more, so I waited."

"And?"

"She said, 'I hate to be the one to tell you, Lance, but have you seen what they're saying about Andy online at that true crime website?'"

"Of course, I hadn't, so I asked her what website she was talking about. She said it was called 'Crimes of the Century.' So, I thanked her and sent her on her way. After she left, I looked it up on my phone. Jill, it's awful. It's one of those places where amateurs who are obsessed with crimes go online and post stuff. I studied the site, which had several articles. One title screamed, 'Andrew Madison: Suspected Murderer, Held Without Bail.'"

"Who owns the website?"

"That's just it. No one admits being responsible for it. I scrolled all the way to the bottom, and there's no place to even find out who writes it. Going back to the article, I read it twice. It's full of lies and innuendo. Remember the terrible newspaper editor we had last year?"

"Yes. Thank goodness she's gone."

"Well, this is just as bad. Yellow journalism at its worst."

"Can you tell how many people read it or follow it?"

"Two K."

"Oh, no. Two thousand? Was anyone quoted in the story?"

"Of course not. Well, 'sources say.' But Jill, it's terrible."

"Hang in there, Lance. I'll go online and check it out."

"Thanks. I don't know that we can do anything about it, but I feel better now since someone other than me knows about it."

"I'll bet a lot of folks in Apple Grove know about it."

After ending the call, I looked at the paper pad where I'd printed the name of the website. I hesitated, then typed it into my laptop. It came up, and what I saw made me gasp. I could feel my heart pounding with anxiety. What heartless people.

Chapter Fifteen

I was still angry about the amateur sleuths website the next morning when I went to the *Apple Grove Ledger* office to see Victoria Kemp. I'd tried to reach Tom to tell him about the true crime website, but he never answered and never got back to me. He must have been researching something that was taking up his time, or he was somewhere with his phone off. As I thought about it, I wondered if Clint Anderson had leaked some of the information in that awful website.

The *Apple Grove Ledger* was situated at the south end of town on Main Street, and it had changed hands several times in recent years. Newspapers were having a challenging time hanging in there, and the owner, Jefferson Canary, had sold it a few months ago to someone from Peoria. We all waited, holding our breath, hoping it would remain a small-town newspaper. I parked in the lot, locked my car, and plodded toward the building.

Just then, Martin Stewart came out, a paper in his hands.

"Hi, Martin."

"Jill, great to see you. I hear you have a funny show coming up at the art center."

"Yes, *The Canterville Ghost*."

"From what I hear around town, it's going to be hilarious."

"We're having great fun. Stop in and pick up tickets. They're going fast, and it's a couple weeks away."

"Will do." He started to leave, then turned back to me. "Say, I'm so sorry to hear about Andy's problems. I heard he was in the county jail."

"Thanks. He's certainly been on my mind."

Martin folded the paper he held and stuffed it in his pocket. "I know how hard that is, your parents being gone and all. Even after years, grief sometimes sneaks up on you when you least expect it. Now this just brings it all up again."

I thanked him for his empathy and walked through the entrance to the newspaper office. Compared to earlier years when the newsroom was a bustling enterprise, the office now seemed practically deserted. At the front desk, I saw a familiar face. Jerri Endolak, who I remembered from high school, was staffing the desk, answering the phone, and nodding to me with a finger up as if to say, "Hang on, and I'll get to you."

I looked around, thinking about the past with this place while I waited for Jerri. Doors to offices were closed, while copies of today's newspaper sat on the counter. I knew the old printing press, huge and lumbering, was out in another room, its noise and clatter stopped cold by the digital age. Nowadays, the newspaper was printed in a town two hours away by people who knew nothing about Apple Grove or its history.

After another minute, she wrote something down, and ended the conversation.

"Good to see you. Now, what can I do for you, Jill?"

"Hi, Jerri. I'm looking for Victoria Kemp."

"She's probably in the newspaper archives. Let me see if I can raise her." She punched a button on her phone and held the receiver between her neck and shoulder while she unwrapped a cough drop. "Yeah, Victoria. Jill Madison's here to see you. Send her down?" She paused for a moment, listening. "Okay." Turning to me, Jerri said, "You can go on down. Take the stairs over there and turn left when you get to the bottom."

I carefully stepped down a narrow, wooden stairway thinking about Ivan and the railing on the steps to the art center basement. That's where he'd broken his leg. These stairs weren't much better. Turning left, I followed a narrow passage that led to a bright light. Hmm. Just like the future end of my life. The lower I was on the stairs, the mustier the air smelled.

"Jill, I'm in here," I heard a voice call out.

Victoria was sitting on a stack of boxes that held all kinds of ledgers and stacks of newspapers in the middle of a room. My heart fell as I realized how totally disorganized this place was.

"Hi. Looks like you have your work cut out for you," I said.

Her round, cherubic face, with white, curly hair encircling it, peeked out from behind yet another set of boxes. "Don't let the total chaos fool you. I know where everything is. It's called job security. No one else has any idea how this is organized."

I found a chair and sat next to her. "What are you working on?"

"Finding information on the Lowry building. Isn't that what you mentioned to me on the phone?"

"Yes. Thanks so much for helping me out."

"Ya got a pencil and paper handy?"

I pulled a notebook and pen out of my bag. "Sure do. Fire away."

Victoria had several open newspaper ledgers sitting in various places around her. She reached for one and said, "Apple Grove began in the mid-1830s when the government opened the territory so settlers would come West."

"I'm particularly interested in the Lowry building and who owned it."

She nodded. "I'm gettin' there. The guy you're trying to find is Daniel Lowry. He came here from Pennsylvania after the war and brought his young wife with him. See this paper here?"

I leaned over and examined the article she was holding. There was the name, Daniel Lowry. The date was April 1866.

"He bought a tract of land that contained an apple grove, hence the name of the town. He cleared out all the trees and began constructing the Lowry building you currently occupy. Look at this article." She pointed to some paragraphs with the headline, "Lowry Building Receives Steel Girder."

"It must have been the beam that goes from the back to the front of the building."

"I imagine. It came all the way from Pennsylvania. What a trip that must have been. Well, he completed the building in 1870. See these lovely illustrations? From the upstairs windows you could see the Square with horses and buggies tied up to hitching posts, and there's the maple tree still there. A bit smaller back then."

"Amazing."

"I'd guess this Lowry must have been thirty or so years old when they completed the general store. He and his wife, Rosemary, lived above it on the second floor. Once they decided it was time to start a family, disaster struck."

"Oh. What happened?" I asked.

"Here's another short article, probably because they were prominent citizens. She died in childbirth. Wasn't unusual back then. Buried them both in the Catholic cemetery just north of town. Pretty sad. She was twenty-six."

"How awful."

Victoria nodded. "You asked me to see if there was any scandal or gossip connected to the building or the owner."

"Yes, I did." I sat there, my pen poised to get this part down.

"There was a great deal of speculation in town about where Daniel Lowry got the money to build his store. It was soon after the war, and money, as well as labor, was hard to come by. A few years after the store opened in 1870, a city slicker from Missouri showed up asking questions about the Lowry store. He wasn't around long. No other explanation."

"How did this Daniel Lowry die?"

"Twenty years after that. Homicide."

"What?"

"See here." She held out another newspaper ledger. "The headline said, 'Local Businessman Murdered.' Looks like a robbery gone bad."

"Amazing. In my art center."

"Yup. There you have it."

"Could you make some copies of those stories for me?"

"Actually, you can do it yourself. We have the archives online. Just thought you might like to see the originals."

"Thanks, Victoria. This is a great start. How did I not know that? About the archives?" I asked.

"I keep quiet about it. Remember? Job security for me!" Victoria said and smiled.

When I left the newspaper office, I saw a sheriff's car sitting across the street from the parking lot. Jeeter was in the front seat. Darn him. This was harassment. I wasn't going to let him intimidate me. I got in my car and drove out of the parking lot. Looking in my rear-view mirror, I saw him leave his car and walk toward the newspaper office. Was he following me? Checking on what I was doing? Why did he keep turning up in places where I was researching?

That evening I was home when my phone rang. The *Law & Order* theme.

"Where have you been, Tom? I've been trying to get hold of you all day."

"Had to drive over to the prison and see if I could talk with Parsons' cellmate."

"Any luck?"

"Yes, although if Jeeter checks it out, he'll see my name signed in. The guy's name is Roy Mason. He was in for burglary. Quinn's cellmate for his last two years, he likes talking. I couldn't offer him anything, but I told him our hard luck story about the accident. He knew all about it from Parsons."

"What was your take on him?"

"Oh, he seemed pretty affable. He wasn't in for anything that involved violence. I guess he and Parsons struck up a friendship, stayed together, and kept their heads down. He didn't have anything to lose by talking to me. He's out in a few weeks."

"What did he say about Quinn?"

"Now there's the interesting part. Remember Parsons talking about the brakes not working on the car?"

"I do. At the church."

"He told Mason he'd realized that under hypnosis. Strangely, he didn't remember stepping on the brake pedal. It was as if he heard someone say the brake pedal wasn't working."

"That's weird." I thought about it. "So, he might mean someone cut the brake lines?"

"It's possible. I'm going to check what happened to the car. I'm sure it's long gone by now, but it's possible one of the cops I know who worked the scene will be able to tell me about the car."

This made me consider another line of reasoning. "If someone cut the brake lines, it would have to be a person who had it in for Parsons. We'd need to know what was happening in his life around that time. Andy might know a thing or two. They were in the same class in high school."

"A good thought. There was something else he remembered Parsons saying. I'm not sure how true it is, however. Quinn might have been making it up or trying to find someone else to blame."

"What?"

Tom paused. "He told Mason when he was hypnotized, he vaguely remembered he was not driving the car that night."

"What? That's crazy. The investigation clearly said it was Parsons. It was his car. He took the blame for it." I thought for a moment. "If not Quinn, who could have been driving? O'Brien? Branson Green?"

"It's an answer we don't yet have."

Chapter Sixteen

Friday morning, I was in the gallery watching Evan Shelly direct a few of the seniors in a very funny scene from the radio show. Six chairs sat on the platform stage, two of them holding Chad and Winston, who were studying their scripts. Evan resembled your stereotypical director: a blue scarf tied around his neck, navy beret on his head covering a sparse clump of gray hair.

"Places, everyone. Chad or Sir Simon, you're sitting in the chair rubbing your knees because a suit of armor just made a fearful crash and hit your knees. Your face is fillllllllled with agony. The twins—once they're able to rehearse after school—are on the stairway with peashooters out to pelt you. Their father, Hiram—he nodded at Winston—pulls out a water gun and aims it at Sir Simon."

"Criminy," said Chad. "I had no idea I'd be under attack in this part."

"Oh, yes," chuckled Evan. "The twins will pelt you with lots of ammunition. In this case, frozen peas."

Chad sat on the chair behind him on the stage shaking his head. "Do they have to be frozen? They could put an eye out."

When Evan put his hands out like he was saying, "So?" Chad added, "They're my neighbor's kids. They'll love this."

Evan waved his hands. "You'll need to enunciate. Take a deep breath, blow it out slowly."

I watched Chad taking direction, a pained expression on his face.

"Again," said Evan. "Slooowly."

Chad followed his instructions.

"Mrs. Otis comes to the microphone—that's you for now, Molly—and has her line about something for Sir Simon's indigestion. Victoria isn't here, but said she'd make the next practice."

Chad looked up from his script. "Then I stand, act like I'm furious at her modern American advice, hear footsteps, and leave with a deep churchyard groan before the twins can get me."

"Yes, yes," said Evan. "Let's hear your groan."

Chad groaned softly.

"No, no," said the director. "It must be a loud, scary, churchyard groan. Try it again. Very loud. Very scary." He said the last line with gusto.

"Okay," said Chad. "Like this?"

As he opened his mouth again, a horrible deep groan came from the rafters of the gallery. Everyone froze.

I looked at Chad and he stared back at me.

"What was that?" Evan asked, once the silence had gone on for moments.

I shook my head. "No idea. Could we all have imagined it?"

"I doubt it, but it was a great groan. Whichever of you did it, do it again. We could use a groan like that."

Another deep groan flew through the rafters and down to the stage, followed by a quiet chuckle.

"All right. Which of you is a ventriloquist?" Evan asked.

They looked at each other, holding out their arms and shaking their heads. Evan turned to me, a question on his face.

"Is this some kind of trick?" he asked.

"Not that I'm aware of," I said.

"Who's on the second floor? Chad, see who's up there," the director said.

Chad laid his script down, walked over, and climbed the stairs. "Here we go again."

We all sat waiting, wondering what or who could be doing this. After several minutes of footsteps over our heads, Chad came back reporting, "No one."

"Hmm. We need to get that recorded. It's a great groan," said Evan. "Well, enough for today. Jill, I trust you'll try to figure out where this is coming

110

from?"

I nodded. "Sure, Evan."

As people grabbed their water bottles, scripts, and coats, I thanked Evan. I adjourned to my office, thinking about the conversation I'd had with Angie. We figured the spirit of Daniel Lowry was haunting this building for some reason. Why was he here? What did he want? I sat at my desk, folding my arms while I told myself I was crazy thinking about a ghost.

The night before, I had looked through Andy's yearbooks again. Darnell, Parsons, Green, O'Brien. I called Tom, who'd agreed to stop for me at the art center today, and run over to Finnegan and Sharon O'Brien's house. So here we were, drinking coffee in Tom's car, looking out at the O'Brien house. It was a modest, lower-middle-class ranch, the sidewalks and driveway cleared, with tiny Christmas lights still hanging from the eaves. The house had seen better days. A gutter was hanging loose on one side of the roof, and the trim around the front windows needed paint. I imagined it was difficult to keep up the house with Sharon working full-time and Finn in a wheelchair.

"Strange," I said. "Usually, Jeeter shows up wherever I go, but today he seems to be conspicuously absent."

"Give him time," muttered Tom.

We knocked on the door after skirting around the incline built for Finn's wheelchair. Sharon answered, a worried expression on her face and a cigarette in her hand when she saw Tom. I didn't worry her one bit.

"Hi, Sharon. Mind if we come in and ask a few questions?" Tom said.

I could see it in her expression. Wary, worried. She glanced behind her. "Finn's asleep, but I suppose I can talk to you."

We walked in and took off our snowy shoes, placing them on a mat.

"Thanks," she said, ushering us into a small living room.

I gazed around the room. Country style was the theme of the day, but things didn't really match. The furniture had seen better days. With Finn in a wheelchair, I imagined Sharon had to support them with her job as a waitress downtown at the Orchard Diner. I couldn't imagine how bad the medical bills must be, but maybe Finn got some sort of disability.

"What can I do for you?" she said after we were all seated, Tom and me on a sofa and Sharon across from us in a wing chair. She lit another cigarette from the earlier one, taking a deep inhalation.

"Well, we'd like to talk with Finn, but perhaps you could answer a few questions we have about the night of the accident, seven years ago."

She blinked several times, putting her cigarette in an ashtray next to her. "Most of the information about the accident has been in the newspaper. I don't know anything more, except it changed our lives forever. We were hoping to have several kids by now, but that ended with Finn's paralysis." Her eyes were cold, her hands in her lap squeezed together tightly. I noticed she was speaking very slowly as though she were carefully controlling her voice. Their childlessness was a topic she probably didn't like to discuss.

Tom waited to see if she'd say more. When she didn't, he asked, "Do you remember the accident? It's been a long time."

She cocked her head sideways. Again, I could tell she was thinking carefully about what to say.

"Yes, it's been years, but I still remember the shock. Two policemen appeared at my door to tell me Finn had been in an accident. They took me to the hospital, where we weren't sure if he was going to live." Her eyes narrowed. "We've had many days since then when we both figure it would have been better if he hadn't."

I was trying not to be judgmental. I could understand her bitterness. "I'm sorry. I know it's been a terrible event in your lives. Our family was devastated by the same accident." I paused. "Did you see or talk with Quinn Parsons after he came back?" I asked. I watched her, but she refused to look at me. When she did, I saw disgust written all over her face.

"Oh, yes. I did see and talk with Quinn. I also slapped him across the face."

Tom sat up. "Why?"

Sharon wrung her hands before she answered. "He made a pass at me. I never liked Quinn Parsons, but for him to come back here and do that after he'd put my husband in a wheelchair, well, it shows you his character. I laughed when he spoke at that church whining about what a changed person he was. He hadn't changed at all. He was always scum and he died scum.

Whoever killed him deserves a note of thanks. I hear it's your brother."

Before I could say anything, a door opened, and Finn O'Brien wheeled himself into the living room. As he smoothly glided across the wood floor, he smiled and offered, "Sounds like you're talking about our favorite person."

Tom rose, wandered over, and shook his hand. "Finn. My sister and I were asking a few questions. We're wondering if the accident had anything to do with Quinn's death."

"I can't imagine it would," he said, bringing the chair to a halt next to Sharon's chair. "But as to that night, I don't remember a lot. I woke up in a hospital room with no feeling in my legs. They said I hit a tree."

"Do you remember who was in the car with you?" Tom asked.

"Sure. Quinn, Green, and me."

"Quinn Parsons was driving?"

I watched Finn. He stared off past Tom's shoulder, then rubbed his jaw with his hand. "Yeah. He was the least soused of the group. We took a vote. He won."

"You and Green were in the back seat?"

"They were," Sharon said before Finn could answer.

Finn suddenly lifted his head, looked at us, and smiled. "I was the lucky one, as you can see."

Attempting to change the subject, I said, "I imagine the medical bills are outrageous."

At this thought, Sharon sat up straighter. "Actually, we have an angel helping."

"How so?" Tom asked.

"Each month some money is dropped in our bank account. We don't know who does it, but it comes regularly on the first of the month."

"We tried to have it traced at one point," said Finn. "I hate to take charity. But whoever it is covered his tracks. We could only trace a bunch of holding companies, but we couldn't find the original owner. I don't understand it all. Makes it impossible to give the money back."

"How long has this been going on?" I asked.

Finn looked at Sharon. "What would you say?"

"Ever since the accident. The payments started a few months later."

Tom stood and I followed. "Sounds like you do have a guardian angel. Well, if you think of anything else, please give me a call." He handed his card to Sharon. As we strolled toward the door, he turned, asking, "By the way, where were you the night Quinn was killed?" He had directed the question to Sharon.

"Right here," she said, glancing at Finn.

I was about to move in front of the door as Tom held it when I noticed a small wastebasket next to a loveseat. There were torn pieces of paper in it, and a few were on the floor next to the basket. Blue. That was the color of the handbills Quinn Parsons was passing out for his church talk.

When we reached Tom's car and got in, I turned to him, telling him about the blue pieces of paper. "So, what did you think?"

He started the engine. "I think they were lying through their teeth. There's a lot they're not telling us. How about you?"

I sighed. "The same, especially when you asked him about who was driving. Sharon jumped right in there."

As he pulled out into the street, Tom added, "The money could be guilt payments, or it could be a warning to keep their mouths shut."

That evening, Priscilla's was humming when I walked in with Sam. It was becoming our regular meeting place to talk about Andy's case. Lance, Tom, Angie, and I sat at a table off the dance floor while Sam went after a couple of beers. He'd had a long day. I figured he needed a bit of camaraderie to cheer him up. When he arrived with our beers, I gave him a kiss.

"Thanks, Dr. Finch." He sat next to me.

"Please, do you have to make out in front of the whole world?" Tom said, laughing.

"Yes," I replied, giving Sam a second kiss on the cheek.

Tom said, "Down to business. I assume Jill has told you about the website of the true crime idiots?"

"Yes," Angie replied.

"I didn't tell Andy about it, and I'm not going to," said Lance. "He can't see it in jail anyway."

Tom's scanned our faces. "I think someone's leaking information to whoever's the website technician. Now they say there was a thread from Andy's sweater sticking to the stair railing at Darnell's cottage. How would they know that? If it's actually true, maybe it's why Jeeter wanted Andy's clothes from that night. But who's leaking this stuff?"

"I put my money on Jeeter. I'll check with Andy the next time I see him. I'd think he'd remember if his sweater got snagged on the stair railing. The red sweater's one of his favorites," Lance said.

"If he didn't," I said, "then Jeeter may be manufacturing evidence."

Tom studied me. "Jill, I think you and Angie should do some checking on Paul Darnell and his wife, Buffy. As I remember, he was always around those guys. The night of the accident, he said he was at the Eagle's Nest but left to go home separately. I'd bet he knows more than he's telling."

I took a swig of my beer. "Actually, I checked Andy's high school yearbooks. He left them at the house. All the pictures of Parsons show their group— Parsons, Green, O'Brien, and Darnell. I thought it was a bit strange Paul was not there with them that night."

"But," said Sam, "he was on a totally different path than those losers. Working at the bank, and, as we now know, making his way up to vice president. He was on a career path the rest of them couldn't hope to follow."

"Still doesn't exonerate him," said Tom.

"True," said Lance. "But sometimes things are stranger than fiction. Sometimes our assumptions are totally wrong."

I thought about the possible ghost of Daniel Lowry in the art center. Truer words were never spoken.

Before Sam dropped me off at my house, he reached over and put his arm around me, sealing it with a soft kiss. Then, pulling back, he said, "I'm glad I'm not a criminal with the Madison family in pursuit."

I laughed. "And why is that?"

His head turned sideways as he thought about his answer. "You all seem to have a very strong connection, and you work well together when you have a goal in mind."

"You should see us when we're arguing. Totally different story. Especially when Andy does something stupid."

"That's true in any family. I like your family. Wish I could have met your parents. But, knowing you, I'm sure I would have liked them." He sighed. "Too bad I met you after their accident. Timing is everything, isn't it?"

"You wouldn't have met me. I'd have been in Chicago trying to become the toast of the art scene and failing miserably."

"I can't believe that," he said. "I've seen some of your work. It's amazing. You have your mother's genes."

"I wish. She was always a tough act to follow. Sometimes I wish I hadn't gone into painting for a living because I could never live up to her reputation."

He took my hand. "I doubt she'd have thought that."

"My dad was always there to make me laugh. Nothing ever went wrong for him. He loved his life, and, selling insurance, he knew everyone in town. Sometimes I wish I'd inherited his gene for calm. That's what I remember the most about him. Nothing fazed him. Patience was his middle name. If something went wrong, he could fix it. If a plan didn't work out, he modified it somehow so it would work." I shook my head. "Well, it's all right. We're doing fine. We'll get Andy out of this fix."

"You're right. You have every reason to be self-confident. I've seen you in action. This, too, will pass."

I turned his face to mine, kissed him again, and thanked God he was in my life.

Chapter Seventeen

Louise and I had spent the previous day and this morning installing the artwork for the show. Three volunteers had helped. We used four sculptures, twelve oil paintings, eight watercolor paintings, and six mixed media works. All very ghostly. Angie and I waited until Saturday afternoon to visit the Darnells. And this was why...

Unlike Finn and Sharon, the Darnells lived in a nicer part of town, not in a McMansion, but only a small step below. I knew Paul had moved up to vice president at the bank quite quickly. I didn't care much for his wife, Buffy. She struck me as a Lady Macbeth type, ready to do anything to push her husband to the top. Would she have killed to keep secrets?

The Christmas decorations were gone, but the kids had built a snowman and what looked like the remains of a fort. I looked up at the top of the house. It probably had a cathedral ceiling, as there was a high peak in the front. Could be the living room. A three-car garage was attached on the south side. It was quite a contrast to the O'Brien house.

We rang the doorbell, which played *Auld Lang Syne*, leftover from New Year's. Nothing happened. Maybe they were gone. We glanced at each other. I rang it again. This time we heard footsteps. Paul came to the door in sweatpants and a T-shirt soaked with sweat, using a towel to wipe his face and neck. He looked startled to see us. Then he regained his wits.

"Sorry," he said. "I was working out in the gym. Hi Jill, Angie. Come on in." He opened the door and ushered us into a hallway, where we took off our shoes. We followed him down another hallway to a huge living room with a glass chandelier that hung yards down from the ceiling. Turning left, he said, "Buffy isn't here today. Took the kids to see her parents."

Angie and I glanced at each other behind his back, relief filling our faces. We followed him into the spacious living room with white carpeting and all-white furniture. He indicated a sofa and we sat, watching him move over to a chair. He looked like a bank VP. His hair was starting to go silver above the ears, and he obviously worked out, so he stayed in great shape.

"Can I get you something to drink? Coffee? Hot chocolate?"

"No thanks," I said. "We won't take a lot of your time." I was thinking I could easily spill a cup of hot chocolate over the vision of whiteness that was their stylish living room.

"Hey, that was some art board meeting for my first one. I wasn't quite sure what you did at those meetings, but I was impressed. Very organized."

"Thanks. I try to keep them organized and professional, but Ivan Truelove is a bit of a thorn in my side."

"I'll say. Wow. He doesn't find a lot good to say about your job, yet you do amazing work. Your art center is jumping. Always activity going on. If I were in charge, I'd have to have at least one assistant to keep it all organized. I'm impressed you manage to deal with such a full schedule."

"As you know," I said dryly, "we're on a limited budget. I use multiple whiteboards." I gently laughed.

"Sure, sure. I get that. You know, I've known Ivan for many years, since we're both in the financial sector in town. He's not had an easy life."

Angie sat up suddenly. "Really? I—we"—she turned to me—"don't know much about his life. Why do you say, 'not easy'?"

"The way I understand it from some of my colleagues, he went to Wharton School of Business, a difficult school to get into, graduating near the top of his class. Got married, took a job with a big financial services company in Connecticut. Wasn't married long when his wife died. I think she was in her mid-twenties. She had been an actress and quite beautiful, I've been told. Skiing accident. Not sure he ever got over it. Could be why he's grumpy all the time."

I stared at Paul. "I didn't know. So maybe I should cut him some slack."

He nodded. "You might."

Angie asked, "How did he get here to small-town Illinois?"

Paul cocked his head, thinking. "You know, I'm not sure." He stood. "I think I'll go grab a bottle of water. I'm parched after lifting. Sure I can't get you anything?"

We both shook our heads and watched him walk out into another hallway.

Whispering to Angie, I said, "He's very interested in making a good impression."

"He's hiding something. But what?"

I looked around and saw several framed photographs sitting on a white baby grand piano. They drew my curiosity, so I walked over to the piano and Angie followed. Most were of the Darnells and their two kids, while one was a wedding photo of them. Two were obviously extended family. But in the back of the group sat a five-by-seven photo of Darnell, Parsons, Green, and O'Brien. I picked it up, studying the faces. It must have been shortly after high school graduation. They were in a room I didn't recognize, their arms over each other's shoulders.

Angie studied the photo over my shoulder. "They look so young there."

"We were."

I jumped at his voice. He came over to the piano with a bottle of water in his hand and took the photo, studying it. "I think that was the summer after we all graduated. Wow. Long time ago. Hard to believe two of us are dead. I'd never have imagined or foreseen such a thing." He glanced at the photo again. "Wish I had all that hair now." He placed it back on the piano.

"It's really why we stopped by," I said, as we walked back over to the sofa and sat. "We wanted to ask you about that night, the night of the accident when my parents were killed."

He gave me a sympathetic nod. "So long ago I can hardly remember. I'm sorry, Jill. That was quite a night for your family. I remember your parents fondly. And now it's too bad Andy is caught up in all this. I've always liked him. How's he doing?"

"Well," I said, "probably as good as someone could be who's in jail, which is to say, not well."

"I'm sorry to hear that. And my old buddy started all this. That's the thing about Quinn Parsons. As time went by, I distanced myself from him. He never grew up in a home like the rest of us. His dad was a terrible drunk, and Quinn often took off for days at a time when his old man beat his mother. We knew him from grade school on and let him hang out with us because we kinda felt sorry for him."

"I can't imagine it was easy," said Angie. "I've heard rumors he might have hung out with some unsavory people too, and possibly gotten involved in drugs."

Did I notice a flicker in Paul Darnell's eyes? Not obvious, but brief.

He shook his head slowly. "I didn't ever see him do anything like that, you know, where I'd notice him taking stuff or selling it. Guess I wouldn't put it past him. It's true, he did run around with lowlifes, but when he was with us he was fine. Unfortunately, you know, when you come from a home like his, it's hard to take the home out of the kid. It was only a matter of time till he'd get into trouble." He hesitated, like he was considering carefully what to say. "Sometimes I blame myself for not being there for the guys that night."

He took a long swallow from his water bottle before he continued. "We all did our share of drinking together. Even smoked a few joints, but as time went by, I pulled away from the other guys because I had to maintain a public image. Working at the bank was long, hard hours with Buffy at home watching the kids, but I managed to move up and all those hours paid off. I couldn't afford to get into some kind of scrape with the guys. I guess we kind of drifted away."

"I'm surprised you weren't with them the night of the accident," Angie said.

"Oh, I was."

"What? You weren't in the car," I said.

"No. In fact, I sat in on a couple rounds of poker at the Eagle's Nest and then went home. I was a little concerned because they'd been drinking quite a bit." He paused, and I could tell he was considering what to add. "After the accident, the police talked to me. I had lots of alibis, since people in the bar saw me there and saw me leave. Like I said, I had to watch my image in the community, so I left early for home. Not sure what time, but it was long before they left. In fact, I didn't even know about the accident until the next day."

"That must have been an awful shock," I said.

He nodded. "Yes. Frankly, it just proves the old wisdom about being careful who you hang with. I think Quinn's story about the brakes was hogwash. He was drunk, and he didn't want to take responsibility. Just like him."

I watched him carefully. He might have been talking about strangers. No emotional reaction whatsoever.

"And Buffy?" Angie asked.

"My wife? Oh, she wasn't with me. She was home and could vouch for me...when I got in. It was much earlier than the accident. Like I said, I learned about it the next day on the news."

Silence hung on the three of us. Angie said, "Well, we'd better get going. Thanks so much, Mr. Darnell."

"Paul," he said, as he rose from his chair.

Once we left the house and got in Angie's truck, I said, "How did he strike you?"

"Like a cold fish." She turned to me, excitement in her voice. "He was quick to throw Quinn under the bus, denying his newly found brake story. I don't trust him. Too much worry about his own innocence."

"I'm not quite sure what to think. He spent a lot of words telling us he had an alibi. Like he said, lots of people saw him that night. He must not have driven to the bar with the other three since he left separately. It seems odd, but I suppose it was possible if he thought they'd be drinking a lot. I can't help feeling we're missing something." I thought for a moment. "He was holding back. Sometimes I thought he'd practiced some of those words. Then he almost added something but stopped himself. A man of self-control."

I'd put in the afternoon at the art center, often thinking about Andy. How safe was he, especially with Jeeter around? Now, I pulled into my driveway just in time to see Tigger Hastings walking his dog, Wingate, between our houses. His first name came from his mother, who thought it would be cute

121

to think of him in the Winnie-the-Pooh stories. I'd have strangled my mom if she'd done that. At the very least, I would have gone to court and changed it legally. I thought of him as a mysterious figure, staying in his house most of the time, leaving mainly to exercise Wingate. Now, in the winter, he'd pulled his vest collar around his neck so you could hardly see his face.

"Hi, Jill," he said, moving toward me on the sidewalk with Wingate.

I moved gingerly down my driveway, being careful not to slip on the snow-covered cement. I could imagine slipping in the snow and falling flat while Wingate came over to lick my face.

He'd come to a stop, Wingate sniffing around the snow. I'd say Tigger was in his mid-twenties, tall, and slender. I'd seen the movers carry in exercise equipment when he first moved in. Actually, slender wasn't the right word. He had muscles on his muscles. A slightly musky scent filled my nostrils, and I wondered what it was about men and aftershave in this town. He had black hair, and wore a short beard, also black, but no moustache. A puffy vest over a T-shirt was all he had on to keep him warm, well, that, and a stocking cap over his head. I watched him. The vest sure did nothing to hide those biceps. Sometimes I thought he was mysteriously not at home because his lights must have been set on a timer, going on at the same time every night. A real enigma right next door.

"I saw the news about your brother. I'm sorry."

"Thanks. We're trying to help him, but it's slow going."

"I imagine your other brother, the detective, is on the case."

He sure knew a lot about me without having had much conversation in the past. "He does what he can. Right now, I'm dealing with the aggravation of a sheriff's deputy who seems to keep following me around town. How he knows where I am, I'm not sure."

Tigger looked down at Wingate and pulled him away from a clump of grass sticking up through the snow. He turned to me. "Follows you, you say?"

"Yeah. So far, he hasn't come close or threatened me, but he's an unsavory human being."

"Hmm." He stared at the eaves of my house, thinking for a moment. "Are there times when he doesn't follow you?"

I considered. "We went to interview a man today without the company of Jeeter."

"How was that different from times when he was following you?"

"Guess I hadn't thought about it. Let's see. Tom wasn't with me, but my friend Angie was."

"Whose car did you take?"

"Angie's truck."

He drew a long breath and looked at Wingate, who had finished checking out the snow and came over to lick my hand. "Were you in your car when he followed you?"

"Now you mention it, yes."

Another long pause as if he were contemplating what to do. "Let me take Wingate in and grab a helpful tool from my garage. I'll be right back."

Now this was an interesting development. What could he be thinking? I watched the dog lead him back to his house, Wingate moving quickly because his little body was ready to be done with the cold. After they'd disappeared, his garage door opened, and Tigger came out with a long pole. He came down his driveway, his boots making crunching sounds in the snow. When he got closer, I noticed a dark clump on the end of the stick.

"And this is for—?"

"It's a tracker detector. Possibly, this guy has a tracker on your car. Come on."

He moved up my driveway, pulling me along behind him, and it felt good to know I wasn't going to slip and slide. I hadn't put my boots on when we went to Darnell's.

"You'll need to open the garage."

I pulled my keys out of my pocket, opened the side door of the garage, and soon Tigger was on his side on my garage floor, poking the pole under my car and shining a flashlight along with it. After a few minutes, he stood.

"Just as I thought."

"What?"

"You have a tracker under your car, attached to the chassis. Here, hold this pole. I think I can just reach it."

I took the pole as he got back to the floor with his flashlight. Examining the pole, I saw a mirror connected at an angle to the end of it. Why would he have a tool to find a tracker like this in his garage? I didn't even know what to call it. Curiouser and curiouser.

"There," he said, getting up from the floor with a grace I sure didn't have. He held out a small object. "He's been tracking you."

"Wow." I took the little box and examined it. "I hate that man."

"I have the perfect idea for where to place his tracker. I have a friend who goes on deliveries—stops and starts his truck a lot. I'll have him stick it on his truck, then later leave it somewhere."

"Perfect," I said, handing it over, along with the pole. "Why would he be interested in where I go?"

"I guess you should ask yourself what he has invested in this situation."

He turned and left as I was considering his words. Before he was out of sight, I hollered, "I'm hardly someone who lives an exciting life where he might want to follow along."

He turned and called out, halfway to his house. "I don't know about that. You don't strike me as someone who's solved two murders in the last year or two."

Suddenly, I stopped thinking about my quiet, small-town life. What? How did he know that?

When I looked up, he was gone.

Chapter Eighteen

I took off my coat and all the winter paraphernalia, hanging it in the closet. Even though we weren't open at the art center quite as long on Saturdays as on the weekdays, I dropped onto the sofa with a deep sigh. What a week. I needed to see Andy again, but it was too late now. My eyes wandered over to the front door. The mail.

I had a mail slot in the door, and there were multiple circulars and pieces of junk mail lying in a pile on the wood floor. A white envelope peeked out through the junk. I picked it up and wandered back over to the sofa. Most of it could go in the recycle bin. But then there was this long, legal-sized envelope. My name was printed on it in block letters. I opened it, unfolding the paper inside. Someone had written in smudged lead pencil, "Good Shepherd Medical Building...parking garage...seven o'clock tonight...Come alone...Andy will be thankful."

What the heck was this? Some kind of kook? A social media nut gone crazy? I knew where the medical building was, about twelve minutes from my house. Small town. Every location is close here. I was about to dismiss it as the work of a true crime nut from that awful website when I studied it again. Andy. They had mentioned my brother. I glanced at the clock on the wall. Six-forty. Twenty minutes. This is dumb. It reminded me of a stupid book character who went alone to meet a sociopath who would kill her.

But they mentioned Andy. Andy, my brother, who was so lonely and scared in that jail cell with Jeeter and Clint making sure he was frightened. What if an "accident" happened? What if he didn't make it to trial? Someone out there didn't want him to push for the truth. Maybe this was a way to help him.

I grabbed my coat and car keys, then headed out the door again. I stopped and circled back to the kitchen and opened a drawer. Tom had given me a small canister of pepper spray. I grabbed it, stuffing it into my coat pocket. If this was some nut, I wanted to be armed. At least this time Jeeter wouldn't be coming along. Imagining him following the delivery truck, I giggled.

I drove past the coffee shop, its owner locking up for the night. Next door, lights were shining over the big parking lot of Greko's Grocery. A bunch of high school kids were "Freezing for Hunger," huddled together at the end of a large truck with opened doors and yelling at passing cars. Their charitable donations from passersby would help stock the local food pantry. I remembered doing that in high school. I have never been so cold since.

Three traffic lights and a police cruiser later, I was thankful I hadn't speeded. I crept into the parking garage, ticket in hand, with a few minutes left. But where was I supposed to go? It was a Saturday night, and the garage wasn't very full. I parked in the first space I found on the second deck, turning my lights off. Or should I leave them on? I had no clue, since I'd never had a rendezvous with a mysterious person before. I kept my keys in my hand, figuring I could use them as a weapon. Andy, this had better be worth it, I mumbled to myself.

I wasn't sure what to do, so I leaned on the hood of my car waiting for... what? I scanned the entire area. It was really dark. Several of the lightbulbs were out on this level of the garage. An occasional forlorn leaf or two from autumn, hanging around to remind me of warmer days, rustled as the wind picked up. The whole area was desolate and cold. I heard voices, but they must have come from the lower deck. I was totally alone. The thought of a stupid book character came back to me. But I was armed with my car keys and pepper spray. I'd added my mauve scarf—my favorite—to my winter jacket to give me courage.

Looking all around, I wondered how long I should wait. I checked my phone. Six fifty-nine. Dropping it in my pocket, I noticed again how dark it was all around me. Shadows filled the corners, their vague outlines undoubtedly recognizable in the light of day. I was sure I saw a brief movement over by the door to the elevator. Something moving. Then, nothing. My imagination. The longer I waited, the more my breath came in short spurts of misty fog. I wrung my hands together and thought about leaving. This was crazy. Whoever it was could be a maniac.

I did see a movement. Over in the corner, a dark shadow detached itself from the wall, taller than me in a long, black, unbuttoned coat with a hoodie pulled up over his head, a black stocking cap, and a mask covering most of his face. Was it a man? I wasn't sure. Could be a tall woman. Moving toward me slowly, he kept his hands in his pockets. I felt the canister of pepper spray in my right hand. Could he have a gun in his pocket? I held my breath momentarily but stayed silent. I couldn't find my voice.

The figure said a muffled, "Jill Madison?"

I nodded, too scared to speak.

The black figure came closer, checking all the shadowy corners. But we were alone. He stopped about eight feet from me. "I know you're worried about your brother. Me too. I owe Tom."

"Who are you?" I had found my voice again.

"I can't get involved in this mess. But because of my situation, I can't hesitate and see an innocent man railroaded. That's what Crockett will do. He'll plant evidence. Don't trust him."

"Believe me, I don't," I said. "But what can I do?"

"Keep digging. People are getting nervous."

I felt relieved, my breathing loosening from the tight lock it had been under. "Now *that* I can do. But where should I look?"

He glanced around the deserted parking garage again. "You need to follow the money."

"Follow the money? What money?"

"Long ago." He began to melt into the shadows again.

"Wait!" I called. "How can I get in touch with you?"

"You can't. I'll reach out to you if I have more."

Now he was backing farther away.

"Wait!" I called again. "Who are you?"

I heard a chuckle come back from the darkness. "Call me Deep Throat."

Deep Throat? Weird. What was that? "Follow the money?" What a stupid thing to say—probably copied from some mystery novel.

But he was gone, moving back into shadows. I closed my eyes, trying to remember what they had momentarily seen. A glint of metal? Silver maybe? Around his neck. Focus, Jill. Close your eyes. Focus. Picture it. A cross. A small one, but still a cross necklace.

Chapter Nineteen

"So, the first rule it states is if you see a ghost, don't move. Stay perfectly still. Don't breathe."

"Don't breathe? How can I do that? And why should I stay still? Running makes more sense." Angie and I were sitting in my office at the art center on Sunday afternoon trying to figure out this ghost thing.

"Not sure. It doesn't say why," she answered, holding her copy of *Ghost Hunting for Amateurs.* "Maybe it's so you can get a good picture. It says to take a lot of photographs, but don't let the lens of your camera click too loudly."

"Hmm. I'm not sure we're getting the best advice here. What's next?"

Angie read a few lines to herself. "A flashlight. You need to have a flashlight at all times."

"That rule makes some sense. After all, the lights could go out."

"The third rule says if you see a ghostly phenomenon, you're supposed to contact other members of your team so they can corroborate what you see."

"Team? All right. We can make a pact to do that!" I reached over, slapping her hand. "Done, my friend."

Angie looked up at me from her reading. "What do we do if we see a ghost? It doesn't explain what happens after we see it."

I thought about it for a moment. "I guess we'd want to talk to it. Maybe ask why it's haunting the art center."

"Did you find anything when you researched the history of the building?"

"Actually, I did. Not sure it tells us much except facts. Victoria Kemp gave me some stuff too."

"So, what did you find?"

I pulled a notebook out of my drawer. "I think history's much more interesting when it's about people rather than buildings, but here goes. Daniel Lowry was the owner and builder, who came here in 1866. His photo is out in the main gallery. This space was an apple orchard, which is why Apple Grove is the name of the town. Lots of apple orchards. The building was done in 1870 and called Lowry Brothers General Store."

"Ah, that's nice. A family enterprise."

"True, but I only saw one name on the court records. It sounds like he owned the building until 1890. It was put up for auction. Some guy named O.M. Wright bought it and opened a pharmacy downstairs with a reading room upstairs."

Angie looked at me. "A room to read in? Why would they have such a thing?"

"I wondered about that too. So, I checked it out online. Reading rooms were very popular in the 1800s. They were more like libraries today. You could go there, read newspapers, and learn about all the latest 'domestic skills' in the ladies' magazines."

"Sounds like a dull existence, if you ask me."

"Remember, ladies back then weren't allowed to do much except wear corsets, nibble food, marry, and have babies."

"Thank God we live in now. What happened next?"

I looked back at my notes. "I think this Wright owned it until 1939. Could he be retired or something. He sold it to another pharmacist named James Mills, who continued to have a pharmacy until 1950."

"Boy, that's still ancient history," Angie said and blew a bubble with her gum. "When does your mom's art center come into the picture?"

"Soon. We're getting there. Three bankers bought the building and opened a department store. Those stores were popular in those days. You could buy all kinds of things in a department store, like a mall today. But malls are now closing all over the country. I guess our future shopping is going to be all internet."

"That's too bad. I wouldn't mind being able to one-stop shop right here."

"This brings us to the end of our building history. In 1992, the department store closed. The building sat empty until the Marsden Trust bought it in 2015. But I found out a lot about the builder—Daniel Lowry." As Angie listened, I explained the history of the guy who Victoria had researched.

"That must be the ghost. Love, death, tragedy, homicide. That has to be the groaner." She closed her ghost how-to book. "It would be so interesting to find out the history of buildings. Of course, Wiley built Priscilla's, so we don't have any history. But you could research the history of your mom and dad's house. How old do you think it is?"

I thought about that. "I think it might have been built right after World War II."

"Oh. More ancient history," Angie said, disappointment settling on her face.

Chapter Twenty

I spent most of Monday morning working with the radio show cast at Apple Grove College's theater department, finding costumes for the show. It was so much fun trying on dresses from the Victorian period in England. Fortunately, the college didn't use dresses that needed those horrible, tight corsets, and their current production was from the modern period.

Mrs. Otis and Virginia would wear heavy silk dresses with the skirts swept up into a small bustle in the back. High necks with lace were the fashion, topped by a hat with feathers for Mrs. Otis, secured by a hatpin. Stiff petticoats would normally be in style, but since the women would be sitting down several times, we decided petticoats without the usual stiffness would work better. Their sleeves were in big puffs near the shoulders. Virginia, being a teenager, would wear a blond, long-haired wig with bows. Mrs. Umney, the housekeeper, would wear a very plain, dark outfit with an apron over the skirt and bodice. The narrator would be dressed like Mrs. Umney in a dark outfit, but no apron.

Then, there were the men. That would be the American minister, Hiram B. Otis; his son, Washington; and Virginia's beau, the duke of Cheshire. They'd wear knee-length topcoats made of sack cloth. The trousers were topped by shirts with winged collars and ascot ties. The daytime scenes would need neckties, which were much less formal. We'd have to have some practice tying the ties. Bowler hats would be fine for casual daytime wear. We wouldn't need top hats because there were no formal scenes. Hiram would need a dark-colored smoking jacket and leggings, since he'd appear with the ghost in some night scenes. The boys, Stars and Stripes, would mostly be in trousers and shirts with long, boy's nightgowns for night scenes.

The ghost, Sir Simon, was more difficult. Since he'd died in 1584, we needed him to be in the style of that time. We found Chad a linen shirt with a high collar and wrist ruffs. Over the shirt he'd wear a sleeveless jerkin that dipped in a V-shape in front. Kind of like a vest. We also needed stockings and boots.

"Nah. I'm not going to prance around in stockings," Chad complained. "I'm just a bit too old to be wearing tights. It's not dignified."

We tried to talk him into the tights, but finally gave up. Instead, we found him some taupe trousers, along with boots that went partway up to his knees. A soft hat, gathered at the crown, completed the outfit.

"You'll have to wear a beard," I said. "That was the style back then."

He looked at me, an expression of disdain on his face.

Who knew Chad could be so stubborn?

"I doubt I can grow a full beard in time for the play."

"That's no problem," said Missy Felton, the costumer. "We can attach a beard that will work just fine with your complexion."

Chad looked at me, and I lifted my eyebrows.

Once everyone had changed back into their own clothes, we gathered up the costumes. "Well, that's it. Help me carry these out to my car, and we'll load them in the back seat."

And that's how I spent my Monday morning. It was joyful, especially seeing the faces of these seniors, who were having a great time with this project. We laughed many times when we tried to figure out how things snapped, buttoned, or fastened. It sure wasn't like living in the twenty-first century. Everyone was so excited, and our laughter spilled down the hallway of the theater department. At one point, a student walked in and said the professor wanted us to quiet down because we were interrupting his class. We'd forgotten classes were in session.

After we loaded the costumes into my car, the whole group insisted on coming to the art center to put the costumes away in the weavers room. I was so pleased that we'd used Chad's suggestion to start a senior group, and these seniors were hardly the trope of ageism, sitting in rocking chairs, knitting, or watching television. Their energy was infectious.

Louise and I had both had lunch and were in my office as I told her the story of our costume expedition. Chad's objections were the funniest of the stories. My phone went off and I casually reached for it on my desk. It was Lance. He sounded breathless.

"What's wrong?" I said immediately.

"Jill, you gotta get over to the hospital. Andy's in trouble."

"What?" I immediately looked for my purse and keys. "What do you mean in the hospital? What trouble?"

Louise lifted an eyebrow and listened to my end.

"Jeeter put some Neanderthal in his cell, and he beat Andy up."

"What? How could he do that? How bad is it?" Louise was holding my heavy winter jacket out so I could put my arms in the sleeves.

"I don't know. I'm going there right now. Eddie Brant, the deputy, called me. Otherwise, I'd never know what happened."

"Okay. I'm calling Tom. Be there in a moment." I punched off the call.

"Don't worry. I'm here. Go take care of your brother," Louise said. She hugged me. I grabbed my scarf and headed out the alley door, tears in my eyes. What next?

I tried so hard to stay under the speed limit to the hospital, but it was tough. Sam was working today in the ER, so maybe he'd know what was going on. I called Tom through my car screen, telling him the scant details I knew. Jeeter Crockett. I hated him even more now. How could he do such a terrible thing? Was it because Tigger found the tracker and made a fool out of him? He'd hate being bested. Maybe this was my fault. The stoplight turned red, and I waited for what seemed like an eternity.

"Come on, come on," I muttered. Finally. I stomped on the gas pedal as if it were my archenemy.

I found a spot to park in the hospital parking lot and ran to the front entrance. Once in, I asked for Andy's room at the main desk.

The receptionist quickly looked it up on her computer. "Room 457."

"Thanks." Racing to the open doors of the elevator, I pressed the fourth floor and was relieved to feel it lift immediately. The door opened on the fourth floor, and who was there but Jeeter Crocket. He smiled.

"If it weren't illegal to hit a police officer, I'd make short shrift of your face, Jeeter," I burst out.

He smiled even more widely. "Ah, Jill. I know you like me. You're so cute when you're mad." He walked into the elevator and held open the door. "Jail, you know, can be scary. If your brother hadn't killed someone, he wouldn't be there in the first place."

Before I could summon up a retort, he let go of the elevator door, it closed, and he was gone. I hit the wall with my fist. Oh, I hated him. I turned and looked for a sign to 457. Right and down the corridor.

I saw Eddie Brant outside Andy's room before I even found the room number. "Is he going to be alright, Eddie?"

He nodded. "I think so. You can go in. Tom's already here."

I walked in and saw curtains hanging around his bed. Steeling myself, I tiptoed over and pulled back the edge of the curtain. Tom was sitting in a chair next to Andy's bed, and he rose when he saw me. I looked over at Andy. Oh, my God. This was awful.

He was asleep, an oxygen tube in his nose. One arm was in a soft cast, bandages wrapped around it, and his face had numerous bruises and several butterfly Band-Aids. His eyes were closed, but he seemed to be softly breathing. Worst of all, they had handcuffed his free arm to the steel side railing of the bed. I just stared at the entire, horrifying picture, my heart pounding. Tears came into my eyes and trickled down my cheeks. Oh, Andy. When will all this nightmare end?

Tom put his arms around me, and we were both crying. My detective brother seldom cried. The last time I saw him weep was at our parents' funeral seven years earlier.

"I can't protect him," he whispered.

I pulled away, wiping the tears from my face. "Has he been able to talk?" I asked softly.

"Not since I've been here. They have him sedated from the surgery on his arm. They had to put a plate and stitches in. Lance is downstairs getting some coffee. Eddie Brant is outside. I trust Eddie to keep an eye on things, but he can't always be here. I think you or I or Lance or Angie should be with him until he's able to get out. Sad to say, but I don't trust the sheriff's department to keep him safe. Obviously. Who knows what other 'accidents' Jeeter has planned?"

"How did this happen?"

"Jeeter was around when I got here, and he said they had to add a guy to Andy's cell because they're up to full occupancy. Of course, I don't know if that's true. He implied Andy should have kept his mouth shut."

"Oh, please. He's blaming this on Andy? Last time I talked with Andy he said there were lots of empty cells."

"Yeah. You know Jeeter. And that's why we'll need to take shifts. I've already called Mary. I'll stay until midnight, and then Lance will come in. And Lance will call Andy's lawyer too. We'll figure out the rest."

"Sounds good." I glanced over at Andy, who was now softly snoring. "This is just awful. He doesn't deserve this. He didn't do anything wrong, and he certainly didn't kill Quinn Parsons."

"I know. Sometimes justice takes a long time." He put his arms around me in a hug. "I won't let that happen. It can't happen. I'll come up with a plan."

"I'm not sure how long he has with Jeeter in the picture. Who knows what he'll try next." I felt a lump in my throat. "I'm so scared for him, Tom. This is a perfect example of Andy not living long enough to be tried. And even if he did, what future does he have with life imprisonment hanging over him? There aren't any good outcomes here. I'm so worried."

"You go home and get some rest or go back to the art center. Lance and I will get this figured out and call Angie. If Eddie Brant is on during the night, we might get by with being here in the daytime only. We'll see. I'll talk to Brant."

"Have you talked to Sam?"

"He was here for a few minutes, but then he was paged to go to the ER."

I could tell that was true since there was the faintest scent of sandalwood in the room.

I looked at Andy again, sleeping soundly away, his left eye becoming increasingly purple. I walked over and gave him a kiss on his forehead and left, hoping this was the worst it would get. I held it together on the elevator down to the main entrance. As I walked out the front door, I began sobbing. It was a long walk back to the car, and I couldn't stop crying.

I unlocked the car and got in. I sat there and thought about it all. I came back to Apple Grove and found my family again last year. After losing our parents, we'd drifted apart for a while. Now that I'd come back and we were working out our lives without our parents at the head of the family, it seemed a lot harder than I thought it would be. But even though there had been ups and downs, the feeling of being part of a family again made me happy I was home. If nothing else, the sight of my brother there in that hospital bed made me determined to find out who killed Quinn Parsons. And I knew it was not my brother.

Chapter Twenty-One

"Okay, so it didn't work. Let's try this." I typed in another name and took a sip of my wine. After working at the art center all day, I had decided to do a bit of research on Daniel Lowry and find out more about the man who had built my art center. I knew Lance was at the hospital with Andy, and I'd stopped by after work. My trusty laptop sat on my dining room table. I'd already found his birth certificate on a genealogy site. He was born in 1834 to David and Arabella Lowry in Covington, Pennsylvania. More digging uncovered he was the eleventh of twelve children. Wow! Two had died while still young. I also found a form showing Lowry had joined the Pennsylvania Reserves in 1863.

He must have survived because he married a woman named Rosemary Pike in 1866. I found three death certificates. In addition to Daniel's, I found one for Rosemary and one for an infant named Daniel in 1871. How sad. She was only twenty-nine. Same date as her son. That gave me pause. I questioned whether I wanted to know any more unwelcome news. But I trudged on. A much later death certificate existed for Daniel Elliott Lowry on February 25, 1890. A gunshot wound. Homicide. Could that be the ghost who might be in the building? The one who let out those awful moans? And homicide?

I sat back in my chair, examined the death certificate on my laptop, and tapped on my lips with my finger. Homicide. Victoria was correct on everything. Why would someone kill him? It seemed ironic I was trying to save my brother from being unfairly accused of a homicide, and here's Daniel Lowry, the victim of a homicide. I needed to find out more about this.

I began tapping on the keys, searching for more information on his death. After a glance at my empty wineglass, I rose, trotting to the kitchen. A refill would be helpful! My cell phone rang with the generic ringtone that indicated no one I knew. I was about to leave it ringing but my curiosity made me check it out. A number I didn't know. I touched the accept button.

"Jill Madison?"

"Yes. Who's this?"

"It's your contact, Deep Throat."

"Seriously? Aren't you carrying this a bit too far? How did you get my cell number?"

He ignored my questions. "I have information. Come or not as you please."

I took a deep breath. "Same place?"

"Sure. Twenty minutes." A click. Not a cell phone.

"Well, thanks for hanging up on me." I dropped my phone in my purse, closed my laptop program, and grabbed my coat. "I hope this is going to be more than 'follow the money,'" I muttered.

This time it was freezing cold as I parked in the garage at the hospital. I waited for a minute or two, putting on mittens and pulling my scarf tighter around my neck. I got out of the car and waited, my toes and fingers like ice cubes. This had better not take too long or I'd have frostbite. Brr.

I saw a shadow move near the elevator doors. The same hooded, masked person—maybe the same? —walked toward me. He stopped once again about ten feet away.

"Did you follow the money like I told you?"

"How can I? I don't have any connections to banks or financial institutions."

"That's where you'll find your answers. But there's another place you might look."

"Oh? Where?"

"Parsons' minister."

I stomped my feet, trying to keep from freezing. "Why would he be willing to talk to me?"

"You'll never know till you try."

I scowled. "These seem like wild-goose chases. And what money should I follow anyway?"

"Darnell's, Parsons', O'Brien's, and one more."

"Who?"

"You can figure it out. If you want to save your brother, get on it." He backed away and was lost again in the shadows.

I got back in my car, thinking about how much of a waste this all was. Follow the money? Talk to the minister? Why couldn't he tell me what I needed to know? Who was this guy, anyway? I didn't recognize his voice.

As I drove back toward my house, I decided to take a detour. I turned into Priscilla's parking lot. I'll bet Angie and I could figure this out. Walking into the bar, I gave a wave to Wiley and walked toward my friend.

"Angie, I need to talk with you. It's urgent."

She was wiping some glasses she'd washed, but she put them down and followed me over to a booth away from the bar. The jukebox was playing some country music, so it would be loud enough no one would hear.

After explaining the Deep Throat scenario to her, I said, "I don't know how we can do that. 'Follow the money?' I don't have any way to get into anyone's bank accounts. Even if I did, it would be illegal. Not only would Tom kill me, but I'd also find myself in jail. It seems counterproductive to end up in jail when I'm trying to get Andy out of jail."

"Hmm. Talking to Parsons' minister—what was his name? Clump? Crump? Frump! That was the name. How could I forget?" Angie said, chuckling.

"Yeah, I believe so. I'm going to call the church tomorrow morning and see if he'll speak to us. He isn't prohibited from talking by some kind of seal of confession like Catholic priests are. Maybe he could answer some questions about what Quinn was thinking before he died."

Angie shrugged. "The worst he could say would be, 'no.' Parsons is dead, so it's not like he's repeating gossip about someone still alive. I say go for it."

I sat back and thought about it. "Financial stuff. Who do we know who'd be willing to hack into databases?"

"I have no clue. No one I know could do that. Wiley knows nothing about it, and even someone like Paul Darnell wouldn't do it. He's a bank vice president."

"Angie, he'd be one of the people we'd need to find out about. He could be up to his neck in this situation with Parsons' death. And it was his lake cottage. His fingerprints would already be there. What if he was involved in the car accident somehow and Quinn was blackmailing him?" I tapped my fingers on the table. "Surely there's someone in this town I know who could help us. Let me do some thinking about it. I'll check back with you once I call Frump." We both giggled all over again.

My phone jingled with a text from Tom.

The doctor visited Andy and he's doing well.

Good. At least that was a bright spot.

On the way back to my house, I decided to stop by my office and grab a copy of *The Historical Archives of Lincoln County*. Victoria Kemp had loaned it to me after I asked her about the Lowry building. I parked and went in the side door. The night lights were on and sound effects equipment was scattered on the stage. It was almost ten o'clock and Chad had finished cleaning. I locked the door behind me and reset the security system. It was eerie walking in here now, especially after the moaning howl the other day when the seniors were rehearsing. I felt in my pocket. The pepper spray was still there. Would it work on ghosts? I scanned the gallery. It seemed quiet enough. No objects like my pencil were rolling around on the floor.

I went into my office and found the book quickly on the loveseat. I grabbed it and walked back out toward the side door.

A deep voice came out of the gallery. Male. Not Chad.

"Aren't you going to talk to me?"

I stopped cold, my hands shook, and I dropped the book. I felt my legs tremble. No one should be here except me. Fighting the impulse to turn around, I took several deep breaths.

"I tried to get your attention with the writing implements in your office. You seem like someone with whom I could converse." Deep voice, almost sonorous.

I slowly turned around, my eyes stopping on a figure in the shadows of the stage. I was about to reach for the light switch when the figure said, "No, the electric lights bother me, and idle passersby might look in."

He was about ten feet away, sitting on a chair on the stage.

My hand flew to my chest. I think I must have gasped. He was dressed formally in a three-piece suit. The short, single-breasted, kohl-gray jacket looked like it was tweed. A dark vest covered a white shirt with a high collar and bow tie. Dove gray pants rose from tall black boots. He had the appearance of someone long ago, with short, black hair parted on the left side, a generous moustache, and a pointed beard. A scar ran down his left cheek, but otherwise his face was unblemished. His posture was relaxed, one leg crossed over the other, his arms crossed also, a contrast with the formal nature of his clothes.

"How did you get in here?" I asked once I found my voice.

He uncrossed his arms, raised his hand slightly, and said, "I have always resided here. This is my building. You are the one who is trespassing. But I must say, it is invigorating watching your work." He glanced around at the walls. "However, I find some of these paintings strange indeed."

I rubbed my eyes. No, he was still there. I pulled my phone out of my pocket and punched 9-1-1 to report a prowler. But there were no bars. Strange. His voice stopped me.

"Your pocket-whatever-it-is won't function momentarily."

He was right. I put it back in my pocket. It struck me—his identity. I'd seen his photo on the genealogy site. "Daniel Lowry?"

He stood and bowed. "At your service, madame."

"But this is impossible. You're dead. You've been dead for a hundred and twenty-five years or more."

"Alas, I am despondent about that unfortunate occurrence. But I try to make the best of it."

I studied him. "How can you be here? How can I see you?"

"I can be here because I am. You can see me because I allow you to do so. If you would sit, madame, it would allow me to do so also." He waited.

I looked around the empty gallery, walked over to a chair, and sat. "There."

"Thank you. Now, as to my trespassing. I built this edifice and opened it as a general store in 1870. I believe I have ownership by prior occupancy. Some decades have been uninteresting, but, as I believe I stated, your multitude of projects has been entertaining."

Multitude of projects, I thought. That's an understatement. Read my whiteboards. "I read about you this evening."

He tilted his head slightly. "Really? People may read about Daniel Lowry?"

"Oh, yes. I found your birth certificate and your record of fighting in the Civil War." I was about to say more but figured it might not be good to bring up death certificates. Could ghosts be aggressive or hurt people?

"Ah, yes. The early years. I had far more brothers than you have."

"I know. Six to be exact."

"Oh. You have done your inquiries. They are gone now. All my siblings. Two, quite young, the rest in the past hundred years or more. I miss them and wish I could accompany them into the great beyond."

"Just why is that?" I asked. "Why are you hanging around here?"

"I assure you," he said, brushing a speck of dust off his jacket, "if I could join their company I would do so. But a poorly planned judgment on my part has left me in this limbo for over a century. As a result, it is a bit solitary with no one to talk to."

"Why are you choosing to talk to me?"

"Simple. We both have brothers we love. Yours is currently in trouble. I sense a kindred spirit in you, Miss Madison. Also, you are doing this whatever-it-is about a ghost. Another kindred spirit. And, frankly, I admire your hard work ethic and intelligence. Maybe you can aid me in my quest to return to my wife in the afterlife."

I sat back, feeling myself relax now that I thought he wasn't planning to kill me so I could join him. Curiosity got the better of me. "So, what was it like, fighting in the Civil War?"

"Horrid. Ecstatic. Terrifying. Prideful. An adventure. Death and destruction. My brother, James, and I joined the Pennsylvania Reserves together. He was child number twelve, while I was eleven. Our father owned a farm, not a particularly good one. Too rocky. But we were all cheap help, year after year. James and I desired to see more. When the war broke out, we found it a contrivance to get away from that back-breaking work. One by one, our siblings left, at least our brothers. We joined in 1863. July."

"And was it an adventure?"

"At first, yes. But in the fall, we marched to a town called Chattanooga on the Tennessee River. Our leaders were told it was a place of habitation where four railroads converged, and if we could control it, we would keep the Rebs from being able to get victuals or ammunition.

"The first night in camp was peaceful. My brother Jimmy and I and a gentleman named Williams from New York stole away and foraged in the countryside, looking for food. We were always hungry. We came upon a deserted farmhouse. Hadn't been deserted for long because there was still food in the kitchen, which we ate like animals. We found a spot in the floor of the barn that appeared to have been disturbed recently. Why? Were the home dwellers hiding something? So, we dug and found a treasure—silver candlestick holders and a hoard of silver money, not those Confederate graybacks. I believe they knew they would have to save their valuables with armies invading their territory. But they were rebels, so I felt no remorse if we stole their goods. We needed a plan. We moved the strongbox out of the barn, took a shovel, and reburied it about a half-mile from that place. Jimmy made a map we copied so we each had one. We figured after the war we would return to recover it if we all survived."

The bell on the alley door jangled, causing me to jump again. It was Chad.

"Saw you in the window and wondered what the heck you were doing sitting here in the dark. It's late. I was driving home from having a few drinks with some pals."

Panicking, I glanced at the ghost and saw him smile. "It's fine. The man can't see me or hear me."

"Well, that hardly seems fair," I said.

"Nothing fair about it," said Chad. "You sure you're all right?"

"Yes. I stopped by to pick up a book." I pointed to it on the floor where I'd dropped it. "I started thinking about the radio play and sat here to see how the stage would look from the audience."

CHAPTER TWENTY-ONE

"A clever prevarication," said Daniel Lowry.

"How's the stage appear to you?" I said to Chad.

"Same as we left it."

The ghost was right. Only I could see him.

Chad handed me the book. "Why don't I see you out to your car?"

"Sure," I said.

"Farewell, Miss Madison," the apparition said.

"Goodnight."

Chad opened the door. "Goodnight to you too."

Driving home, I decided I was losing my mind. Talking to ghosts. My imagination was working overtime after all the research on Daniel Lowry. Angie would tell me I was imagining things. This week, worrying about Andy, the hospital, and Deep Throat guy—it had all been too much. Suddenly, it hit me. I knew someone who could get me financial information, and he lived right next door. I was going to go home, have another glass of wine, take a long shower, and go to bed. Tomorrow it would all seem like a crazy dream.

Chapter Twenty-Two

Angie and I sat in my car outside the Babbling Brook Community Church the next day. The church was a brand-new building with a huge cross rising above the roof. And yes, a brook would babble next to the parking lot, but it was frozen for now. I was beginning to feel guilty I had left Louise at the art center by herself so often. I hoped the board didn't get wind of this. Especially Ivan Truelove.

"Did you talk to Andy yesterday?"

"Yes," I said. "I went to the hospital. The doctor had been in to once again pronounce his surgery a success. I guess Andy will be there for a few more days. I actually think he's safer there."

"I'm on a short shift to stay with him tomorrow afternoon."

"Thanks for your help. Poor Louise is putting in overtime keeping her eyes on the art center." I took a sip of my coffee in its to-go container.

"Did you tell Tom we're going to talk to Pastor Frump?" she said, giggling.

"You have to get over your laughing when you mention his name," I scolded.

She put her hand on her mouth and said, "I'll try. Maybe call him 'Pastor.' What's the plan?"

I tapped on the steering wheel considering her question. "I think we need to get him to trust us, show him we aren't trying to blacken Parsons' name, although it would be nice. We want to know if he told the good reverend some information that might help us with our investigation. Let him ramble on for a while."

"Sounds good to me."

I had called the minister's office earlier this morning and asked if he could see us. He was clearly interested. So, here we were, escorted to his study and seated in chairs by a stern-looking secretary. I bet she never giggled at his name. The clock on the wall ticked loudly as we waited for him to show. He had a huge desk, covered with papers, a large Bible, a concordance, and several other books about biblical research. I figured he was working on his Sunday sermon.

Angie rose and walked around behind his desk, looking at some items on a bookshelf.

"Jill," she whispered, signaling me to come join her. "Look at this."

I walked over and watched as she lifted a framed photograph from the shelf.

"Aus-tra-lo-pith-e-cus?"

I looked at the photograph she was holding. A much younger Pastor Frump was standing next to a set of bones that looked like it had been a primate. A huge primate.

"What is it?" She turned it over and scanned the back. Then, she read, "Some kind of genus of ape-like animal from two or three million years ago. It says the good pastor was in a museum in Africa. Suppose he's interested in studying this kind of thing?"

I nodded, worried that he might return and find Angie in his stuff. "Put it back," I whispered.

"He must be weird."

She set it down on the shelf again, but it wouldn't stay upright. Three times it fell down.

"Angie, hurry."

"I can't get it to stand up."

I scowled. "He's going to come in any minute."

She looked at me, a thoughtful expression on her face. "I've got it!" She took her chewing gum from her mouth, stuck it on the back of the framed photo, and pushed it against the back of the shelf. "There!"

I rolled my eyes, hoped the minister wouldn't pick his prize photograph up to show us, and motioned her back to the chair beside me. Just as she sat, the door opened. I let out the breath I was holding.

In strolled Pastor Frump. Up close, he was a short, slender man in his fifties, scholarly. His glasses hung on a cord around his neck while his face was only beginning to deepen into wrinkles. Dressed in a dark suit. I couldn't imagine him in a sweatshirt or T-shirt. He seemed like kind of a formal guy.

We stood, introduced ourselves, chatted a bit about his church, and explained Angie had no church affiliation while my family went to the First Methodist Church on Granger Avenue. Actually, I managed to make it occasionally when my niece and nephew had a program, but I didn't think it was necessary to mention that. Then it was time to get down to business.

He moved a folder to the side of his desk and asked, "What might I help you with today? I had the impression you were concerned about Brother Quinn Parsons, may he rest in peace."

I had my own opinions about where he should be resting but decided to put them aside and smile my best smile. "We are interested, Pastor Frump, with any information that might help us understand his mental state prior to his death. As you may know, my brother, Andy, has been arrested for his murder. While I'm sure he's innocent, I thought it might help us to know any little details helpful to his case."

"You believe someone other than your violent brother might have done this?"

Angie and I glanced at each other, both thinking about the same word in his question. "Oh, I can assure you," Angie said, "I grew up around Andy. He wasn't violent. He was a wonderful older brother to me. I'm afraid he'd had a few drinks before he attended the meeting at your church. Perhaps the alcohol guided his lack of a forgiving countenance."

"Countenance?" Did I hear Angie right? She really was studying her dictionary.

"Spirits never belong in the house of the Lord," he said quietly.

"Actually, Pastor Frump," I said, "my brother has always been a kind person, but I'm afraid he was overcome by his sadness in missing our parents."

For a moment he stared at his desktop. His face softened as he said something remarkable, an idea I'd never thought about. "You know, Ms.

Madison, I can understand the process of grief with your brother and the rest of your family. When a thoroughly unexpected tragedy jolts us, we can only feel that tragedy. Nothing else matters. We become numbed, saddened by our own plight. With distance and time, our minds begin to see the tragedy in the plan of our whole lives. I will pray with time, you'll come to terms with this misfortune brought upon your family."

I sat there stunned by his insight. It was true our parents' deaths had affected the past seven years. It was a jolt, totally unexpected.

"Well," he said, nodding. "I understand your kind of grief. Often, I deal with it when counseling my parishioners. I can tell you, I suppose, Quinn Parsons was quite adamant he was not driving the car the night of his unfortunate accident."

Angie leaned forward. "Did he say, perchance, who might have been?"

I turned, giving Angie a quizzical look shortly after "perchance." Where had my best bud gone?

"That he couldn't remember. But he was quite clear it wasn't him. He was equally sure the brakes on the car didn't work. He grabbed the steering wheel to try to keep from crossing the center line of the highway."

"Did he think the brakes had been tampered with?" I asked.

He nodded. "The group of boys had decided to let someone else drive who had not been drinking. Certainly, theirs was a responsible decision. I know—in fact I'm certain—he was not only telling me the truth, but he felt terribly guilty and sad at the pain the accident caused several families, including yours."

"Why didn't he say this at his trial?" I asked.

The good reverend sat back in his chair, his hand to his mouth, considering. "I, too, asked him your question. It made no sense to me that he would take the place of someone else responsible for the accident. If he weren't driving, why not admit it?"

"Did he have an answer?"

"Yes. At the time of the accident, he had been drinking. His memory was not at all what it should have been. The accident itself, the horror of it, affected his memory. Several people suggested he was driving. The other two young men in the back seat couldn't have been in the front. No one else was at the scene. He naturally assumed he was driving but couldn't remember. That is, he couldn't remember until he was hypnotized in prison. Then, he knew he wasn't driving, but he still didn't know who was." The good minister shook his head slowly. "So many times, I've seen alcohol cause misfortune."

Guess I'd better not mention Angie's and my wine consumption.

As if to speedily change the subject, Angie said, "Did you have the impression he wanted to find out the driver's identity once he was back here?"

"Oh, yes," he answered Angie, gazing at her intently. "I had the impression he'd narrowed it to one person. He was planning to question him or her, but he never told me whom he suspected."

Angie and I studied each other. I knew we suspected the same person.

"Is there anything else you can tell us, Pastor?" I asked.

He shook his head. "Afraid not. Quinn Parsons was a man of secrets, and I am sure he didn't tell me the deepest secrets hiding in his heart. He appeared to be on a mission, but who the subject of his mission was, I do not know. I can tell you this. I believe he knew this driver quite well because when he talked about fixing the past, he hesitated to tell me the name. I had the feeling it was someone I might have known. Just a hunch."

I stood. "Thanks so much, Pastor. You've helped us immensely."

As we left, Angie and I plodded through the snow saying nothing. I glanced up just in time to see a sheriff's car driving slowly down the street. Clint Anderson was behind the wheel, and he stared at us through his window before moving on. Once in the car, I flipped on the heat, put on my seat belt, and turned to her. "Are you thinking what I'm thinking?"

"I don't know. You first."

"Who isn't accounted for in the Parsons' car? Who said he was there with them earlier in the evening."

"Paul Darnell." Angie thought for a moment. "But he has an alibi."

"Alibis can be faked. I think we should put Tom on this. Maybe people at the bar that night can remember when Darnell left and how he left."

"But if Darnell was driving the car, how come he didn't get hurt? How come he was at home when the news broke?" She shook her head.

"Above my pay grade. Tom will figure it out. If we solve another murder before him, I'm afraid he might kick me out of the family."

After dropping Angie off at her house, I drove to the police station to talk with Tom. I didn't have the pieces put together, but I felt like we were getting closer. One of those pieces I hadn't mentioned to anyone was a conversation with my next-door neighbor, Tigger. "Follow the money" Deep Throat had said. I gently probed Tigger about his many talents, and hacking was one of them. Explaining I needed to know about the finances of Darnell, Parsons, and O'Brien, he acted like it was child's play.

"You realize this is totally illegal, right?" he'd said.

I nodded. "But then there's my brother Andy sitting in jail." I could tell he was reluctant, maybe because he didn't know if he could trust me. "Could the police figure out what you do?" I asked.

He chuckled. "Nah. I'm really good at it."

"What if the FBI or CIA show up to arrest you?"

He laughed. "If they show up, it would never be to arrest me."

I stared at him for a moment, considering what that meant. "I'm willing to pay whatever the going rate is."

"Why, Ms. Madison. I do believe you're a natural-born lawbreaker."

"Let's just say my friend Angie and I have had a little experience."

The conversation ended when he assured me he'd make an attempt to find the goods on those three. Maybe it was going to be helpful to have such an expert living next door to me.

At the station, I spoke to several of the guys Tom worked with, went to the front desk, and asked whether my brother was in.

"Sure is," said Jake Singleton. "Just a minute." He picked up his phone, punched some numbers, then let Tom know I was coming. "You know the way. He's been really grumpy lately. Good luck."

I smiled. "Haven't we all with my other brother in jail?" I strode through the depressing institutional gray hallway to Tom's office. My artist's brain said it could sure use a more cheerful color. Possibly a few murals. Morale might improve. He came out the door as I got there.

"Wow. It's been a while since you've paid me a visit at the shop. What's up?"

We moved into his office and sat, he at his desk and I flopping into an uncomfortable, well-worn chair across from him. It was generic—the office, that is—with file cabinets, a plain desk, a lamp and florescent lights in the ceiling. Lots of piles of papers occupied his desktop.

"I think I have a possible lead."

He leaned back in his chair, folding his hands behind his head, observing my face. "A credible lead? An idea I can work with without Jeeter showing up?"

"Yes." I told him about our conversation with the minister. "Don't you see, it has to be Paul Darnell who was driving Quinn's car."

He shook his head. "He has a solid alibi."

"When you say 'solid,' do you mean his wife?"

"Sure, but also some of the people at the Eagle's Nest said he was there that night but left before the Parsons' crew."

I stared at my hands in my lap for a moment, then back at Tom. "Here's a 'what if.' What if he left, went out to his car, and waited for the others to leave? He might have thought about the shots they'd been downing, had second thoughts, and offered to drive. He could easily take Quinn's car back to the bar and leave it there. Go get his own car later. He didn't plan for faulty brakes or an accident."

"But why would he offer to drive them?" Tom sat up straighter with his usual skeptical expression on his face.

"Because he felt bad for Quinn. He told Angie and me. Maybe he didn't want to see him get into any more trouble than he was already in. I have the impression Parsons was selling drugs. That would be bad enough. Darnell felt sorry for him because he came from such a terrible home. What if he were driving the car, had his seat belt on, and got out of the accident alive? It didn't happen far from the Eagle's Nest. He could easily have circled back there, picked up his own car, and left. His wife, the social climber, would lie about the time he got home."

Now Tom was thinking. I could see the wheels turning behind his eyes.

"I've been checking on Parsons' background prior to the accident. We had a lot of folks at the station wondering if he was engaged in the drug traffic at the high school. I can't imagine Darnell would be involved in drugs, but it does add to what we know about Parsons and what motivated him. What if he remembered it was Darnell driving and threatened to turn him in? Or blackmail him? Could his threat be the reason Darnell loaned him his cottage at the lake? If he threatened Darnell with exposure, could Paul be the one who pushed him down those stairs?"

"Now you're thinking."

"But how to prove it?"

I sat back, putting the pieces together. "I have an idea. Even if Darnell left the Eagle's Nest early, then changed his mind and decided to drive the guys, might one of those witnesses have seen Darnell's car still in the parking lot, although Paul had left some time earlier in Quinn's car?"

Tom nodded. "It's worth a check. I'll go back over the accident report to see which witnesses they questioned at the bar. I'm sure some of them are still alive. But are they around?" He jotted notes. He looked at me. "It's a start, Jill."

I brushed my hands together, my grin a smirk. "All in a day's work."

Chapter Twenty-Three

After an uneventful day at work, I had a Friday night alone. Sam had drawn the short end of the stick on shifts. What should I do? Angie was working. I could go over to Priscilla's, but without Andy and Lance it wouldn't be much fun. Stay home and read a book or watch a movie? Neither option appealed to me either.

I thought about my conversation this afternoon with Lance. He told me Andy's doctor was in and pronounced Andy good to go back to jail, probably tomorrow. I wish he didn't heal so fast. The hospital seemed like a safe haven.

I sat on my sofa eating strawberry cheesecake ice cream straight out of the carton. It was one of the perks of living alone. My mind wandered to Daniel Lowry. He was extremely attractive. I pictured his face in the shadows, with the strange scar on his left cheek. Well, he was good-looking, but also—I reminded myself—dead. Besides, I had Sam, who was very much alive, handsome, and worked too many hours at the hospital. But what good was a boyfriend who was alive if he was never available?

My phone pinged. "Ivan, for the love of God could you please leave me alone? It's a Friday night. You're off duty."

Lighting. I'm very good at light clues. No problem with making rehearsals.
Ivan F. Truelove III, CPA

I took a deep breath. What was going on with him? And "clues" must have been "cues." Why this interest in helping when all he'd ever done was criticize me? I texted back, "We're fine on the lights, but if we need more clues, I'll check with you." There, that should puzzle him.

Frustrated and restless, I put the ice cream carton back in the freezer and glanced around my living room. What pretext could I produce to visit the handsome, interesting, but dead guy in my art center? OMG. Am I hearing my crazy self? Talking about a dead man? A ghost? I threw my hands in the air and rubbed my tired eyes. My nefarious brain came up with an excuse. My phone said nine thirty, so Chad would be done working. I grabbed my coat, gloves, scarf, boots, and car keys. Boy, it was demanding work to live in the Midwest in winter. Putting on all the winter gear took longer than driving downtown. It would only take me a five-minute drive to get to the art center. I'd park out back.

The streets were deserted, the traffic lights blinking at the intersections on Main Street. I drove past the post office outside boxes and dropped some bills in the chute. At least I felt I was doing something productive on this crackbrained mission. See a dead guy? I couldn't tell anyone about this ghost. Angie. I hadn't told her. Some part of me wanted to hang onto Daniel Lowry and not share him. This was too harebrained even to tell Angie. I smiled, humming a happy tune. It was exciting having a secret of my own. I parked my car in the back, away from the streetlight and in the shadows. This would keep anyone who knew me from wondering why I was here late on a Friday night.

Opening the alley door, I reset the alarm. I strode in, stomping my boots on the entrance carpet to keep the snow off the hardwood floors. I casually walked back to my office, turned on a light, and took off my coat and winter paraphernalia. On my desk were the programs for the radio show. I pulled scissors out of my desk drawer and cut open the twine holding the package together. Pulling out the top program, I stared at the cover. It was amazing. A huge old English castle, Canterville Chase, reimagined. I swelled with pride at my decision to create it and place it there.

Inside were the acts of the play, the names of the seniors in each part, and the sound effects and stage prep people. They'd be so excited. After that came the pieces of artwork scattered around the walls along with a few well-placed ads for businesses supporting us. They were filled with ghosts and goblins. Each piece of artwork had a brief description of its origins. I paged through the photographs, marveling at how it had all come together. I'd take a copy to show Andy. Normally, he would have done the photos, developing them in his home lab. But sadly, he was unavailable for this event.

Putting the program with my coat, I roamed back out into the gallery. He was there in the shadows, and I stood quietly admiring his profile. Standing in the far corner, he gazed at a painting of ghosts rising in a cemetery. What was he thinking? About his own inability to rise?

"Daniel?"

"Yes?" He turned around, a pensive look on his face.

"You're still here."

"Of course. Where else would I be? I am condemned to dwell in this building."

I wandered over to the middle of the gallery.

As I did, he leaned back against the wall, his curiosity showing. "Why did you return tonight?"

I considered his question. "I thought you might need some company, and I wanted to pick up a program for my brother, the one who's in jail."

"Ah," he said, and paused. "What about your young man, that blond bloke?"

"Sam? He's working tonight."

He considered this statement. "He seems to labor a prolonged time."

I tilted my head slightly. I agreed with his point but felt a need to defend my guy. "Sam's a doctor, so he works long hours."

"Ah, a sawbones."

"Well, I'd say medical procedures have changed considerably since you were alive. Both of us are terribly busy with careers," I added.

"Women laboring. You should be at home, married, and having children."

"Fortunately," I said, "we have a few more options these days." The conversation stopped. Maybe I'd spoken a bit more harshly than I meant to. "So, tell me what happened when you were in the war. Last time you spoke of it, you said you'd buried a treasure. Did you ever find it again?"

He walked over to a chair or seemed to walk. Now that I saw him closer, I could easily see through him. Like one of those holograms of three-dimensional displays in museums, he moved quietly. Then he sat. I pulled up a chair too but left the lights off so no one would see us. The dim night lights were enough.

"I had been contemplating that very subject. Conversing about it with you unlocked memories I believed I had forgotten."

I didn't say a word, just waited for him to continue.

"Well, fate obstructed my path. Our regiment lined up the following morning to engage the enemy in an encounter they later called the Battle of the Wilderness. It transpired in Spotsylvania County, Virginia. A fierce, horrible fight it was. Jimmy and I attempted to remain in unison. I desired to keep him safe."

I thought about Andy, who I'd hoped to keep safe also. Sitting back in my chair, I focused again on his story.

"It was insane chaos. We had to discharge our rifles and reload, praying no one would dispatch us to the next life in between. The smoke was so thick you could not see whom you were charging, and in many cases, you killed your own men. We commenced the morning in a line, but anon, it became total chaos. When the battle concluded, I was captured by a group of dirty Rebs. That was where I got this." He pointed to the scar on his ghostly face. "I did not know what had transpired with my brother. We were marched to a prisoner-of-war camp. Later, I heard there had been twenty-eight thousand deaths in our battle, and over three thousand soldiers captured. Hard to even envision so many. Those numbers. So senseless. I was fortunate to be among the living. But what of my brother? Was he a casualty?

"For days I was in discomfort from scrapes, swinging rifle butts, and a sword that had grazed my cheek. But none of those brought me any great consideration. I desired to know what had befallen Jimmy. Without him, I fell into a despair like I'd never known. I was supposed to take care of him. I had promised our mother when we left.

"Several of the men in my unit were also in this camp, and one said he

157

had seen my brother. Hope. I thought, if he is right, Jimmy must be alive. I searched as I could for days, and finally found him. He had been wounded in the leg, and I could see no healing. But with aid from some of my soldier-friends, I returned him to our group of men, and tried to help him as best I could. One of the men had been a doctor's assistant. He contrived to find some cloth to bind the wound. Eventually, it healed, but Jimmy still shuffled with a limp. Then, the next year, we were moved to another camp, a newer and larger one they had constructed called Andersonville."

"That seems miraculous you found him. But Andersonville? I remember studying the camps in school. It was a hellhole."

"I could have told you myself. Every day, we lived in filth, vermin. We attempted to shape a mud shelter with bricks and blankets. Four of us stayed in it, getting weaker and thinner. Having lived through your time with your Vietnam War, I know more soldiers died of disease in my war than yours died in battle."

"It seems so senseless, doesn't it?" I said quietly. "My custodian, Chad, was in the Vietnam War."

He sat there a moment, saying nothing. I wasn't sure he'd heard me at all. "Yes, I am aware. I hear him betimes singing songs about that war." He paused again, thoughtful. "At night, Jimmy and I would discuss returning home when the war ended. We agreed to strike our way out West. We would find a small town and build a general store. I could envision the sign and described it to Jimmy. 'The Lowry Brothers General Store,' we would call it. We could use the treasure we had buried to begin the business. I'd looked for the Williams fellow, but never found him, so I surmised he had been killed."

"You came up with the idea to create this building. How wonderful you had this dream, and you made it come true."

He didn't answer right away.

He sighed. "Fate has a way of changing things, I fear. Yes, I constructed the Lowry Brothers store, but not exactly the way I had imagined it. Jimmy and I stayed together, but he succumbed to sickness. Dysentery, they called it. I attempted to keep his spirits elevated in that hell. But it was not to be. Finally, he died, holding my hand. He made me vow our dream would come true. He was interred in a grave—more like a deep hole—with hundreds of others."

"I'm so sorry. How terrible, but at least you were there with him at the end."

"I was, when he took his final breath. This tragedy made me enraged for an interminable time, but eventually I did not have the energy to be so unbalanced. I did not figure I would make it out of there either, but in 1865, when the war ended, we were released to travel home. I was little more than a skeleton. My recovery took months. My mother nursed me back to health, day after day, hour after hour, month after month. But I never ceased to forget my brother or how I would have given a ransom to have taken his place. Nor did I fail to recall the treasure we had secreted in Tennessee."

I wasn't sure what to say. His voice had such a plaintive tone.

After several minutes, he said, "Tragedies like this are presumed to happen to dastardly people. I thought we deserved what we were given. Our pain and suffering came because of our sinful behavior. But my brother was not that kind of soul. He was a kind, warm, generous, righteous man. I never saw him do a single act of evil. As I pondered his end, I understood he could not have lived through the war. It brought out the beasts in men."

"I see. I think all bets are off when there's a war. That's a great description of my Andy too. But I can't believe this mess he's in is going to kill him. We'll all fight to free him from this predicament. He didn't do this terrible murder. I have to believe life will be fair to him."

"Fair? Life? Good fortune with that."

He was bitter tonight, recalling the past.

As if he guessed what I was thinking, he said, "I consumed a lengthy time questioning why this happened to our people. What did we do to deserve this ruthless, violent end? But I began asking instead, 'So this has happened. What am I going to do about it?'"

I glanced at my phone. It was midnight. As I watched Daniel, he faded into the air. Maybe he sensed he'd said enough for one night.

I left the art center, driving through the darkness to my house. I'd thought it would be exciting to spend some time with my ghost. But he'd put me in a

159

reflective mood. His words kept echoing in my head. I began asking instead, "So this has happened. What am I going to do about it?'"

Chapter Twenty-Four

"I brought you a program for the radio show and art exhibit. Eddie Brant checked it out to make sure I hadn't hidden an AK-47 within the pages."

I had hoped my humor would make Andy smile, but he didn't. He sat slumped in the hard, plastic chair of the visitors' room. Now I knew he had lost weight. It was obvious in the loose fit of his clothing and the hollowed-out cheekbones of his face. Lance and I were the only visitors in the visitors' room on Saturday afternoon. Andy had returned from the hospital this morning. Tom had threatened Jeeter with a lawsuit if he put anyone else in Andy's cell. Even so, Tom and Lance would be at the jail often, checking on his safety.

"We need your help," I told my brother.

"Not sure what I can do to help while I'm stuck in here. What difference does it make? Jeeter has had it in for me for years. He's not going to let this slide." He stared down, refusing to look at me.

"Have you talked to Bill Gatesmith, the new attorney?" Lance asked.

"Yeah. He's been to see me several times."

I looked at Andy. "What did you think of him?"

"He's good enough. Unfortunately, no matter how expansive and positive he is, he can't get past my motivation to kill Parsons, declared in front of a large segment of the town. Since I left fingerprints and tire treads at the scene of the murder, I'm not sure how he'll get around it."

"We know lots of people who have volunteered to come in as character witnesses," Lance said quickly. "That has to count for something."

My brother lowered his chin to his chest and let out a long, low sigh. "It won't matter."

Several moments went by until Lance said, "How's your arm?" He obviously wanted to change the topic to a more positive subject.

"It's better," Andy said. "A magnet will now stick to it since I'm full of metal."

I chuckled, hoping to lighten the mood. "No more international travel for you."

"Probably not."

More silence. Stupid me. That had been the wrong thing to say. I needed to think before I spoke.

"Say, how come you're here on a Saturday afternoon, Lance? Who's minding the store?" he asked.

"I had to make an executive decision," Lance said. "I hired a high school kid to come in on Saturdays so I could make some time to see you."

"How could you? Our margin of profit these days can't be much."

Lance studied me. "It's okay. Jill is helping us a bit with his salary."

Andy didn't exactly explode. He didn't have the energy, but I could tell he was not happy from his facial expression, his pursed lips, and hands knotted into fists. Lance stood and said he'd go out for a breath of air. He disappeared out the door once Eddie let him out. I wasn't exaggerating if I said I noticed a thick tension in the room. Andy was feeling guilty he had brought it to this.

"That's all we need," he said, after Lance left. "I'll never forgive myself for getting us into this mess. How he's going to manage the store once I'm gone is a good question I've been weighing over and over in my mind. I'm never going to get out of here. Jeeter's going to see to that. I blew it, Jill."

I saw tears rolling down his face. Andy seldom cried. He was always the happy-go-lucky life of the party.

"I blew it," he repeated. "And now I'm going to pay for it the rest of my life. I won't see Lance except through a glass window. What will happen to the store? I won't see Jim and Emily graduate from high school or college and get married and have kids and..." He ran out of breath and started choking.

"Stop it, Andy! You're not going to be gone."

He stared at me, and his eyes filled with tears. "You don't know that, Jill. There's no way out of this even though I didn't lay a hand on that idiot, Parsons. Jeeter's had all the time in the world to add to the evidence he already has. I've got nothing. I was stupid enough to go out to Darnell's cabin. Now I'm the perfect target. I won't get out of here, Jill. I've lost it all—Lance, my family, the store, my freedom. I'm stuck."

"Oh, Andy. I have faith this new attorney will get you out. It's all circumstantial. No one can put you at the bottom of Darnell's stairway."

"Unfortunately, they also can't put anyone else there either. So, I'm the one. I have over two months to sit in here and think about the rest of my life in prison. I don't know how I could take that. I'm so scared, Jill."

He stared at me. I could see desperation in his face. Never in my life had I seen Andy like this. I wanted to hug him and tell him it would be all right. I wanted to lace his fingers in mine and make sure he knew we'd never let him down. My shoulders drooped, and I was sure mascara was running down my face. How to turn this around?

I leaned over the stained, ugly table. "Andy. You can help with this. Tom, Angie, Sam, and I are working on other suspects. Tom seems to think whoever killed Quinn Parsons must have done it because of some motive going back to the time before he went off to prison. Someone had it in for Quinn. Once he returned, he became a target. What can you tell me about the guys around him? Darnell, Green, O'Brien?"

He gazed down at his shackled hands. "I'm not sure I know anything that would help. They spent their time together in a tight group. If Quinn wasn't driving the night of the accident, one of the others would have to be. My money's on Darnell, but Tom says he has an alibi."

"We're—that is, Tom—is working on his alibi. Can you remember them in high school? Tom said some of the older policemen told him they came to the attention of the police as possible drug sellers and users. Do you know anything about it?"

Lance came in quietly, closing the door behind him. I quickly caught him up on what we were talking about. Andy glanced at him. I could see a look between them that said Andy's anger was over, and Lance had forgotten it already.

My brother's eyes came back at me. "I know Parsons was selling because I saw him take money from guys and hand them small bags at the high school. O'Brien and Green too. But I don't remember Darnell being a part of any of that. He was clean. I didn't see him getting mixed up in drugs. He was always smarter. Well, maybe since he was smarter, he was running the operation. I can't imagine the other three having the brains to sell drugs and not get caught. 'Course, Darnell's married to a wife who will do anything to claw their way to the top of the food chain. She's been to the store several times, and it's always about the best, the most expensive. Sometimes, I feel a little sorry for Paul. I'm sure he has a lot of pressure on him financially."

"That helps a lot, Andy. I'll tell Tom what you've said. He has his suspicions about Darnell as I do. Paul's on my art center board. Our relationship is strictly art board business. But his name keeps coming up when I research Quinn and the others."

Eddie Brant came in and told us time was up. I sighed, worried about my brother. Then, Eddie did a strange thing. He shut the door, staying on our side, an act that puzzled me. We were about to say our goodbyes when Eddie indicated we should wait a second. He walked over to my brother, unhooking his handcuffs from the ring in the table. Looking at Andy, he said, "Go ahead, hug them. The cameras are off. It can't hurt as long as no one sees but me."

My heartbeat raced, and I grabbed Andy with trembling arms. He put his arms around me clumsily with the handcuffs on, his hands behind my neck. I whispered, "Don't give up. We'll get you out of here, so help us." I let him go so he could hug Lance too.

After I dropped Lance off at his store, I drove on to my house. It had snowed a little last night, but the wind had gently blown the white, fluffy stuff off my driveway. I got out of my car in the garage and headed toward the back deck door. I felt rather than saw a presence behind me. The hair lifted on my neck. Could Jeeter have been following me? No. It was Tigger Hastings. He didn't have Wingate with him, but he carried a bulky folder.

"Hey, Jill."

CHAPTER TWENTY-FOUR

"Tigger. What's up?"

"Got the information you asked me to check, but you didn't get it from me. No one will find out what I was doing. Strictly off the record whatsoever and scrubbed from my laptop. If possible, shred it." He placed the folder in my hands.

"How do you get information like that?" I asked, puzzled.

"Ah," he said, rubbing his hands together. "We hackers have our secrets, just like Houdini. Oh, and I included a business card you can keep with my cell number."

"I see," I said. "Don't worry, my lips are sealed. I'll be talking with my brother, but he doesn't need to know where I got information. Was there anything?"

He shrugged. "I believe you will notice some surprises. I circled and noted peculiarities in the financials."

I sighed with relief. "Thank you, Tigger. If this helps my brother, I'll be forever grateful."

"We aim to please," he said, with his mysterious smile. He turned and shuffled down the slick driveway, his shoulders hunched against the cold, a cold I felt in my bones.

I tromped into my house through the back door, leaving my boots in the mudroom. Hanging up my coat and hat, I went out to the kitchen with the folder and stuck the tea kettle on the stove to heat. This was definitely going to be a long, tea-warming night searching for clues. I dropped the folder on the kitchen table waiting for the kettle to shriek. Wine tonight might muddle my thinking. Andy needed me totally sober.

By midnight, I had some answers, information we'd never have found by conventional means. I gasped several times, went back, and rechecked all the numbers. If Tigger was right, they pointed to one person who was paying people off. But did it connect to Quinn Parsons' murder? I was sure once I gave the information to Tom, he'd make all the dots fit together. It was too late to call him, but I'd get him here in the morning. Of course, I'd have to think of a way to explain how I got this information. Illegally. He didn't go much for that.

Before I fell asleep, I remembered my brother's face, tears in his eyes, fear in his voice. Had I—or rather Tigger—found the key to prove Andy's innocence?

Chapter Twenty-Five

It was Sunday afternoon before I could catch up with Tom. Lance and I drove to Tom and Mary's house to have a war-planning session. We'd put our heads together so we could decide what direction to take next. Tom and Mary lived in a two-story, Naples yellow-sided house that screamed "solid, conservative." The windows were framed with jet black shutters that matched the roof. At least Tom had taken the Christmas lights down, though a wreath hung on the front door.

Something was different. It took a few minutes for me to figure it out. "Where are the kids?" I asked Mary, listening to the quiet house.

My sister-in-law smiled. "Emily had a sleepover for a birthday party with one of her friends. Jim's at the high school shooting hoops and practicing his free throws. Tom helped him with his shot, so now, knowing Jim, the perfectionist, he has to practice it five hundred times." She gave me an exasperated look, then left to bring in coffee and a wonderful dessert. My sister-in-law was an amazing cook. I knew she'd supplied Andy with some of his favorites while he was in jail. I didn't know how much he'd eaten since he seemed so thin, but at least she'd tried.

"Have you talked to Andy when you drop off food at the jail?"

Mary glanced at me after she set a cup of coffee in front of me. "Yes. I know he's discouraged, but I assured him we were working hard on his case."

Tom walked in, carrying a notebook. "Hey, you two. I think I've rounded up some people to question about the accident night. Did you find anything, Jill?"

"Amazing stuff, Tom. But it may be more about the accident than about

Parsons' death. I don't know. We'll see."

Everyone sat around the table, coffee cups in hand, forks ready to dig into Mary's lemon poppy seed bread. I'd smelled the lemon the moment I entered the house.

Tom began. "Well, I examined the files to see who was at the Eagle's Nest on the night of the accident. The police interviewed quite a few people. Like you, Jill, this is all about the accident rather than Parsons, but as time goes by, I realize the people closest to Parsons were in the accident. If we're right in theorizing the past connects somehow to Quinn's death, this might be the ideal place to start. Jeeter can't protest that I'm working on the murder. Instead, I'm rechecking the accident investigation."

Lance listened carefully and asked, "This goes back to the Eagle's Nest. Who did the original interviews with these witnesses?"

"Ned Fisher."

Lance took a sip of coffee, considering the name. He asked, "Do you trust him, Tom? Think he does a quality job?"

Tom nodded. "Absolutely. He's still around if we need to question him. I'll ask about his take on the witnesses and their answers. 'Course it's been seven years, but his interview notes would help jog his memory if we wanted to ask more."

"Great. So, what did he get from those guys?" asked Mary.

Tom opened the file and began perusing the information. "Of the people they interviewed—all men and one woman—five have moved to warmer climates, left town, or died. That still leaves four other people, oh, plus the owner. I haven't talked to them yet because I thought it would be good to consult you all first. I only got the information yesterday, since it had to be located, then boxed up. But I did find out Darnell drove a silver BMW. His car would stand out in the lot at the Eagle's Nest."

"What's your plan?" asked Lance.

Tom shoveled a piece of poppy seed bread in his mouth. "Man, this is good, Mary." Washing it down with coffee, he continued, "I think I need to ask specifically when each witness left. They might not remember the exact time, but they'd be able to estimate. Back then, no one considered asking that since Darnell had an excuse for leaving in his own car. If Darnell's car were in the lot rather than gone as he claimed, I think they'd remember it. According to Fisher's notes, the lot was not full at all. Only a handful of cars. Sally Helms is a smart cookie. She owns the place, and I'll get over to see her right away. She'd remember if Darnell's car was there when she closed."

I watched Mary and Lance. "Our theory is Darnell left with Parsons, plus his crew, driving them home because he wasn't under the influence and they were. He didn't expect an accident, so he figured he'd drive Quinn's car back and park it, then get into his car and drive home. But he told the police he'd left earlier. His wife is his alibi, but she'd lie for him."

"In a minute," Lance said, scowling.

"What about the brakes?" I asked.

Tom shook his head. "I don't know. If someone cut the brake lines we'll never know since the accident demolished the whole front of the car, and the vehicle would be scrap metal by now. But if someone did tamper with the brakes, they had it in for Quinn. That motive might still have been in play when Parsons showed up here searching for a place to call home."

"Yeah, like a warm welcome was going to happen," I noted.

"I've located all of these witnesses, so I'll get on it tomorrow," said Tom. "Lance, I know you've talked to Andy's lawyer, Bill Gatesmith."

"Yes. He lets me know he'll be at the jail to see Andy, and I usually sit in."

"Good. Let him know what we've found."

"I will."

"What do you have for us, Jill?"

I took a deep breath and passed out copies of what I'd found from Tigger's folder. Rather than give them Tigger's originals, I'd summed up everything pertinent. No use having Tom see how official the financial pages were.

I looked Tom square in the face. "Now, Tom," I said. "You can't ask me where I got this information. I know you won't be able to use it in court unless you can get the case opened again."

My brother, the law-abiding detective, gave me a stern stare. "What do you mean? What have you done now?"

I protested my innocence. "I have a source who gave me some financial information on this group. Like I said, after we talk about it, we need to chew it up and swallow it, or put it in the closest shredder."

"I won't be a partner to illegal actions," Tom said.

I glanced at Lance and Mary. "Look, Tom. Hear me out. However I came by this isn't important. It gives us a place to start as far as thinking about motives and suspects. If you get your witnesses to produce information implicating Darnell in lies about that night, you could reopen the case. Once that happens, you could find this information yourself through legal channels."

He gave me a pained expression. I could tell he wasn't happy with me.

Mary gave him a disgusted look. "We want to prove Andy innocent, don't we?"

He paused, thinking about it for a long, long minute. "All right. What've you got?"

"Oh, *good*, Tom," Mary said, with great exaggeration. We all laughed at my brother's discomfort.

I sat up a little straighter. "If you study this summary of what my source found, you'll see Quinn Parsons had a large infusion of cash prior to his death. Five thousand dollars. Turn the page. This other person had a debit from his account the day before for exactly the same amount. Now, look at this other account. Every month, it receives two thousand dollars on the first of the month. No one else's account matches an equivalent debit of two thousand a month, so the question is where that money is coming from. Someone feeling guilty?"

"What about similar bank records from back when they were younger?" Lance asked. "You thought this might go back to high school."

I nodded. "Sadly, bank records aren't kept back so far. Even my mysterious source couldn't get information from that long ago."

Mary glanced at me. "If I'm reading you right, we're seeing some possible blackmail going on among these people."

Tom took a deep breath, folding the papers and creasing them. "I understand your enthusiasm to get into peoples' bank accounts illegally, Jill, but if anyone finds out about this, you and your source are toast. I'd have to worry about both my siblings behind bars."

Mary put her hand on his. "Tom, let's shred these papers. See if you can get the case reopened with your witnesses. If you can, this information will be available to you legally. I applaud Jill for her tenacity in going after these people. We all understand you must follow the rules, and this kind of information isn't helpful unless we can open the case again in another way."

They all handed their copies to me. I collected the pile. "Yes, they go in my shredder."

"Tonight," Tom said, "and don't speed on the way home. I never saw this information."

"Yes, Tom."

"And," he added, "good job."

On the way to Lance's house, I heard him sigh.

"You doing all right?" I asked.

"I'm feeling a lot better after tonight. We may be no closer to finding Quinn Parsons' killer, but I believe we're on the right track thanks to you and the phantom accountant."

I chuckled. "At least you can cross Ivan Truelove off your list for an accountant-suspect. He'd not lift a finger to help Andy, I'm sure."

"Not if it were a request to do something illegal. This is dynamite information. Make sure you creep along slowly on your way home."

"Don't worry, I will. And Lance—"

"Yes?"

"I'm so thankful you're here. All those years when Tom, Andy, and I were growing up, we always had our parents around—front and center—talking us through our problems. We could never get into too much trouble because everyone watched out for us in Apple Grove. Back then, that made me mad. I couldn't get away with anything. As soon as Angie and I drove a bit too fast down Windish Street right after I got my license, a cop stopped me. When he looked at my name on my license, he gave me a warning. But he mentioned he'd see my dad at Rotary later that week, so I'd better tell him what happened before the cop did."

"And did you?" Lance asked.

I sighed. "Yup. But I don't know if the cop really told Dad. He never said anything to me about it after that Rotary meeting. It just makes me think now about what it was like growing up where people watched out for you. Now, I feel like we're watching out for Andy in their absence. So, thanks again."

I dropped him at his door, then thought about his last words. It was a good thing Jeeter could no longer follow me because of his tracker. Whew. That would have been awful if he'd stopped me with this information. It was going in the shredder the moment I walked in the house.

Shredders and subterfuge brought me to another thought. Who was this Deep Throat? He'd said to "follow the money." His hunch might turn out to be right. He seemed to know everything going on in town. Could he be Deep Throat? Whoever he was, he must be someone with an inside track on this case. But who?

Chapter Twenty-Six

S unday evening, I was sitting in the back of the gallery where the chairs would be set up for the radio play. The seniors wandered in one at a time or in groups for the radio play rehearsal. I opened the first page of our program to see how the Cast of Characters looked.

The Cast of Characters
Narrator: Alisa Segura
Sir Simon de Canterville: Chad McKenna
Hiram B. Otis, American minister: Oliver Winston
Mrs. Otis: Binky Asbury
the Current Lord Canterville: Bradley Murphy
Washington Otis: Shawn Raglan
Virginia Otis: Molly Ripple
Stars & Stripes: Jimmy & Johnny Raglan
Mrs. Umney, Housekeeper: Liz Goodwin
Cecil, Duke of Cheshire: David Marlow
Director: Evan Shelly
Sound Effects by Tango and Foxtrot
Set Construction: Chad McKenna, Tango, Foxtrot, Oliver
Winston, Molly Ripple, Andrea Palmgren, Jason Smith, Donna
Filbert, Liz Goodwin
Lighting: Alexander Brandywine
Costumes: Missy Felton

Perfect. All the names were spelled correctly, and everyone had been recognized. Evan Shelly called the group to order. He took several minutes to explain his plan for the rehearsal.

"Now, we don't have a lot of time until the real play on Friday and Saturday. Dress rehearsal will be on Thursday evening at six thirty. Full costumes, sound effects, and lighting that night. Tonight, we'll run straight through it, and add the sound effects for the first time. Straight through, and I'll make notes to give you at the end of the play. Places, everyone. Let's get started."

I watched as the actors found their spots, the sound effects guys moving to the back, where all the equipment was sitting on a table. They'd be doing these effects out in the open where the audience could see them. Chad had recruited two of his Vietnam buddies, known simply as Tango and Foxtrot, to do the sounds.

Tango and Foxtrot. The former was short, five foot seven, with an enormous stomach, long, gray beard, and round, frameless glasses. He reminded me of someone who might be wearing a motorcycle gang jacket, but after meeting him, I realized his appearance hid a teddy bear. Foxtrot was the opposite. Tall, thin, clean-shaven, with big ears. Seriously, his long, narrow ears stood out from his head like flaps in the wind. He favored army fatigues. Both had come to the art center to practice, and Chad was satisfied they knew what they were doing. My own brain was familiar with all the thunder, lightning, and chain-rattling, since they'd driven me nuts practicing.

Glancing up at the rafters, I saw Daniel sitting on a beam, watching all the proceedings. He'd been curious and attentive at the rehearsals. Staring up at him, I'd seen multiple expressions on his face, especially laughter. No one heard him but me. I'd prevailed upon him not to do any shrieks or moans. We had all the sound effects covered. By now, I'd think he'd be sick of the same story over and over at every rehearsal, but no, he hung around. Literally.

The next thing I knew, someone had slipped in the door of the gallery and come over to sit next to me. Ivan Truelove.

"Ivan. What are you doing roaming around tonight?" This was not good.

He was undoubtedly here to make some negative judgments about the play.

"I thought, Ms. Madison, I'd stop in and see how the radio play is going. You know, one of my duties as president of the art center board. I take it this is a rehearsal."

"Yes," I said quietly. "You have to whisper. We'll rehearse every night now until the play on Friday."

He spoke quietly. "Need any help?"

I thought for a moment. "No, I think we have every job covered. You're welcome to stay and watch. They'd love to have an audience."

"Perfect," he said, although I heard some disappointment in his voice. He reached over to a bag he'd carried in. I watched him set the tote next to his chair. He pulled out a couple of paper bags and handed one to me. "Popcorn?" he asked.

I took the bag he handed me, puzzled. Was this the Ivan Truelove, CPA, who had made my life miserable?

"Plays and movies are much better with popcorn to munch on," he said, and began munching as he watched the performance.

I was floored. Between a ghost in the rafters, and Ivan eating popcorn next to me, this was turning into one weird night.

I went back to concentrating on the actors, but also found myself pushing popcorn into my mouth.

Mrs. Otis, played by Binky Asbury, noticed the red stain on the floor near the fireplace. As an American, she didn't know what it meant. She mentioned it to the housekeeper, Mrs. Umney, played by Liz Goodwin, who said, very dramatically, that "blood had been spilt on that spot." Her line should bring a laugh from the audience, I thought. Next, key up the dastardly story of Lady Eleanore de Canterville, murdered by her husband in 1575. Later, he disappeared under "mysterious circumstances," and his spirit haunts the Chase. When Washington Otis, played by the oldest of the three Raglan boys, declared Pinkerton's Champion Stain Remover and Paragon Detergent would remove it, a terrible peal of thunder, followed by a flash of lightning, lit the room. Tango rippled the plastic sheet and Foxtrot rolled the crash box around on the table. Alex flashed the lights on the stage.

It was perfect. The whole cast started laughing, applauding the sound crew. Tango and Foxtrot bowed, people couldn't stop laughing, and then Evan got it back under control.

"This is why we're using the sound effects tonight. To get you used to them. You can feign fright or hysteria about the storm, but for goodness' sakes, don't laugh."

And they all laughed again. It took a few minutes to go on.

I found myself thinking about Andy. He'd have loved to be in this show, especially doing the sound effects. I sighed. Oh, well. Another day.

Now, it was one a.m. in the play, and the ghost was shaking his chains in the corridor. Foxtrot grabbed the chains, shaking them with enthusiasm. I was watching him when suddenly he fell backward off the stage. Oh, no! I thought. Someone screamed, maybe Binky or Molly. When he didn't stand up, all the cast members near him began to move over to the floor to see what had happened. I ran to the front and saw Chad sitting beside him, talking quietly, but Foxtrot didn't seem to be able to move. I rushed over, sat next to his head and told all the seniors to back off. Give him some room to breathe.

"Foxtrot? Are you okay?"

He moaned and shook his head. Chad asked him where it hurt, and he replied, "All over, but right here in my left hip is bad."

My eyes met Chad's. "I think we should call an ambulance. He needs to be checked out at the ER."

Tango reached into his back pocket. "Yeah. Got it." He pulled out his phone, dialed 9-1-1, and we all waited in hushed silence.

Foxtrot was moaning in terrible pain.

"Chad, I think it would be best if they took him out the alley door. Closer, less jostling," I said.

"Yeah, you're right." He was hanging on to Foxtrot's hand like he couldn't let go. I saw tears streaming down his face. He wiped them with his sleeve.

"I'll go out in front and steer them around to the alley," I said.

"Good. I'll stay here with him. Tango and I can talk to him, try to keep him conscious while we wait."

The ambulance arrived much quicker than I thought it would. It's so hard to see someone in pain, and as I'd gotten to know Foxtrot, I'd liked him for his sense of humor and funny ears. Everyone watched as I led the paramedics in from the alley. Sam wasn't with them. They loaded Foxtrot on the gurney, raised it from the floor, and wheeled him out the alley door. Chad said he'd go with him. This accident had sobered everyone.

After they left, I made a mental note to go to the hospital tomorrow and check on him. Evan rounded up everyone, and they took a vote. They'd continue with the rehearsal, but have Evan read Chad's part for now. After tonight, he'd search for someone to take Foxtrot's spot. It was only four days until the dress rehearsal. I hoped Foxtrot's condition wasn't as bad as it looked as I had watched him on the floor, writhing in pain, but we'd have to figure out what to do if he couldn't return. A quiet voice spoke next to me.

"If you need my help with the sound effects, I'd be glad to learn his part and be a stand-in until he gets back."

It was Ivan Truelove, my archnemesis, who'd handed me popcorn tonight. Was I living in *The Twilight Zone*?

I turned to him, checking for any subplots or treachery. All I saw was an honest expression on his face, an actual desire to help. I made a split decision, nodding quickly. "Thank you, Ivan. Yes, we'd love to have your help. I'll check with Chad, who can train you with the props, and we'll get the two of you together. Maybe tomorrow?"

"That will work just fine. I'd love to help. Thank you for the opportunity."

What was going on in my world? Ivan, who had been nothing but critical of my work at the art center, was coming to my rescue? There must be some nefarious plot beneath his words. I'd have to be on my highest alert, keeping an eye on him.

Chapter Twenty-Seven

Monday afternoon, I stopped in to see Foxtrot at the hospital. Poor guy. He gave me a weak smile and explained that they had to order some hardware that was being shipped at the speed of light. They'd operate tomorrow. He was keeping his hopes up, certainly cheerful for someone getting ready for a hip replacement.

I'd texted Sam that I was going to be at the hospital, so he stopped in and we went down to the cafeteria for coffee. We'd been people-watching, drinking coffee, and talking about the play at the art center. There was so much he couldn't tell me about his job, so the play was the subject.

"Your guy's going to be all right. That's about all I can say," he said, putting his hand on mine.

"Seems like I'm seeing you at the hospital a lot," I said, stirring some cream into my coffee.

"Well, you know, with the hours I keep it makes sense to track me down where I work. But I'm thinking about a plan for that. We'll see what happens. Nothing to report yet."

I nodded. "Is this something about your idea that plans can be modified to work better?"

"Absolutely." He smiled at me, his beautiful smile with perfectly aligned teeth. I found myself thinking that someday I hoped our children inherited his smile. It was beautiful. I glanced at my watch.

"Probably need to get back to the art center. Louise has been doing way too much overtime lately. Good thing she's patient, and, I thought, it's wonderful that Ivan can't track me down since I can use a cell phone anywhere. He wouldn't be happy with my time away to help Andy."

"What is it you say? He can 'go stick his head in a bucket'?"

"I'm trying to be nicer to Ivan since he seems to have had a sea-change."

"Good to hear. All right. I need to get back too. Love to see you during the day, however."

We both stood, and he leaned over and gave me a kiss. Just a brief one in the middle of the cafeteria. Nice.

"You never forgot the buried treasure," I said, telling Daniel Lowry where we'd interrupted his narrative about the past. It was Monday night at the art gallery. I'd worked straight through dinner, making sure details for the radio play and art exhibit were on course. I could leave no steps to chance.

Daniel was sitting on a chair in the weavers room at the back of the art center, while I sat at a table counting tickets and doing a few odd jobs as he talked. The longer I saw him, the less transparent he became. I'm not sure why. It was as if he were a living human now. He stood at the end of the room, where a small kitchen held our store of water bottles and wine. Why he was more like a solid human since the last time I saw him, I didn't know. But it only made his rugged good looks even more attractive.

He smiled. "I take pleasure in talking to you, Jill. You're the most attentive listener I have spoken with since one of the pharmacists who labored here in the 1940s."

I felt myself blushing, chided myself for acting like a lovesick teenager, and stared at him with an expectant expression. "Carry on."

"I do not believe I disclosed meeting my wife."

I arched one eyebrow. "I believe I'd remember if you had."

He nodded his head slowly.

"Rosemary and I—Rosemary Pike, that is—were introduced after I recovered. I never knew if it was because too many soldiers did not return. The few of us who did were in need of wives. We were companionable. I courted her for several months. When the time was right, I petitioned her to be my betrothed. However, to be proper, I revealed I was intending to leave civilization and depart for the wilderness. After the war, I had an abundance of time to reflect, and I concluded I was done with my fellow man for a time."

"I can understand after all the killing you'd seen."

"Ah, yes," he said. "Our war was an uncommonly brutal, vicious one, and I found myself mistrustful of people. At times, I suffered from nightmares. Loud noises frightened me. She understood and kindly accepted my courtship. But first, I made a solitary trip to Tennessee with a wagon pulled by a team of horses. I had constructed a secret box under the seat of the buckboard."

"Weren't people a little suspicious of a Yankee so far down South?"

"I pondered that. My plan was to travel in the daylight on the principal roads and always stay with the wagon no matter where I encamped. I avoided large population centers, not that there were a lot after what the war had done to ravage the area. During the war, I had carried a one-shot musket. I wished I had one of those clever Spencer carbines that fired seven shots without reloading. After I returned home, it was one of my first purchases, so I carried it with me on the trip. It was an uneventful journey. Finding the spot where we'd buried the treasure was simple with the torn and dirty map I'd carried with me throughout the war. Returning home, I buried the loot until I could redeem it for money."

I watched his animated face as he finished his tale. Once he was over his war wounds, had found a wife to love, and had sufficient capital to set out on an adventure, I imagine he felt he had the world at his fingertips. "So, she agreed to go with you to the middle of the country?"

"Unreservedly. She was not one of those addle-brained girls who loved fashion and gossip. By the time we met, she was twenty-six, settled, filled with common sense, searching to start a new life with a husband. I loved her."

Holding my breath, I remembered what would happen down the road. Poor Daniel.

"Her father was a minister, so he read our vows in the parlor of their home. I had a momentary twinge of guilt compelling her to leave her family. Her mother was devastated, but the two of us would be on this adventure together. We departed for an area just short of the Mississippi River. I had heard travelers talk about that part of the country opening, especially for soldiers after the war. While it was a long, arduous journey, we attained this tiny town, Apple Grove, which was beginning to expand, particularly with war survivors. I still retained the money I had carefully guarded, and soon I had a plan to build the general store, designating it for my brother and me. Between lack of materials and labor after the war, the building took four years. Finally, we threw open the doors. I knew my brother would have been euphoric to spy our names over the front door—The Lowry Brothers General Store. Just like we had planned."

I heard footsteps. Who could be in the gallery? Daniel glanced at my face, saw the concern, and disappeared.

He returned saying, "The soldier is back. Chad." I relaxed.

"Jill?" Chad called out.

I regarded Daniel, who could easily have disappeared again, but he decided to stay so I could be confused about who was talking when.

The footsteps came closer.

"Out here in the weavers room, Chad."

His face appeared above the top stair. "What the heck are you doing here?"

I smiled and lined up tickets. "I was trying for a change of scenery while I do these mundane jobs for the radio show."

His face said he wasn't quite buying my explanation. Skeptical. Frowning. Finally, he said, "I was hoping you'd taken my advice and gone home."

"He is a tetchy employee with the advice, is he not?" said Daniel.

I frowned at the ghost, then back at Chad. "It's fine, Chad. I'm almost done. Besides, I'm a grown-up. You don't have to worry about me."

Chad scanned the room as he sauntered down the stairs. "I was sure I heard voices."

I feigned an innocent look. "Nope. Just me and the ghosts."

At that reply, Daniel laughed, but Chad's expression didn't change, so I guess he couldn't hear the laughter this time.

"Want me to stick around?"

I stood, stretched, and said, "Nah. I'm fine. Almost done. But thanks for stopping in to check."

He nodded, looking around again. "Okay. See you tomorrow."

Turning, he went back to the gallery. I could hear his steps receding, then the door closing.

Daniel studied me. "It is interesting the way the gentlemen in your life want to protect you, much like my time."

"Not interesting. Exasperating. First my brothers, now Chad. I must look like I need protection."

"In my day, ladies always needed the protection of a strong father or husband."

I was so tired, I didn't even bother to mention my world was different. Looking at my watch, I said, "I must go home soon. Please, finish your story."

He settled into a chair at the other end of the table. "It is good to conclude where I did, because all is disaster after Rosemary and I began the running of the store."

I thought about his observation and glanced at him from my ticket piles. "You know, I've often heard it said no one is promised a life free of pain or disappointment. Right now, with my brother, Andy, I'm definitely in a valley. But I've lived long enough to know life will get better. At least I hope it will."

He stared at his hands in his lap. "Ghosts cannot predict the future, only understand the past."

"I think ghosts have it better than humans!"

He paused thoughtfully. "Williams appeared."

"The man who helped you bury the treasure?"

"Unfortunately. I do not know how he found me. He had been to Tennessee and discovered the empty hole where we had buried the treasure. He desired half of the money since James had died. Williams was residing in St. Louis, had married, and fathered two children, both sons. I did not know what to do. I had spent our treasure on the building, and I discerned no way to repay him what I owed him. He threatened me with ruin, going to the newspapers and telling the treacherous story. By now, I was a well-known, respected member of the Apple Grove community. Rosemary knew nothing of my nefarious past. What could I do? My heart ached just contemplating it."

"Money. It always seems to be at the root of motives for violence. That's

182

what my brother is dealing with right now. 'Follow the money,' my secret source said. I think he's right. Over a century between our lives, and the story is still the same, isn't it?"

He looked guilty. "Aye. A steep price we pay. I reasoned I would have to dispatch him, so I lured him to my office one night, attacked him with a knife, and buried him in a stretch of land a mile from our home. You understand, as a callow lad of eighteen before the war, I could never have done that. But I had seen the worst in men." He stared out the window thoughtfully. "Yes. I had been able to slay without a moment's thought to protect what was mine. After several fortnights, I could breathe easier, but my conscience still weighed heavily on me. I called to mind the picture he'd shown me of his widow and two sons, who would now grow up without a father. Whenever I passed the ground where he lay in death, my stomach roiled and my heart pounded. What had I done? My conscience was a terrible, constant reminder."

Had his looks changed? No. But had my thoughts changed after hearing his tale of murder? Maybe. How could he do this?

As if he'd read my mind, he said, "Yes, I was a coward. I did a terrible thing. And I have had decades to contemplate it. But life does not let you get away from an action like that. I ended a life. I left a widow and orphans. I knew I would receive my comeuppance."

"Your comeuppance?"

He nodded. "I could not get away with murder scot-free. Life exacted compensation for what I had done. With that situation ended, I soon got Rosemary in the family way. When it came time for our son to be born, his birth went terribly amiss. My Rosemary died, as did my boy. We had planned to name him Daniel after me. But instead, he lies out in the Catholic cemetery north of town next to his sainted mother, who had done nothing wrong. It was my fault, my grievous fault. I knew what I had done to deserve that. God was punishing me for my sins of cowardice and greed."

I'd seen this coming, but now that it was here, I didn't know what to say. Quietly, I murmured, "I'm sorry you lost your family."

"We pay a price for what we bring upon ourselves with our ill-considered actions."

"Well, you have me there, Daniel."

He was silent, his head down, his shoulders hunched over.

A new thought came into my head. "You said the radio play we are doing called you into the present. Why?"

He took a deep breath. Slowly, his head came back up. "I have watched your people do the story practices. Is not the subject of the play forgiveness?"

"Yes. The ghost has to be forgiven by someone weeping over his sins."

"Those concepts intrigued me. Forgiveness is a foreign concept to me."

"For the moment, me too," I confessed.

"My understanding is in order to be forgiven, so I can join my Rosemary and Daniel in the afterlife, I must reverse my act of cowardice. I must perform some act of bravery."

"Oh," I brightened. "That makes sense. I think you could do a brave act."

He shook his head. "Here? In this building where I have been since 1890? No scenarios of bravery come to mind at the moment, nor have any for a hundred and twenty-seven years."

I sat silently staring at the table. "I can see why that would be frustrating." I glanced at the time on my phone, shaking my head. "It is late."

"May I ask what has befallen your man who was doing the sound effects?"

"Oh," I thought. "Yes, I was going to ask you to do a favor for me."

"Anything I am capable of performing."

"Foxtrot, the man who was hurt, is in the hospital. Looks like he may need a hip replacement, so he's not going to be available for the show. We have someone to fill in."

"Ah, yes. The unhappy, socially inept man who is your boss. A hip replacement? Is that possible?"

His words seemed like a decent description of Ivan. "Yes, in our time it's possible. However, when Foxtrot fell, he broke the audio we were using for groans and shrieks. Suppose you could fill in on those?"

His eyes grew big, he smiled, and nodded his ghostly head. "I know precisely when to do that. I have watched every practice. But how will you explain my actions?"

"I'm going to tell people I have an app on my phone that will make those sounds when I hit one of two buttons."

"An app? Hit buttons?"

I was too tired to explain modern technology to a nineteenth-century ghost. "You don't need to understand. Just do the groans and shrieks."

"Oh, marvelous!" he said. "I will get to perform with the group! Thank you."

What was it about people wanting to be part of a play production? First Ivan, now Daniel. I hesitated, hating to leave because it was so comforting to talk to this handsome...ghost. Handsome, intelligent, maybe not so kindhearted, but definitely dead.

Chapter Twenty-Eight

I stared at the map of St. Michael's Catholic Cemetery north of Apple Grove. Since I woke early and couldn't get back to sleep, I decided to do a little exploring. This cemetery was huge, and I'd stopped for a map at the office. I'd never be able to find the Lowry graves without a map. I reminded myself it was Valentine's Day. This seemed like a strange way to begin a romantic holiday. Turning the map around, I finally figured out where I was and where I needed to be. I got back in my trusty Austin Mini and slowly drove through the cemetery roads to reach the very south end. The oldest graves were there.

I was the only one coasting slowly down the one-car road. Yew trees lined the way and gathered in bunches at the edge of the cemetery. I could hear the crunch of my tires on the rocks of the road. On either side were small and huge tombstones, many with names of families I knew from growing up here. Except for my tires crunching, silence dominated. Not even a breeze blew to break up the stillness.

GPS didn't help one bit in this situation. Stopping occasionally to check the map, I finally reached the area where the Lowry plots were supposed to be. Ah. There. I stopped my car, zipped my jacket, and got out to examine the ancient headstones. They were so different from the kind we have in this century. Time and erosion had also darkened them to a kohl gray. Fortunately, the wind wasn't too bad this morning. There had been a weather forecast for thawing.

There was Daniel Elliott Lowry's grave. Born November 15, 1837, and died February 25, 1890. A Civil War private in the Pennsylvania Reserves.

Strange, I told myself, to realize his bones might be lying here under this stone, but his spirit is alive and well in my art center. I scratched my head. What would happen if he ever got to leave the Lowry building? Did his spirit join his body here or go to some other afterlife, forever separated from the bones that held his body together? For a moment, I thought I should slap my face for digging into this deep philosophical argument. But it would make a hilarious conversation with Angie later.

I moved over to the next stone. His wife, Rosemary Pike Lowry, born July 7, 1842, died June 8, 1871. Beloved wife of Daniel, mother of Daniel Pike Lowry. Seeing the names made me understand this was real. The story Daniel told me happened so long ago when my own ancestors were coming West. What heartbreak he must have felt to lose his wife and child in an instant. Finally, next to Rosemary's grave was a small stone for Daniel, the little boy they held for only moments. Standing there, I bowed my head and said a prayer for the family. Then I left a penny on the gravestone as a symbol of respect. This made it even stranger that I was talking to a ghost who had spent several days telling me about the history behind these markers. I shook my head. At some point, I was going to have to share this with Angie, but for now it was my own little secret.

I sighed, looking at the engraving on the stones one last time. Such a sad story. And this woman and baby had been waiting for over a century for their husband and father to join them in the hereafter.

I turned and walked back to my car, starting the day a little rattled. Once back at the art center, I dug deep into the details for the radio show this weekend. Louise was working full throttle, too, making sure the hospitality committee had ordered enough refreshments for the intermission. I was about to leave to go to the bank when my phone rang. It was Tom.

"Morning, Jill."

"Hi. Everything falling into place?" I asked.

He paused. "Yes. Heading in that direction. I interviewed three of the bar patrons from the night of the accident and called two others who've moved out of town. Your hunch was absolutely right. After a bit of digging, it became apparent the three witnesses remembered Darnell's car being in the parking lot, empty, after Quinn and friends left. No one asked them about that the night of the accident. I can see why. It wouldn't have occurred to anyone to talk about Darnell because he wasn't found at the scene of the accident. As far as anyone knew, he wasn't involved. One guy even said he figured Darnell was sleeping off the booze he'd drunk or worried about going home to his wife."

"Great. Our theory may be closer than we realize."

"Yes. When I talked to the bar owner, she said the car was gone when she closed. This means Darnell is unaccounted for in a window of time when the accident happened. It's enough to reopen the case, call Darnell in for questioning, and see if he was driving that night. It would also give us a motive for Quinn's murder, especially if he were blackmailing Darnell."

I'd recruited Darnell because, as VP of a bank, he knew all about finances, a subject that always came up at a nonprofit, and he knew everyone in town. But he was up to his neck in this, and his bank statements had suspicious withdrawals. I considered the possibility. "Maybe you should call Lance. Let him know what you're pursuing. It might give him a bit of hope on this gray, damp morning."

"Thanks, Jill. Your help has been immeasurable."

"I aim to please." Then, another thought hit me. "You know, Tom, if Quinn wasn't driving the car, my anger and hatred have been misplaced. I've never forgiven him all these years. Looks like I may have to eat those feelings."

"Likewise."

Our conversation gave me a second wind, since we now had a direction that could pay off. I knew from Lance that Andy's lawyer was working on sorting out motives of other suspects. I went through the afternoon with a smile on my face and a song on my mind. Martin Stewart had stopped in and bought the last two available tickets for the play. I imagined he could use a little humor in his life. It was great to feel my spirit lift out of my earlier funk at the cemetery, especially since Sam had invited me to his apartment tonight where he would cook dinner for me. Valentine's Day. And, wonder of all wonders, he was off work.

By eight that evening, I was sitting on the sofa at Sam's, having an after-dinner cocktail and feeling extremely stuffed. His apartment was warm and cozy. I was feeling that pleasant euphoria where the problems of the world subsided, and a gentle calm waved over me. He'd grilled filet mignon out on the balcony. I'd tossed the salad. He'd added the baked potatoes. I let out a long sigh. I was so full of food I'd not have to eat for a week.

Sam was in the kitchen making dish-cleaning noises while I waited for him to return. I'd offered to help, but he said I should relax. I glanced around his apartment. Minimalist was an understatement, but he was at work twenty-four, seven. He had a galley kitchen, living room, bathroom, and two bedrooms. Tastefully decorated in modern colors and design, the apartment reflected his neatness. Although he was gone most of the time for work, when he was home, he took care of business. I liked that, although this place was sure the opposite of my office at the art center. Or my house.

"All done," he said, walking back to the living room. He sat next to me, putting his arm around my shoulder. Soft music on the stereo added to the cozy, romantic ambience, and he'd taken a sip of his own drink. He touched my arm. "Finally. Some time alone."

I yawned, stretching out my arms. "Life has been way too busy and fast lately. I've worried about Andy so much my mind is scrambled most days. We've had some last-minute problems with the radio play, but I think they're solved now." I paused. "But I've been looking forward to this evening. Nice to see you so relaxed."

He smiled. "I know I haven't had much time off work. It's as upsetting to me as it is to you. Sorry. I'm going to do better."

"I think your vow is a great start."

He reached over and kissed me, holding my hand. "I've wanted to kiss you at all times and places lately. But we're never together." He sighed. "What do you think? Would you like me to figure out a way to have more time for us?"

"Of course," I said. "Are you planning to blow up the hospital?"

He laughed softly. "That sounds more like devilment you and your partner-in-crime- detection, Angie, might plan." He rubbed the back of my hand. "I'll have you know I have a new contract coming soon. These long hours

189

are going to finally pay off. The hospital board sees me as indispensable, but my work is going to come with a price. I'm going to push for fewer shifts and more regular hours."

I sat up and looked into his eyes. "Really? Can you do that?"

"I'm gonna try. I have more leverage, since I've been there for some time, and they've been quite satisfied with my work."

I chuckled. "They should be. You're always there."

"Correct. Now I won't be. I think the powers-that-be are interested in keeping me happy, so I gave them a plan of my own for the next contract. We'll see what happens, but I'm almost sure they'll be willing to grant me more leeway about my hours and shifts. I should know in the next few days."

"Sam, that's wonderful. Yes, a change in your hours would make me much happier."

"Good. It's settled." He sat there for a moment thinking. "I also got you a tiny token of my esteem and love for this special Valentine's Day."

I watched as he pulled a small box out of a drawer in the side table next to the sofa. It was small. Could be jewelry. My heart began to pick up speed. Beautifully wrapped, it looked like a store wrapping job. Not Andy and Lance's wrapping paper, so he must have wanted to keep it a secret. He handed it to me while I sat there for a moment.

"So, may I open it now?"

"Absolutely," he said, smiling and expectant.

I'd already given him a new watch before dinner. When he didn't reciprocate, I wondered what he had up his sleeve. Hmm. The package was too beautiful to unwrap.

On second thought, I tore into it.

Opening the small box, I saw a necklace with two hearts intertwined.

"Check out the back," he said.

I turned the hearts over and read, 'J With Love From S' and the date.

"Oh, thank you, Sam. This is absolutely beautiful." He helped me put it on, and I admired it in the mirror across the room. Perfect.

Coming back to the sofa, I wrapped my arms around him. "I love you, Sam."

He kissed me once and said, "I love you too." There was a long, definitely-not-peck-on-the-cheek kiss.

Chapter Twenty-Nine

I was sitting in my office Wednesday afternoon thinking about the next few days. Tomorrow night we had a dress rehearsal for the radio play. The actual production would take place on Friday and Saturday nights. Several of the actors had come in today excited about the upcoming performance, wanting to talk about it. Chad was in, of course, making sure everything was exactly where it should be. There was an air of expectancy about the approaching show. We were sold out for both performances, and after we'd paid for the refreshments, we'd still make an excellent profit. I was so proud of Chad for his suggestion we have a senior group. Who knew how successful it would prove?

I thought back to my restless night. Of course, I was nervous about how the weekend would go, but my uneasy sleep was disturbed by a memory. Something Deep Throat mentioned had slipped right out of my mind. It was one of those "ah ha!" moments. I called Tigger once it seemed like a respectable hour this morning and made one last request. Then, I said a brief prayer that Deep Throat had given me the key to Andy's predicament.

I thought again about my brother. It seemed like he'd been in that jail for ages. I'd stop by and see him, if only for a brief conversation. Even though I was busy with the play, he was always on my mind.

Louise had been to the post office and brought back the mail and newspaper.

"Jill," I heard her say as she came into my office. "I need to leave early today. I hope that's all right."

I stared at her. "Seriously? After all the time you've put in for me with

192

Andy's disaster? Of course, you can leave early."

She smiled.

"Another hot date?"

She hemmed and hawed a bit. "Well, maybe not hot, but could be a possibility."

For Louise, a toad would be a possibility. She'd had so many online dates. "Go for it, Louise. Take all the time you need. Just let me know the outcome tomorrow. I live vicariously through your online dating episodes."

"Perfect," she said. The bell jangled on the front door. She stuck her head into the hallway. "Looks like your buddy, Angie."

"Great. Go ahead, take off."

I rose and went to the gallery to meet Angie. She had an oblong package in her hand.

"What's up?" I asked, pointing to the box.

"Hi, friend. I stopped in about a couple prime pieces of information. You know the website Lance mentioned to you."

"Sure, the hideous, gossipy, nonfactual, true crime thing. What about it?"

"There's a new story online. You might want to check it out."

"Follow me."

Louise was just leaving. She greeted Angie and took off. I walked back to my office, pulled up my homepage, and typed in the address. There it was. She was right. A new story was online about Paul Darnell, along with a photo of him. I read it aloud. "Paul Darnell, local banker, voluntarily arrives at the Apple Grove Police Department for an interview with local authorities. He's called a 'person of interest' in the 2010 accident that killed three local residents. Could this also be in connection with the recent death of Quinn Parsons, the driver in that accident? We're on the case and will have more details soon. Check back for live updates."

"What's going on? Has Tom said anything to you about this?" Angie asked.

I shrugged. "I know he's been trying to figure out the timeline for the night of the accident, and whether Paul Darnell participated in the disaster. He's careful not to connect his investigation with Quinn Parsons' death, but this stupid blog is doing exactly that. I hope Jeeter doesn't know about this.

At least if the website is talking about Darnell it takes some suspicion off Andy."

"I imagine it will momentarily."

I stared at her, noticing the long box on the floor next to my love seat. "What's that?"

Smiling, she pulled the box up on her lap and opened it.

"A Ouija board? I thought we had ruled out using one after the great Ouija board disaster."

"Your mom's not here to remind us, or clean up the mess, so I figured this might give us a head start. People are talking. They're seeing lights on at unusual times here in the art center and wondering about them." She scanned my face, her eyes narrowed. "Is there something you're not telling me?"

It was impossible to lie to Angie, but I tried. "Old buildings like this often have curiosity attached to them."

"Soooo? What aren't you telling me?"

I moved around uncomfortably in my desk chair. "I've occasionally noticed a creak in the floors, and I told you about my turquoise pen. I can't find it even now."

She gazed at me intently. "Come on, give."

I shook my head. "Not sure what to tell you." Trying to hide my secret, I didn't look in her eyes. I still wanted to keep Daniel close to the vest.

"Humph." She leaned over, opened the box, and took out a Ouija board. "Just one way to find out. If someone's here who shouldn't be because he or she is not breathing air, we should be able to raise the spirit with this little beauty. It's the deluxe version. Come on." She rose and told me to follow her out to the gallery, where there was a table set up with several chairs. We'd been using it for counting programs and making notes about the hospitality committee. I followed her reluctantly.

"All right. Sit across from me. Let's see if we can talk to this spirit."

I let out a long breath. I took a surreptitious glance up toward the rafters. Daniel was sitting up there on a beam smiling down at me. He signaled with his hands I should proceed. This would be a disaster. She'd figure out my secret for sure.

"So," Angie began, "we each put one finger on this little triangular piece called a planchet. It moves around the board stopping on letters so it spells words out. Or it can also point to 'yes' or 'no.' You ask it a question."

"I remember now."

"Oh," she said, "we have to invoke friendly spirits first." She closed her eyes and chanted, "Oh, friendly spirits, please have your messages ready for us. And if you're an evil spirit, please leave right now."

"I'm sure that will work," I said, dryly. I glanced up at Daniel, who had a mischievous smile on his face.

"Now," she said, "close your eyes. I'll ask a question. Keep your finger on the planchet."

"Perfect." I closed my eyes, listening to Angie.

"Are there any happy spirits who would like to speak to us this afternoon?"

We waited. Nothing happened. I was about to upset the whole board, figuring it was a disaster, when I felt the planchet move. I opened my eyes and watched.

"Yes," Angie said as the planchet moved to the word "yes" on the board. The darn thing moved. "Wow! Did you see that, Jill?"

I waited until she looked back down and stared up at Daniel, shaking my head. He put his arms out like an innocent, but lying, teenager.

"Yes," I said to Angie. "We're on a roll."

"What shall we ask him or her?"

"How about asking if they have a message to tell us?" I asked loudly.

"Sure."

We both put our fingers on the planchet. Angie asked the question. Slowly, the planchet began moving under our fingers.

Angie repeated the letters. "'B...O...O.' Well, that's crazy. They have a sense of humor at least."

I took a deep breath. She had no idea he could hear her.

Let's ask the ghost's name. Then I can stop saying, 'him or her.'" She spelled out, "What is your name?" The planchet moved again.

"D-A-N-I-E-L," Angie repeated. "Daniel. Isn't that the name of the guy who built the Lowry building?"

"What a coincidence."

"Let's ask him why he's here," Angie said.

I nodded, but figured we'd get a humorous answer. Daniel was in that kind of mood. I listened as Angie read the letters the planchet pointed to. "To keep an eye on Jill."

"What? What's going on? Jill? Have you been holding out on me?"

"Me? Of course not. Try again."

This time the planchet rolled around the board very quickly. Angie spelled out the answer. "C...O...D...E...R...E...D. What? It's our signal for hot guy in the vicinity. Code Red."

Suddenly a gale of laughter rolled down from the ceiling, and we both looked up, seeing different things. Angie followed my eyes to an empty ceiling, and I saw Daniel disappearing.

"Jill?" She glanced at me with accusation in her eyes. "What was that? What have you not been telling me?"

"Oh, all right. It's a story. I haven't told you because I figured you would think I was hallucinating. But we have to go to my office." Once in my office, I whispered to her about Daniel Lowry, our conversations, and my trip to the cemetery to verify his story. The longer I whispered, the more she stared at me like I was from another planet.

"Why are we whispering? And how long has this little romance been going on?" she asked.

"He can hear us out in the gallery. It's not a romance. He's just lonely. I think he needs someone to talk to."

"Jill. You're talking crazy. This is a delusion because your boyfriend, Sam, is unavailable way too often. Now you talk to a ghost?"

"He's a really handsome ghost, a widower, and a great conversationalist. It's been interesting hearing about his life. I'd like to help him but don't know how."

She eyed me and said out loud, "Handsome? A widower? A great conversationalist? Are you listening to yourself?"

"Shh! He can hear you," I whispered. "I think so. I've become a little attached, I guess."

Angie whispered, "Attached? What are you talking about? He's dead."

"Well, yes, there is that."

Angie might sometimes lead me into trouble, but when it came to sorting out situations, she was definitely a realist, not a romantic.

Chapter Thirty

As I waited for the doorbell to ring, I sat on the sofa in my living room and leafed through a fashion magazine. Chad was dealing with the rehearsal, so I could take the night off. My mind was elsewhere despite my excitement. Tom had called me earlier at the art center, promising to fill in Lance and me about Darnell this evening. I wondered what he'd found. Did his decision to take Darnell in for questioning have anything to do with what Wiley called "his recent visits, alone, to Priscilla's for drinks."

Was there a side of Darnell I didn't know? Did his sudden appearances at Wiley and Angie's bar mean he had guilt of some sort eating away at him? He sure seemed calm and on top of his life when we talked to him at his house. If there was anything I'd learned lately about the past, it was that you couldn't let anger or vengeance sit in your heart and rot. I'd spent too many years with misplaced anger at Quinn Parsons. Now I found I'd been wrong. What a waste of anxiety and bitterness.

Lance showed up first, grabbing a beer from my refrigerator.

"I went to see Andy today. He's feeling better since we're making progress on his case. He was surprised when I mentioned Paul Darnell. Always thought he was a stand-up guy."

Studying Lance's face, I noticed crow's feet and a few small lines I hadn't seen before. My heart sank. He was exhausted by his fears of this case. Watching Andy in jail, visiting him most days, he was aging more than I realized. Would we look back on this time once Andy was found innocent and brood about the time we'd lost, the fear and anxiety we'd felt, and the anger over my brother's incarceration?

"Paul's knowledge of finance has helped us a lot at the art center. Of course, this is Paul Darnell the adult, and I don't know about Paul back in the bad old days when he was running around with Quinn and the guys. Andy'd know more about it. I was never in high school when my brothers were." I laid the magazine aside and concentrated on Lance, who had plopped into an armchair across from me.

"Frankly, I don't know him. Only his wife. She's something else."

I shook my head. "I know. She's been in to the gift shop at the art center. Not a nice lady. Very into herself and her money. Appearances. Lot of complaints and feelings of entitlement."

"Same at my store. I imagine life with her isn't the easiest for Paul."

The front doorbell rang. I hollered, "Come on in, Tom!"

He opened my front door, stomped his feet on the entry rug, and took off his snowy shoes. "Got a beer for a thirsty detective?"

"Sure." I walked out to the kitchen, grabbed him a beer from the fridge, and thought about his high spirits. Maybe this was a good sign.

"Well," he said, once we were seated around the kitchen table, "I've had quite a day. In the middle of it, Jeeter called to yell at me about treading on his case. But I've been focused on the car accident, so it really isn't his case. He's determined to hang Quinn's murder on Andy."

"Do you think he's getting nervous you might prove Andy innocent?" Lance asked.

Tom nodded. "We'll see what happens with the overlap of the two situations—the car accident and Quinn Parsons' death. Right now, I'm homing in on the car accident. Had Paul Darnell in today, along with his lovely wife. Halfway through, he sent her home. Even Paul could see she was lying through her teeth. I think it made him nervous."

"Did he bring a lawyer?" I asked.

"No. In fact, by the time we were done, I believe he had kept a lot on his conscience for a long time. He was ready to unload. Not sure Buffy has a conscience. She was ready to unload, but mostly at me."

I took another sip of my beer, waiting for Tom to elaborate, but Lance was anxious.

"Get to it, Tom. I want to know Andy's going to get back to me and be gone from that godforsaken jail."

"I can tell you we're into big changes in the car accident. Paul looks terrible. I think he wanted to get it off his chest. Quinn Parsons coming back brought it to the forefront again. He sent two thousand dollars a month to the O'Briens for Finn's medical bills and his inability to work. Paul's wife didn't know. He set it up through a tangled series of accounts she'd never find. It was the only way he could salve his conscience. For the past six years he's been able to pretend he had nothing to do with it. Buffy kept lying for him until finally he told her to leave. As she left the interrogation room, she swore she would call his lawyer, but Paul said, 'Don't bother.' I won't repeat what she said. That's when I knew we were in for new information."

I shrugged. "What could he tell you? Was Buffy lying for him with her alibi?"

"Yes," said Tom. "Total lies from Buffy. Resignation from Paul. Once she was gone, he opened up completely. I think he's been keeping this inside so long it was a relief to get it out." He took another sip of his beer before starting the story. "The night of the car accident, Paul met the guys at the bar. That much is true. It was obvious when he strolled in they were having a great time, drinking a lot, and in no pain. Only Quinn was holding off, but, even so, he'd had a couple beers by the time Paul arrived."

"Were they celebrating?" I asked.

"Oh, I guess Quinn had won two hundred and fifty on a lottery ticket, so they were blowing some of it on booze while they played poker. Paul didn't plan to stay very long. He hadn't hung around with Parsons' group for some time. When Quinn stopped by the bank and told him they were celebrating, he saw it as an opportunity to hang with them again but leave their celebration early."

Lance cocked his head to the side. "Plans obviously changed."

"Yes. Darnell had moved away from the guys since high school and college because he knew appearances were important with his bank job. By then, Quinn Parsons, Finn O'Brien, and Branson Green had solidified into a group without him, and few people associated Darnell with them. He was married, had a couple of kids, and they were running with the country club bunch. But he couldn't resist an invitation from Quinn to hang out briefly and talk about old times."

I nodded. "I can see how that might happen. Maybe he'd had a rough week with the wife and wanted to blow off steam. So, why did he change his plans?"

Tom took another swig of his beer. I could tell from watching his eyes he was thinking about how to talk about this. "I think his story has been lying heavily on his mind for years. If Quinn Parsons hadn't come back, Paul might have managed to get by with forgetting his conscience. The night of the accident, Paul left the bar early and went out to his car. Before he started it, he thought about his friends. It was obvious they were all the worse for the drinking they'd done, and even though Quinn wasn't too bad, Paul felt some pressure to get them home. Call it nostalgia, call it his conscience, call it whatever…he sat in his car trying to decide what to do. Time went by as he sat there thinking about the old days. Finally, he saw them come out, O'Brien and Green staggering quite a bit. He told Quinn he'd drive them home and leave Quinn's car in the bar parking lot overnight after retrieving his own."

I could see where this was going.

Tom could read it on my face. "I know, you and I both realize he hadn't planned on an accident."

"Nor bad brakes."

"He told me he pulled out of the Eagle's Nest parking lot, turned toward town, and began to pick up speed down the first hill. Quinn was in the front seat with him. When they rounded the curve by the Restful Home Cemetery, he realized the brakes weren't working. He pushed them to the floor but felt nothing. Quinn grabbed the steering wheel, but they both lost control, crossed the center line, and hit our parents' car head on. When Quinn's car came to rest off the road, Darnell was dazed. He'd had his seatbelt on but the others hadn't bothered with theirs. Managing to crawl out of the car, he started walking, not realizing where he was going. I suppose he was in shock."

Lance sat up. "He didn't check to see how anyone else was?"

"No. It's one of the thoughts on his conscience. I'm giving him the benefit of figuring he was in shock and wandered off into the woods. He stayed near the road so he could make his way back to the Eagle's Nest. His head was throbbing. He had cuts and bruises from the windows breaking. But he somehow got himself to the bar parking lot entrance, got back in his car, and drove home past the wreck. It hadn't happened that far from the bar."

"How terrible!" I exclaimed. "To think he drove them to keep them safe but then didn't help them after the crash."

Tom nodded. "That's why I think he was in shock. Paul Darnell would never leave them if he were in his right mind. Leave the scene of an accident, especially one with fatalities? That's not him."

"It must have been him the night of the accident," Lance said emotionally. "What if he'd been able to help your parents? Or any of the others? Unbelievable."

"I know." Tom nodded slowly and paused. "Once he got home, Buffy went into action. She asked him questions about the accident, some of which he could remember. But mostly, he could hardly talk about it. She told him to leave it up to her. She'd tell people he'd had an accident making some shelves for their family room. And they waited."

I stared at Tom. "They waited?"

"Yes. He visited Quinn in the hospital..."

"At the hospital? Wow! That took guts," said Lance.

"It became apparent to him quickly that Quinn and O'Brien didn't remember what happened the night of the accident. The police were saying Quinn had been driving. Paul and Buffy thought they'd dodged a bullet. All they had to do was keep quiet."

"And they did," I said.

"Yes."

"What does this mean?" I asked. "Will Paul Darnell go to prison for reckless homicide?"

"I can't tell you yet. I read him his rights. The DA will have to examine the information, then make some decisions. We have no way of proving the brakes did or didn't work that night. The car was demolished long ago. He certainly did leave the scene of the accident, so his actions would come into play. But Tad Hopkins, the DA, will have to order an investigation to decide what's chargeable."

I stared at him. "Does this mean Paul hasn't been arrested?"

"No. He's in jail being held for leaving the scene, but pending charges will take time. He'll probably get out on bail."

Lance stirred. "What does this mean for Andy?"

"I don't know yet. Paul did admit Quinn Parsons blackmailed him for five thousand dollars. He figured paying him off might be more like guilt money. We saw that payment thanks to Jill's work."

"Or if he were going to kill Parsons, it would be the one and only payment," Lance said.

"True." Tom stood and walked his beer bottle over to my recycle bin. "Seems kind of crazy to pay someone blackmail, then kill him. We're forgetting someone."

"Who?" I asked.

"Buffy. More recently, the night of Parsons' death, Paul was at a conference in Chicago. I checked his alibi and it's true. He couldn't have killed Quinn. Buffy was not with him. So, the question is, where was she?"

I shook my head. "I can't imagine she'd think a blackmailer on her doorstep would ever stop demanding money. She's always pushed Paul to be successful since she was used to a certain standard of living." I rolled my eyes, trying not to sound snarky.

"I guess you have more people to interview in the guise of checking on the car accident, not Parsons' death, right?" Lance said.

"Yes. But I'm also thinking ahead about how the two situations intertwine. Whoever killed Quinn—"

"—who wasn't Andy," Lance said.

Tom nodded. "Yes. Could have been Buffy over the blackmail and concern Paul would go to jail, losing his job and reputation."

"Where do the O'Briens fit in this?" I asked.

"That, too, is on my mind," Tom said. "I don't see Finn rolling his wheelchair into the cottage or pushing Quinn down those stairs. But what about Sharon? She was the one who called him out when he talked to the big audience at the church."

"She's very bitter about Quinn coming back to town, especially when her husband is in a wheelchair she blames on Quinn's driving," I said. "And, of course, the question of no children."

"Perhaps Sharon has to do some rethinking now that it appears Quinn was not driving the car." Lance paused. "Do we know that O'Brien can't get out of his wheelchair and walk?"

Tom and I looked at each other. He spoke first.

"Guess I hadn't thought about that."

I sighed. "Sounds to me like you have a lot of work on your hands, Tom. Let me and Angie know if you need help."

Tom stood while Lance followed.

"I could get Angie and her Ouija board working on this," I offered.

My detective brother rolled his eyes. "It would be great if you could find a way for the results to hold up in court," he said as he opened my front door and left, Lance traipsing out behind him.

After they left, I sat and thought about the two incidents. The car accident. Quinn's death. A teeny, tiny thought slithered into my brain. It was something Tom had said to me several days ago. I considered it, put on my coat, and left to speak with a person who'd know—my next-door neighbor who seemed to know everything going on in town.

Chapter Thirty-One

As always, when we had a special event planned, my schedule was crazy. I was trying to balance Andy's situation with the senior group and the radio play rehearsals. But we were finally coming to the last rehearsal before the play. Ivan was working out well on the sound effects. The first time Daniel groaned, everyone was startled, then looked at me with my phone in my hand. "It's the reverberation off the rafters," I explained, hoping they'd buy it.

I was sitting in the back of the rows of chairs we'd set up for the audience, and I had my script of the play in one hand, my phone in the other. Of course, no one knew I wasn't using an app for Daniel's shrieks and groans, except for Daniel. It was working out quite well. Daniel was having the time of his life—or death, however you want to look at it.

Virginia, played by Molly, and the ghost, played by Chad, were having a heart-to-heart about his terrible behavior. Virginia—Molly—was in a long, ivory dress to symbolize her innocence. Chad was explaining he was so lonely and couldn't sleep. He hadn't slept for three hundred years. Virginia, of course, was feeling sorry for him.

He described the Garden of Death. It was a beautiful place to be at peace. Sir Simon explained she could help him get there. She must give away her tears to gain his forgiveness. To open the doors of the Garden of Death to him, Virginia must weep for his sins, and pray for his soul, and her innocence would cause the Angel of Death to have mercy on Sir Simon and allow him to be at rest. The next line was about the powers of Hell unable to win against the innocence of a child. It was Chad's best line as Sir Simon de Canterville,

205

and he played it to the hilt.

Molly, as Virginia, realizes she will pay a price for this. She disappears with him to open the doors of death. Of course, both sat on their chairs on the stage rather than actually leaving.

Alisa Segura, our narrator, described Virginia's absence. The Otis family and Cecil, the duke of Cheshire (who's in love with Virginia), searched for her everywhere. After several days, on the stroke of midnight, she returned alone. Stars and Stripes were excited because the old, withered almond tree had now blossomed outside the window of the castle. The curse was lifted.

Virginia explained the Angel of Death had forgiven Sir Simon and he was now able to sleep in the Garden of Death. The final words of the theme about forgiveness ended the play.

I glanced at Daniel Lowry. He was wiping his eyes. This must have hit a little too close to home for him.

A hush fell over the room, and everyone realized they were done. Tango hit the thunder sheet, and everyone yelled, "The end!" I glanced over at Ivan, and he was yelling with all the rest of them. Even Evan was applauding enthusiastically.

"All right, everyone. If this goes exactly as it did tonight, we'll have a huge winner on our hands. I only have a few notes for you tonight, so listen up." Evan began explaining, while I glanced up at Daniel Lowry. He was watching the cast as they listened to their director. Then he disappeared.

I helped everyone put the costumes away. They left, one by one, laughing and talking about how the rehearsal went. While they were three and four decades older than me, they had such enthusiasm for this event. They were sensational. I couldn't help but think if my parents were still alive, they'd be involved in this play.

I looked around and saw Ivan sitting alone on a chair. Maybe he was waiting for a chance to talk. Chad was upstairs checking the area. I walked over to my foundation board president.

"It went well, Ivan. Thank you for your help. It was kind of you to step in."

He touched his always-present bow tie. "Thank you, Ms. Madison. I know our relationship hasn't always been smooth…"

Smooth? I thought. You've thrown up barriers every step of the way and made me doubt myself.

"...but I want you to know this means a great deal to me."

"I'm happy if you're happy. The senior group is a great bunch to work with."

He began to put on his jacket. "You see, long ago there was someone special in my life, but she passed away."

"I'm sorry to hear that."

"She was an actress. The last production she was in was this one—in New York City. She played Virginia, although she was older than the part. That was my last happy memory of her. So, being a part of this has brought back fond memories of a happy time before the world turned upside down. I am grateful. Thank you."

I didn't know what to say. I was speechless. Recovering, I said, "You're welcome. We're pleased to have you in the cast."

He paused. "I'm aware that your brother Andy is in a serious situation. I haven't mentioned it because I didn't think it was my business. But I hope he will be exonerated. If anyone can help him with her knack for finding dead bodies and snooping into everyone's business, it's you."

I didn't know what to say. "Well, thank you, I think."

With that, he turned and walked out the side door as Chad came down the stairs. "What was that all about? Did Mr. Grumpy have some new complaint?"

"No. He reminded me of how small-minded I've been, and maybe I shouldn't have judged him so harshly. That old saying: you never know what people are dealing with."

"I'll remember that the next time he sends you a nasty text."

"Yup," I said. "I imagine I might get a few more of those."

I told Chad I'd lock up the downstairs. I had a few things to do to finish the final details for the opening tomorrow night. He left, making sure I'd lock myself in until I was ready to leave. Chad was a godsend. Despite his suffocating overprotectiveness of me, I had come to rely on him as much as I relied on Louise. We were a great trio.

Then, everyone was gone. I'd finished the list of what I needed to do before tomorrow night. As I walked out into the gallery, I spied Daniel sitting on a chair on the stage. He was deep in thought, his head buried in his hands, his elbows on his knees. I moved over and sat in a chair in the first row of the audience seats. I waited. After the rehearsal tonight, everyone was relieved and happy the show was in a good place. I wondered if Daniel felt that way too. I waited for him to speak.

Finally, he looked at me. "Your show is a bit over-weighty for me to fathom."

"Figured you would be moved by the ending. If it can happen for Sir Simon, I'll bet it can happen for you."

He cocked his head to the side. "Just feeling pity for myself. I realize I have only been here a century and a quarter, and Sir Simon was imprisoned for hundreds of years. But he is fictional. Not real. Your play put me in mind of why I am here. No one has given me a circumstance in which I may redeem myself. So here I remain. It has been amusing to release a few howls and scare people. Over the decades, I have accomplished that to a highly entertaining degree. But here I remain."

"You haven't told me about the end of your story, how...how you died." Despite that occurrence, I thought it might cheer him up to let him talk about his own life.

"Oh." He studied me with interest. "Where did I stop?"

"After your wife and son died. It must have been such an emotional upheaval."

He nodded. "It was. Terrible. He was so tiny. I only got to embrace him for a moment. Rosemary was spent and died shortly after my son. After I buried them and held a wake, I spent my days and nights deep in my business. It was the only way to forget. The railroads were rushing West, and we were now linked to Chicago, which made it easier to obtain goods. My store was flourishing, though I did not have anyone with whom to share it."

"Did you ever think of remarrying?"

"No. She was the only woman I ever loved. After her death, I squandered money, gambled a fortune away, and inadvertently made myself a target of a person who coveted what I had. One night, I was in my office working on the store accounts. I heard glass breaking. When I tread softly downstairs and investigated the noise, a man had broken in, and he got the advantage of me. When I awoke, I was tied to a chair in my office."

"Did you know him?" I asked.

"No. He demanded I open my safe. I figured if I did as he asked, he might leave me alone. I possessed plenty of revenue in the bank but only a few hundred dollars in the safe. After I opened it, he shot me. Total shock. Why? It was in February 1890. When I awoke, I was still here in my building, but I was dead. Somehow, I had missed out on going to heaven or hell. But I grasped, instinctively, I could not leave until I did a brave act to make up for my cowardice in killing another human being."

I checked my phone. Only ten o'clock. Still plenty of time. I looked at Daniel. "Unfortunately, doing a brave deed depends on an opportunity that's out of your hands." I paused and changed the subject. "Being in a building that changed around you over the years must have been weird."

"Your loud renovation project last year drove me to the edge of madness."

"Me, too." I laughed.

He paused. "You are right. Over the years I have watched my building turn into an apothecary and reading room back in the 1890s. It resumed only as an apothecary until 1950. Three bankers bought it and converted it into a building they called a department store. It has been intriguing to see their mercantile and how the goods reflected the changing times. I was fascinated by motorized vehicles appearing outside the windows in the early twentieth century, and watched liquor sold under cover when it was an apothecary. Now that is an idea I would have contrived."

"I suppose the liquor sales were during Prohibition, when liquor was illegal."

"What? Illegal?"

"The country has changed since you died, Daniel."

"I imagine that is inevitable. I have admired the women's skirts rising higher and higher. Even you and your friends are nothing like the prim wife I cherished decades ago. It is shocking to behold. I am not certain if I like what has happened to women. They seem a bit forward."

Forward? My anger rose in my chest. Calm, Jill. Now how was I to answer his nineteenth-century viewpoint? Of course, women were demure and more subservient in the 1800s. "Times change, Daniel, and thank God, they've changed for the better for my sex. No more corsets, no more staying at home whether I want to or not, no more having children unless I want to. I imagine men loved the nineteenth century."

"At least till those suffragettes appeared."

"Exactly."

He didn't say anything. I suppose he was thinking about how his world was upended.

"I have enjoyed watching your radio play, and I must say it has touched me. Maybe you will put in a few words for forgiveness. Alas, I believe the world could use forgiveness, even now."

I nodded. "It's been a hard concept for me, too. I'm only now discovering I've been angry with someone for years for a crime he didn't commit, one very close to me."

"Does that have anything to do with the pictures in your office?"

"Yes. My parents. They died in a car accident. I hated the person I thought was driving the other car. But now it appears I misplaced my anger. It's left a terrible feeling in my soul. Judging other people, especially when you don't know their motives or reasons, sure gets you into a lot of trouble."

He stood and moved toward me, but a confused expression came across his face when he remembered he wasn't human anymore. "Fortunately, you have discovered your error. You still have time to make amends."

I stared at Daniel Lowry. "Yes," I said. "I'm going to try to do better."

"I bid you good fortune tomorrow night. I will be watching and groaning— at the appropriate time of course."

"Thank you, Daniel. For some reason it's so easy to talk to you. Feels like I'm selfish, since I'd love to have you stick around. But you need to find a way to end this limbo you're in. I have faith you'll find your way home one of these days."

I called Sam as I drove home. He picked his phone up on the first ring.

"You still at the art center?" he asked. "If I didn't know better, I'd think you had some boyfriend stashed away there."

I swallowed and forced my voice to be calm. "Are you kidding? Have you looked at my whiteboard lately? At least when this show is over, I can relax a little. And yes, I'm on my way home. Tomorrow, Tom and I are going to go see the O'Briens. If anyone is taking up my time, it's my loving brother. But I think that will be resolved soon. I hope it will. And yes, I am exhausted."

"Well, drive carefully. Go home. Drink some warm milk and go to bed."

"Is that what the doctor orders?"

"Definitely. I'll send you my bill in the morning."

"Thank you, Sam. And thanks, too, for being so understanding. My crazy schedule will get less crazy soon."

"Good night, Sweetheart."

"Good night."

Chapter Thirty-Two

Tom and I sat outside Finnegan O'Brien's house on Friday morning. The art center hadn't opened yet, so we had plenty of time for what we were planning. Like many married couples, the O'Briens had a language of glances and facial expressions. It would be a better plan to speak to Finn separately from Sharon. He might be the weak link. We knew she left for work around eight, so we waited down the street in my car.

"Talked to Bill Gatesmith, Andy's lawyer. He says the forensic evidence—fingerprints—only shows Andy was there. He could have been there any time. Andy told me he didn't remember snagging his sweater on the handrail. That might have been planted."

"Does he think Andy has a chance?"

Tom nodded.

"So, on to Finn O'Brien. You think we have a better chance of him talking without his wife there?" I asked.

He sipped his coffee. "That's the general theory." He yawned.

His yawn made me yawn. "What do you know about his past?"

"I know he got a job at a bar that caters to Black residents called the Oasis Bar and Grill down on Avalon. Since he's biracial, like us, he talked to everyone, white, Black, brown. But, like lots of folks who work in bars, he began drinking too much. He'd been quite the athlete in high school football and worked out to keep his muscles toned. But after a while the alcohol began to take its toll. By the time of the accident, he was living on borrowed time. Too much drinking, smoking, and running around with Parsons and Green."

A slammed door made us both look up. Sharon O'Brien came barreling out the front door of their house, a tote bag over her shoulder, smoke practically coming out her ears. She pulled up the garage door, letting it hit the top of the garage ceiling with another angry crash. Once she was in the car, her back lights went on, and she reversed like she was being chased by demons. Her car came careening out the driveway, backing into the street with a wide turn that barely missed a car coming from the opposite direction. She took off, fishtailing down the snowy street. If her attitude could be discerned from her actions, she was one angry woman.

Tom turned to me. "Shall we?"

"Why not?" I said, as he waited for me to drive us over to Finn's house.

Tom rang the bell. After several minutes, Finn's angry voice called out, "What now? Forget your work keys or what?" He opened the door and, seeing us, took a deep breath. "Oh. It's you."

"So excited to see us," said Tom, a smile on his face.

Finn pulled back from the door, allowing us room to enter. We followed him into the same living room we'd visited before. He rolled his wheelchair across the room and turned it around to face us.

"How's your day started?" Tom asked.

A scowl lit his face up. "Great before you got here; great once you leave."

"Is there something we can do to help?" I asked in a contrite tone.

"No." He gazed all around and was silent.

It was obvious he was really angry at Sharon. Thus, the car door and the house door slams. Lots of slammed doors today. Tom and I waited. He'd taught me sometimes people will talk if you wait and let them speak once they're ready. Finally, Finn broke the silence.

"I just found out something I'm angry about. It's nothing to do with you."

Tom lifted his chin slightly, stared at Finn closely, and said, "Your wife. Sharon has a problem?"

"No." Again, he paused. "Yes. I found out she may be having an affair." We waited again.

"The night Quinn was killed she was gone."

"Do you know where she went?" I asked.

"She said nowhere near Quinn's house. So what else is there? It's not like she has lots of friends running to our door. Quinn saw to that once he put me in this chair. She's never gotten over it: the accident, the wheelchair, and my inability to have kids. Who wants to hang with someone who's constantly angry?" He pushed his chair back a foot, then pushed it forward again, anything to take his anger out.

"How do you know she's having an affair?" Tom asked.

Finn pulled some magazines off an end table, throwing them angrily to the floor. I supposed he couldn't do much more to show his anger. "She told me, that's how. Do you think it makes me feel good when I'm in this chair able to do nothing? And who caused my imprisonment?"

"I thought it was Quinn Parsons, but now it appears I was wrong. Paul did that," I said.

Tom leaned forward and spoke quietly. "Finn. My gut tells me the present has to do with the past. I feel it. I know it. Tell me about seven years ago when you guys were hanging out, and Paul drove you when you left the bar."

"I can't. I don't remember. When I heard through the grapevine about Paul confessing to driving, I was as shocked as anyone. No memory of the accident whatsoever."

"Do you think Sharon is capable of murdering Quinn Parsons, thinking it was Quinn who put you in this situation?"

"I don't know what to think."

Now, Tom leaned forward again. "Finn, I want to know if Quinn Parsons was dealing drugs back then. What do you know?"

He licked his lips and pursed his mouth. "I can't talk about that."

I heard Tom let out a deep breath. "If you were involved too, Finn, we could talk to the prosecutor about an immunity deal. No one wants to see you go to prison."

"I'm already in prison." It came out bitterly, a reminder of his wife's past comments.

Tom pressed again. "Please, tell me about the drugs."

Finn pressed his hands together, saying nothing.

"Please," said Tom.

214

Finn turned his head toward Tom, then me. "It was Quinn. He was picked up for shoplifting when he was sixteen."

Tom and I waited, wondering where this was going to lead.

"He told me, after that, somebody left a note in his school locker asking him to sell drugs and to recruit a second person. There was lots of money in it. He'd get a good cut. He was curious, especially about the money. Quinn said he was left a blindfold and directions to go to a prearranged place at Peterson Park. Once there, he was to put on this blindfold and wait."

"So, you didn't go with him?" Tom asked.

"Naw. I didn't know nothing about it. At this meeting, the dealer took him out of his car and walked him into the woods. There was a spot in the woods where they would make the drop. The dealer would leave the drugs, and Quinn would leave the cash once he sold the drugs. He had to count to a hundred, and when he took off the mask, the person was gone. Whoever was leaving the stash there was watching him, but he couldn't figure out from where. It was a feeling. He could easily find his way out of the woods, so he knew where to leave the stuff. Talked me into helping, but I wouldn't sell the hard stuff, only weed. He sold the coke.

"We sold the stuff for several years, but never got caught. The money was rad because we'd gotten an alcohol habit by that time. After high school, Quinn landed a job at the local Pontiac garage selling cars. He did okay, but the money on the side from the blow was helpful. I was tending bar at the Oasis when I met Sharon. Branson Green had moved to Chicago but was back in a couple of years. He'd learned the butchering trade and got a job at Strand Market. We still hung around together. Only Paul was not around much."

"Did Paul know you were selling?"

"No. We never told him. It was our own little side hustle."

"Were you still selling when the accident happened?"

"Yeah. But not as much as in the old days."

"The accident ended it," Tom said, as if it were a fact.

"It was the end all right. But just before the accident, Quinn told me he thought he knew who our supplier was. He was going to confront the person."

"And did he?" I asked.

He shook his head. "I don't know. The accident happened. My whole life before that ended, you might say. Life wasn't ever the same."

"I wonder," said Tom. "Is it possible when Quinn came back here, he confronted this person or even tried to blackmail this dealer?"

"If he did," Finn answered, "he never told me about it. Sounds like something he'd do. He always was crazy. Didn't think about what he did before he did it."

"The night Quinn was killed, you were here alone."

"Yes."

"What time did your wife get home?"

"I don't know. I was already asleep." He slowly turned his chair toward the side.

Tom regarded me as if to say, "Anything else?"

I shook my head gently.

"Well," said Tom. "I guess we'll go and leave you in peace. But we may be back to ask more questions. Thanks for your help. We also may need to question your wife."

Finn stared out the window as if he hadn't even heard what Tom said. I guessed he had other thoughts on his mind.

Chapter Thirty-Three

The OFTA group was closing in on the end of their final radio show on Saturday night. I sat watching their well-rehearsed lines and listening to the audience laughing. Friday had gone exactly like this. Sam came for that show, but he was working tonight. We had a full house both nights. The demand for tickets was so high we could have put this on two more nights.

During the intermission, I was approached by Tigger, who'd been in the audience. He suggested we meet briefly in my office. Once there, he handed me a single piece of paper with columns of numbers.

"You were right," he said.

I glanced through the paper. "Thank goodness."

"Remember to get rid of this."

"I should chew it up and swallow it, but for now, I'll stick it in my drawer and lock it."

We both returned, separately, to the gallery, and I thought about the paper he'd given me. It could wait until tomorrow.

Virginia, aka Molly, described Sir Simon's lesson to her. "He taught me what life and death were about." She took a deep breath. "He made me realize love is stronger than both."

Virginia and Cecil moved closer together. The play ended with their love and plans for their future marriage.

The applause was deafening, and everyone took several bows. Chad pointed to me. He used the microphone to ask me to come up on the stage and say a few words. Flustered, I stopped to think about what might be appropriate. I moved confidently to the stage, smiled at our wonderful cast, and turned to the audience from our little town who had supported us so well.

"Thank you so much for coming tonight to support our Old Friends group and the creative opportunities we provide for our downstate community. Each day I thank God we have this community surrounding us with love and appreciation for the arts. We were sold out both nights for this wonderful senior show." I stretched my arms out wide. "We can't thank you enough. As many of you know—since we're a small town—this hasn't been an easy year for the Madison family. When I chose this Oscar Wilde story for our first radio play, I did so with the thought that love is better than hate, forgiveness is better than revenge, and empathy is the best way to approach those who carry burdens we might not realize. So, in the spirit of my mom, who would have loved to be here to see this play, I thank you all for your support of the arts. Thanks to Evan Shelly, our director, and our cast and the many helpers who made this work. Please feel free to have refreshments and enjoy the artwork in the gallery. Some of the pieces are for sale." I stopped, hoping I hadn't missed thanking someone.

The audience applauded fervently following those words, and I watched with a huge smile when everyone stood. From my angle on the stage, I saw Tom and Mary, their kids, Lance, Pastor Frump, Martin and Doris Stewart, and so many others that I knew. The town had turned out to support our little art center. The cast and I took a final bow. I glanced up at the rafters of the gallery. There was Daniel, his hand saluting me, a smile on his face.

Once the audience had cleared out, I went to the weavers room with Angie and brought up eight bottles of champagne. We handed out plastic flutes, filled them, and had multiple toasts to all the people who'd helped—Chad, Evan Shelly, the cast, the crew, and the sound effects people. Sadly, Daniel couldn't have any champagne, but I saw him hanging out watching the festivities.

Now, it was only Angie and me.

"Well, pal, I guess you did it again," she said.

"Ah, this was so much fun. I love those 'geezers,' as Andy calls them. What a fantastic job. They're already talking about when they can do this again. Find a new play, of course. Whew! I am totally exhausted. What a week it was getting ready for all this."

Angie looked at me. "I suppose no one knows some of the sound effects didn't come from the tape you made."

I glanced at the rafters. They were empty. Angie had figured out it wasn't my phone app. "Yes, we had to have Daniel Lowry, our resident ghost, fill in at the last minute."

"And Ivan? I actually saw him laughing. What has happened? Is the world falling apart?"

Taking a deep breath, I sighed. "I think he came a bit in my direction, and I moved a bit toward him. Maybe he isn't so bad after all."

"I'll remind you of that when you get his next text." She paused and began picking up her coat and scarf. "You'll clean all this tomorrow?"

"Yes. Volunteers coming in."

"And"—she paused, as if she didn't quite know how to say what was in her head—"is the ghost here?"

My eyes searched the rafters. Daniel was hovering above, probably waiting for us to leave so he could have his peace and quiet back.

"Yes, he is. Up there." I pointed.

She stared up at the rafters, squeezing her eyes in an attempt to see something, anything. "Oh, please, Mr. Lowry, let me see you just once. I've never seen a real, live—well, not alive—ghost before, only heard one evidently."

Across the room near the hallway to my office, Daniel stood expectantly.

"Oh." Angie's mouth hung open, her hand reaching for it. "Oh, my. You're as handsome as Jill said you were. And what a romantic scar."

He bowed with his usual charm. "Thank you."

Angie stared at him for several seconds. Not taking her eyes off him, she said, "All right, Jill. Now I believe."

I laughed. "I guess I'm not crazy after all."

Daniel disappeared as suddenly as he'd come.

"Whew. How utterly amazing. Wiley will not believe this," Angie said. She put her coat on, tied her scarf around her neck, and came over to give me a big hug. "See ya soon."

"You will." I smiled.

I had put the money for the tickets in our small safe. We'd get it all to the bank on Monday. Out of the corner of my eye, I saw some movement near the front door through my office window. Who could be here at this time of night? Instantly, my stomach recoiled. I recognized the shape. Jeeter. Before I could even think rationally, my fingers dialed Tom's number on my phone. I slipped it into my pocket with the speaker on. Jeeter slunk in the door, its bell silent because I turned it off for the play.

"Jill. Nice to catch you here alone. I have one or two items to talk over with you." He made a huge show of locking the front door. Dread washed over me. Except for my cell phone—my lifeline—I was completely alone.

I stood my ground, didn't move. Making my voice strong and powerful, I said, "Jeeter, I have nothing to say to you. I'm leaving to go home."

"Not quite so fast." He took off his coat as if he planned to stay awhile and hung it over a chair in the back row. "I'm told by my bank someone's been digging into my finances. My banking records. They're investigating. Don't suppose you know anything about that?"

"Why would you ask me?" Trying to sound stupid wasn't a good look for me, I thought, but it was the only ploy I could think of.

"Because you've been a nosey parker throughout my investigation, always going here and there, talking to people, asking questions. Your brother Tom is enough of a pain when it comes to investigating. You had no reason to get involved."

I moved back a few steps as he lurched toward me. I could hear my heart pounding in my head, and I hoped my phone was on so Tom would hear Jeeter's voice. I tried to take a deep breath, but my lungs seemed frozen. My feet couldn't move away from him. Fear paralyzed me.

He kept coming. "What did you find in my bank records?" His movements were patient as if he had all night. That made me feel even more terrified.

"Me? I found nothing. But someone told me a little too much cash for a deputy sheriff." There, I'd said it. Now, he was right in front of me. He reached out and touched my hair. Immediately, I pulled my head back and slapped his hand away.

"Too bad. You always were a looker, but I didn't have enough time to check you out. "Well"—he dropped his hand and glanced at his watch—"maybe there's still some time to check you out tonight."

"Jeeter, don't come any closer. I'll scream."

He laughed. "Really? And who would hear you? It's just you and me, babe."

I needed to play for time. Get him to confess so Tom could hear him. But could I do that before he assaulted me? Maybe appeal to his ego. "Where did all your money come from, Jeeter? I didn't know deputy sheriffs had such a great retirement fund."

He pulled back a bit, crossed his arms. Trying to act unconcerned, he said, "Years and years of supplying dope and blow to the area. The customer base is bigger than I thought when I first started."

I feigned shock. "You sold drugs?"

He shook his head. "Nah. I only supplied the stuff. But I closed it down a few years back when my two best sellers were stupid enough to get into a car accident."

I studied his face. "Finn and Parsons?"

"See?" He smiled again. "You know way too much for your own good. For my own good. Just like Quinn Parsons. I thought I could trust him after all the years he'd made money from my efforts. But no, he came back here looking to blackmail me. I couldn't allow it. I had retirement plans. Somewhere warm with lots of booze, women, sand, and waves."

"You killed Quinn Parsons?" My mind was desperately assessing how I could get help. Sweat trickled down my back, under my arms.

"Of course. I couldn't let him take all my hard-earned cash. So, he had a convenient accident. Your brother was a handy patsy, but now you'll have to have an accident and he's in jail, so I guess we can't blame this one on him. An accident. Okay. Time's up," Jeeter said. "You're coming with me." He rushed over, took my arm, and turned me around in the direction of the hallway, shoving me a few feet. I let out a scream, somehow finding the

221

strength to push out of the suffocating fear of him.

I tried to push him away but he grabbed both arms, shoved me back against the wall, and I could feel his breath on my face. Yuk. Barbecue and onions. What could I do to slow this down? No one could hear me, the doors were all locked, and I was feeling desperate. He was so much stronger than me. Where was Tom?

As if in slow motion, we moved toward the basement stairs. The very place where Ivan had his fall, the stairway that took us to the basement where we'd found a corpse buried. Now it would become a place where no one would find me for a while. Why was this basement always a pain in my neck? I should have filled it with cement a year ago. Never, I'd never let him push me down those stairs.

I tried to fight him, but he was too strong for me. He had both of my arms behind my back and was pushing me through the hallway. My heart was pounding. My arms hurt where he was holding them awkwardly behind me. Trip him, I thought. I tried to push my foot against the hallway wall, but he kicked my leg from under me so hard I almost fell. Wanting to alert Tom on my phone, I screamed, "Stop, Jeeter!" But Tom wasn't here. I could only pray he'd have this message in his head after Jeeter killed me. OMG. Fiery determination coursed through me. I was not going to let him pull me to those stairs without a fight.

He let go of one of my arms and reached around with one hand and felt my pocket. Pulling up my phone, he said, "Ah. What have we here?" Without looking at the phone, he threw it clear down the hallway. So much for Tom being able to hear me.

Despite my efforts to slow him down, Jeeter had me at the door to the basement. He let go of my arms, blocking my retreat with his body. Too strong. He was way too strong for me to push him away.

"Open it!" he yelled, his patience with me ended.

"I can't. My keys are in my office." Anything to slow him down. Sweat was pouring down me now.

He felt my keys in the other pocket. "Liar. There," he screamed.

Pulling out my keys, he passed them to me, and I dropped them on the floor. Whatever I could do to waste time. Tom, where are you? I can't hold out much longer.

"Open the door before I break this arm," he shouted.

I picked up the keys, put the right one in the lock, and turned it. The door opened with ease.

"Hmm. Looks like a long fall with cement at the bottom. Just like Quinn Parsons."

I looked into the darkness, and prayed I could take him with me.

"Time to say your prayers," Jeeter taunted me.

In the silence I heard, "Move right, Jill." It was Daniel's voice.

I dove to the right side of the doorway beyond Jeeter's reach as he went tumbling down the stairs. I watched in amazement as his body rolled over and over, landing with a terrible thud on the cement floor. Then, silence except for my heartbeat pounding in my head. Gasping, I almost fell after him, but strong arms pulled me back and set me on the floor. Turning around, I saw Daniel, smiling. I reached for him, but he dissolved into nothing.

Sirens screamed closer and closer. I pulled myself together and gazed down the stairs at Jeeter, who was moaning on the floor. Well, at least he wasn't dead. For a moment, I thought about the torture my brother had suffered at his hands. At first, I was glad Jeeter was in pain. But I knew he needed help, and taking the high road was better. Then I heard pounding on the front door.

Racing out to the front of the gallery, I opened the door for Tom and two officers. I pointed to the hallway. Quickly, they went tearing past me. I could hear Tom calling for an ambulance. He sent Aubrey, one of the officers, to stay with Jeeter, while he came back to the gallery.

"He'll live. I heard every word, Jill. Good thinking on your part." He put his arms around me and held me close, calming my shaking. "You did a perfect job keeping him talking."

Wiping a tear from my cheek, I said, "Andy's good now, right?"

"Yes."

On the verge of collapse, I blew out a long breath. My legs were wobbly, so he walked me to a chair in the gallery. The tears kept coming and I couldn't make them stop. It was all too much.

Tom moved over next to me, waiting for me to get hold of my emotions.

"What I don't understand," Tom said, "is how you managed to overpower him. He outweighs you by a lot, and he's got huge muscles."

I nodded, still breathless. "You should never underestimate the power of a woman… especially…when she can trip a man at the top of a set of stairs. I think adrenaline kicked in." I looked up at the rafters to see if Daniel was listening to my lie. He was missing.

Eddie Brant walked into the gallery next. "I heard about Jeeter on the radar. Is he all right?"

"I think he's gonna make it," said Tom. "But he'll have a lot of years to think about what he's done. In prison."

Eddie sat for a moment with us. We watched the ambulance driver and another paramedic walk in with a stretcher. "I couldn't talk to you about the case, Tom. It hasn't been the best weeks of my life at the sheriff's department. Every day I kept seeing Andy's situation get worse. Jeeter was on a real tear."

Tom nodded. "I know. But you kept an eye on Jeeter and did what you could."

"I tried. The day Andy got hurt, I was off duty. I guess Jeeter waited for me to be gone. I don't think he trusted me."

The paramedics carefully climbed the basement stairs and shuffled into the gallery with an unconscious Jeeter on the stretcher.

"What do you think?" Tom asked.

"Could be a concussion, but no broken bones."

"Good," said Tom. "I'll be able to arrest him. With immense pleasure. You going to be okay, Jill?"

"Yes. I'm fine. I'll lock up and go home."

"Good. You need to come down to the station so I can take your statement in the morning. It's late, and we're all exhausted."

Tom stood. So did Eddie Brant.

They shook hands and both headed out after the stretcher. As Eddie turned toward me, a beam of light from one of the ceiling spotlights bounced off his open jacket, and I saw a necklace hanging from his neck. A cross. He saw me looking at his necklace.

"Thanks, Eddie," I murmured quietly.

"You're welcome." A cool, neutral expression filled his face. He wasn't going to confess to being Deep Throat.

Once they were all out the door, I locked it. I should have done that to begin with, but in all the hubbub, I didn't think of it. The gallery was quiet with everyone gone. I remembered the laughter and smiles about the fantastic time we'd all had this evening. Then, Jeeter. I wiped some tears from my face. Bonus. I couldn't wait to tell Andy about this. Andy, my brother who'd no longer be an accused murderer.

I walked back to my office, and just before I turned off the light, I looked over at my desk. There was my turquoise pen, the one I hadn't been able to find. Right in the center of my desk. Remembering the strong arms around me at the top of the stairway, I smiled. He'd had it all along.

Turning out the light, I locked the office door and stood there leaning against it. In the darkness, I thought I heard Daniel's voice murmuring, "Thank you, my dear. You gave me a chance to be brave. Forgiveness works. Until we meet again."

Chapter Thirty-Four

"Crockett and Darnell Arrested" screamed the headline in the morning newspaper. Since it was a Sunday paper, it was thick. But this story was on the front page above the fold. It went on to describe how Jeeter was in jail, awaiting a hearing in the attempted murder of Quinn Parsons. I was sure the prosecutor would charge him with distributing drugs too. Of course, he'd be in the town jail where Tom worked, while Andy was still in the county lockup. The second part of the story was about Paul Darnell's arrest for leaving the scene of a crime and lying under oath. I had to smile because Tom and I were both mentioned prominently in the investigation. My detective brother was getting used to being paired with me when it came to solving murders. Ha! I was sure I'd hear about this one too.

On the social page was a review of *The Canterville Ghost*, with accolades for everyone. The acting and directing were superb, the sound effects and backdrops imaginative, and special praise was given to the shrieks and moans of the Canterville ghost. I laughed out loud. Too bad Daniel didn't know he was one of the highlights of the review. I knew several of the actors, including Chad, had gone to the hospital to see Foxtrot after the performance.

I'd gone to Tom's office to give my account of last night, and I was feeling no pain this morning with the right people in jail and the Old Friends group getting deserved praise for their work. In fact, I'd pulled a vermilion red dress from my closet to wear to work. Oh, happy days. Chad had been so right to form a senior gathering for our art center. They were already there as volunteers, so they might as well have some fun too. I'd have to start thinking about what to put on next with this enthusiastic group.

My phone sang the *Law & Order* theme.

"Hi, Tom. Yes, I saw the morning newspaper already."

He chuckled. "I surrender. I'm getting used to your butting into my business."

"How about Andy? Is he out of jail yet?"

"Thought I'd let you and Lance go over to the jail. You can talk to him about it today. Eddie Brant's working, and he'll let you in. I've filled Lance in on what happens next, but Andy should be out momentarily."

I took a huge breath. "Thank God."

"Well, I think we all had something to do with it, too." He paused. "By the way, I've talked to Jeeter at the jail about the car accident. He swears up and down he did not touch the brakes on Parsons' car, but I think he may be good for it. He lies so easily. I know he's a great mechanic. I've seen him working on his own cars. O'Brien and Parsons were unhappy with their share of the trade. Parsons, who'd figured out his supplier was Jeeter, was threatening to quit unless he was paid more. So, having them die in a car accident would be convenient. He could always find another sucker to sell for him."

I thought about it. "Maybe you're right. Keep after him." Something about that scenario didn't quite jibe with me, but I let it go for now. I couldn't wait to get to the jail and see Andy. I'd call Lance. We could go together.

"I'll be interrogating Jeeter again this afternoon. The hospital checked him out, and he's sitting in jail. He's going to be fine. His trip down your stairs wasn't as lethal as I thought it might be. I'm still trying to figure out how you managed to trip a man twice your size."

"A girl can't tell all her secrets." I chuckled again and punched off.

"I was beginning to worry that we'd never see this day," I said to Lance as we closed the car doors. He came over and hugged me, reminding me that we'd all been in this together.

We opened the door to the county jail. Thankfully, Eddie was sitting behind the front desk. No more Jeeter. He rose, came over to shake our hands, and smiled for the first time in a long time. "I told him you were coming over today. He is a whole different person now that he'll be getting out."

"Again, the whole family thanks you, Eddie, for keeping an eye on Andy," I said.

"Well, at least he's still alive, although he has a bit of metal in him now. Follow me. I'll go get him."

We waited in the visitors' room, but it seemed not so ugly or dark as it had. Pretty soon, the door to the cells opened. Andy came out in his jail clothes with Eddie, no shackles or handcuffs. He reached out to Lance and hugged him, then came over to me.

"Guess you're going to have me to check up on you, sis," he said. "I should have been there to protect you."

"I managed without you or Tom, but thanks," I said, not mentioning the help I'd received from my paranormal friend.

"I need to get back to my guitar. All this publicity should bring in a great crowd." He smiled at Lance.

"So," I said, "how do we get you out of here?"

"I have the answer," said Lance. "I spoke with your lawyer and the prosecutor. The easiest procedure is to have a dismissal order signed, and you're good to go."

My brother looked terribly disappointed. He spread his arms out. "That's it? After all this time?"

"Andy! We need to get you out ASAP," I said. "Why would you want to stay here?"

Lance laughed. "I knew this would happen. The prosecutor said you have three choices: First, he files a statement of *nolle prosequi*, with no judge's signature. It means 'Get out of jail free.' They let you out. Or second, the prosecutor takes an order to the judge to sign. He signs it. Done. Finished. Home free."

"And the third option? What's behind door number three?" Andy asked.

Lance sighed. "You could be taken over to the courtroom by Eddie, the prosecutor would make a formal motion to dismiss the charges. The judge would approve it and sign off on it. You would get your day in court."

"Hmm," said Andy, rubbing his chin with his hand. "I think I want the full meal deal. The whole town needs to see I've been forgiven, and there are no longer any charges. I didn't do it. I'm innocent. Let's go with selection number three. And I want my lawyer there too. Also Josie Brinkley."

Lance turned to me and rolled his eyes. He said to Andy, "I knew that would be your choice. We need to have a big, dramatic finish. And because I knew, I already talked to the prosecutor who spoke with the judge. It means you'd have to stay one more night here. Tomorrow morning, Monday, they set a time aside to do that. I'll bring you some clothes early tomorrow. Has your lawyer, Gatesmith, been here?

"Yes. And Josie Buckley stopped by to congratulate me. Also, I would have no problem with staying if Mary could send over some strawberry shortcake. Eddie likes it too, so send enough for both of us. Oh, and lots of whipped cream."

That afternoon, Sam was working—of course—while I was at home doing laundry, making a grocery list, and tackling all the chores I'd let go in the last week since we were so busy at work. I'd just finished my list and was leaving for the grocery store when my phone rang. It was Sam. I could almost hear a smile in his voice. "Hey. Checking in since you're on the downslope of your long week at work. Hope you're relaxing."

"Are you kidding? I've got so much to do to catch up."

"Oh." He sounded disappointed. "I thought you might want to go out for dinner tonight. We're celebrating."

I was intrigued. "Really? What? Celebrating what?"

"I signed a new contract."

"Oh."

"Now, wait until you hear the terms. I will no longer have any emergency room hours."

"What? That's wonderful! No more being on call every other weekend and too many nights?"

"Correct."

"How did you manage to talk them into no more on call?" I asked. This was crazy.

"I'm taking a new position."

"Oh. Please tell me it isn't so many shifts and hours."

"It's a pay raise."

I sighed. "Oh, Sam. That's great. But how will this new contract help us see each other more?"

"It will." He paused and relayed some medical jargon to someone else wherever he was. "Sorry. I'm in the break room and one of the guys needed some information and now he's gone. Okay. I'm going to be what they call a 'hospitalist.' I'll have regular, normal hours, get a pay raise, and work with patients who've been admitted to the hospital. No more emergencies, no more crazy hours."

"Sam! That's wonderful! I can't wait. When does this start?"

"First of the month."

"Perfect. Oh, I love you, Sam."

"Love you too. This will be so much better for us. Can't wait."

"Nor I. Sending you hugs and kisses."

"Back to you."

"And yes, let's celebrate tonight."

We both disconnected. This was such amazing news. Finally, we'd be able to spend time together like real couples. Who knew where that might lead? I was hoping Sam might want to move in with me and maybe consider a ring for my finger. I added a bottle of champagne to my list. Life was looking up.

My phone rang with a text. I turned it over and checked it.

Ms. Madison. Just inquiring when we will be doing another radio show. I have a list of some possible scripts. Will forward it to you.

If a new script contains shrieks and groans, I believe you should hang onto the groan app. It sounds so authentic.

Please address replacing Darnell on the art center board. I will send a list of names to you. Time's a-wasting. Keep on tip of this.

Ivan F. Truelove III, CPA

Well, most of my life was looking up. Some parts I couldn't do much about. And it's "top," Ivan. You'll never understand autocorrect.

Chapter Thirty-Five

Louise had come to work but had left for the bank already. Tuesday morning. I felt a deep sense of depression. It was probably a natural letdown from the radio play being over. Everyone had gathered in the art center yesterday, taken apart the stage, returned the costumes to the college, and cleaned the entire gallery. Every single senior in the Old Friends group showed up to do the job. What an amazing bunch of people I could rely on. I think they loved the art center as much as I did. I sat in my office looking at the stack of papers I needed to go through. I just didn't feel like working on them.

I yawned. Andy had had his court date yesterday morning. He'd practically passed Jeeter in the hallway and done a happy dance to anger the former lawman. Jeeter was arraigned on first-degree murder charges and a slew of other charges. My guess is he won't be around Apple Grove anymore for a long, long time. When the judge said she'd sign the form to get Andy out of jail, he'd thanked her and given her a list of his band dates for the next month. He thought she'd love their music. She struck me more as a classical music type. Oh, well.

My brother was handed over to the loving arms of his family and friends. Both of the lawyers had joined us.

I happened to see Tigger and Wingate. I thanked him for the note he'd handed me at the play—the information on Jeeter's account, and he told me he enjoyed making the world right. But his hacking of websites would have to stay our little secret. I assured him it would. When I mentioned Jeeter's bank was checking out who the hacker was, he said they'd never find him.

Tigger told me he was sure no brother of mine could ever have killed anyone. For a virtual recluse who walked his dog three times a day, he was always aware of what was happening in town. I wondered what his real job was.

Snow was falling steadily outside, and I figured I'd not have a lot of company in the art center this morning. I strolled out to the gallery and watched the flakes drift down, beautiful, fluffy, and delicate. I gazed up into the empty rafters of the gallery and felt my ghost's absence. Although I was glad Daniel had been reunited with his family, I felt his loss. Just like Sir Simon de Canterville and Virginia, his human connection to me gave him the bravery to lift the curse. It seemed to me that the most unusual, loving actions in life were part of being human. The girl who helped Sir Simon, and the ghost who helped me were rewarded with a pathway to "the great hereafter," as Daniel had called it.

What a powerful emotion forgiveness is. I was no longer angry with Quinn Parsons, although I certainly didn't condone selling drugs that ruined peoples' lives. But he hadn't been responsible for killing my parents. Paul Darnell was going to pay a steep price for his part in the accident, but I couldn't find it in myself to hate him, either. He thought he was doing the right thing in helping his friends, who had been drinking too much. But he also had left them at the scene of an accident, so I kept thinking about how much gray area was involved in moral judgments. As I'd told Daniel, judging people might be a human invention, but it was often the wrong thing to do. On the other hand, I figured Jeeter deserved whatever he was going to get. His fate was out of my hands and was a consequence of his bad actions. He was a cold-blooded killer. Not much gray area there.

I could hear my phone playing some tune quietly. I walked back to my office. The closer I got, the louder it was, and I recognized the tune. "Welcome to the Jungle." I smiled. How I'd longed to hear Andy's ringtone in all the weeks he'd been in jail. I grabbed my phone and punched the "accept" button.

"Hi, favorite sister of mine," he said.

"Your *only* sister," I reminded him, as always. Another smile formed on my face.

"Yes, there's that. Say, the band's going to have a last-minute gig at Priscilla's tomorrow night. Want to come?"

"Of course. I've missed your music."

"Nothing like being locked up in a rat-infested, filthy jail with no water all day to give a poor boy guitar player inspiration for new songs."

"Andy. The lockup is not rat-infested or filthy. Boring certainly. And you didn't lack for food or water."

"Testing out my biographical details for when Lance and I become famous."

"I think you'll have to do better. The internet makes it hard to lie—"

"Actually, it makes it easier. But I take your point. I think I'll compose an honorary song in case Judge Cummings shows up for our concert. I issued her a special invitation. Thought we might do some jail songs a la Johnny Cash."

"Don't you think you're carrying this prison theme a bit too far? You never made it to prison."

"Well, okay. You'll come, right?"

"Of course, I will."

"You don't realize how much it means until you can't have it."

I was lost for words. "Andy. Cheer up. You're going to be fine. It was only a short part of your life."

"Just kidding, sis. See you there."

We both disconnected. I considered how beautiful it was to hear his voice on my phone again.

I tapped a few keys on my computer and pulled up the website, Crimes of the Century. There was nothing about Andy. They'd taken their poison to some other "true crime." Some poor woman whose sister had been kidnapped. I shook my head. Social media had some good qualities, but the bad qualities outweighed the good about seventy-thirty in my mind. People could be so cruel, especially when they didn't know the facts or found it easier to make them up.

I sat for a few minutes. Something had been bothering me—an idea I couldn't quite formulate in my head. It was connected to the saga of Quinn Parsons and the car accident. Every time I thought I knew what I'd been trying to think of, it eluded me. What was it? Well, it would come to me. I studied the whiteboards on the wall of my office and thought it was time to start planning our next national exhibit.

For a moment I stood there perplexed. What was that thought?

Chapter Thirty-Six

And the thought came—in a dream.

After talking to Andy yesterday, my mind mulled over the connection I couldn't remember while I was awake. Doesn't it always happen that way? When you sleep, your conscious mind disappears while your subconscious takes over, wrapping itself around the very thought you've been trying to remember.

After grabbing a bagel, cream cheese, and a cup of coffee, I pulled out my laptop and began my research. I remembered Victoria Kemp had told me the archives of the *Apple Grove Register* were online now. I began my hunt for the connection. Research always fascinated me, so I spent two hours examining all the information. I printed off several of the articles and called Tom. He was tied up this morning with a robbery but would get over to the art center. He thought he could meet me right after lunch. Perfect.

And after lunch it was when he came dragging in the door of our mother's art center, a sandwich in one hand, a bottle of water in the other. I ushered him back to my office, explaining I knew how Quinn Parsons' death was connected with the car accident that had killed our parents. I was sure.

"Here, I'll show you." For the next thirty minutes he was intrigued by the research I'd done. He made a phone call, and we left.

"It was when they arrested your brother that my conscience began haunting me."

Tom and I sat back, listening to his story in an interrogation room at the police department.

"We were no longer happy—my wife and I. Eventually, I figured out how to make Quinn Parsons pay. I didn't know he'd have a car full of people when he left the Eagle's Nest that night. I had studied him over several weeks at the bar, and I noticed he was usually there by himself. I took my time, thought it over, and knew it was the only way to get him back for the drugs he'd sold to my boy."

"I assume it didn't turn out the way you figured it would," said Tom.

"No. Not at all. I cut the brake lines on his Chevy Camaro while he was in the bar drinking. Since I didn't show my face that night, I assumed he was there alone as usual. But when I read in the newspaper the next day that not only did Parsons survive but other people died, I was sick. So sick. What had I done? I thought his car would go off the road, killing only him. It took weeks before I could even look at myself in the mirror. I was sick. Couldn't eat, couldn't sleep. But Parsons went to prison, so at least I felt he was paying a price for what he'd done."

"So were the rest of us, losing our parents," I reminded him.

"I know, I know," he said. "My conscience haunted me. They were good, kind, decent people. Your parents. How was I to know they'd be on the road that night, or Quinn Parsons' car would hit them? Or that his car would have other people in it? Andy was arrested for Quinn Parsons' murder, and I figured maybe he'd done it. But now I know I wasn't right about him either. Can't you see what a horrible bunch of errors this whole stupid situation was? I'm so sorry about your parents. So very, very, sorry."

Tom leaned over the table. "We're giving you an opportunity to do the right thing. Now that you've confessed to what you did, at least the story can be straightened out."

He dropped his head, looking down at his lap. Tom pushed a box of tissues across the table in front of him and he took a couple, wiping his eyes. "I couldn't live with myself. I confessed to my wife after seeing the play at the art center. At least that ghost had a chance to redeem himself. I'd done as terrible a crime as he had, but forgiveness isn't in my future. I'm ready to confess. God knows I've lost everything."

Tom stood and knocked on the door. Dominic Aubrey came in with a set of handcuffs. As he put them on the man, Tom said, "Martin Stewart, I'm arresting you for the murders of Howard Madison, Adele Madison, Branson Green, and the attempted murder of Quinn Parsons. You have the right to remain silent..."

Tom finished reading him his rights, and Martin was led away, his head down, a broken man.

I wondered what would happen to him. Blinking my eyes in confusion, I couldn't find it in me to hate him the way I'd hated Quinn when I thought he'd killed my parents. I couldn't imagine losing a son to suicide. That didn't make it right—what he did—but it made it more understandable. Mom and Dad were collateral damage. Wrong place. Wrong time. I thought about Daniel's belief that his sins caused the tragedies of his life. The minister's words about our personal tragedies. Sometimes, I thought, terrible things happen for no reason. They just do. I hated the idea, but there it was.

"Your research was right, Jill."

"Something kept nagging at me. It wasn't Jeeter who cut the brake lines, since he needed his drug sellers. It wasn't Quinn Parsons, since he wouldn't cut the brake lines on his own car. I remembered the day I went to the Stewart farm to take a check for him to sign. He was working on a tractor in the barn, and he told me he could fix anything. You and I both figured someone cut the brake lines over the front tires. But what was the connection between the car accident and Quinn Parsons' murder?

"When I began researching Matthew Stewart's death, I found he'd died from an overdose of cocaine. It was ruled a suicide. He'd left a note. Who sold cocaine at the high school? Quinn Parsons. At least that was what the rumor was. Who was blackmailing Jeeter Crockett? It looked like it was Quinn Parsons. So, Jeeter got the blow, and Parsons sold it to Matthew Stewart."

"Why would Matthew Stewart, who had so much talent, kill himself?"

"I don't know the answer to that, but it does strike me he was an only child, and he wanted his father's love and encouragement. Matthew was an amazing artist, but Martin Stewart didn't see much use in his talent. While Stewart eventually told me he'd come around, he said 'it was too little, too late.' He said that to me when he was talking about his son. I imagine he carried a truckload of guilt about how he'd treated his son's talent. Suicide is such a terrible thing, for the doer and the survivors. But I think the survivors suffer the most of all. It's amazing how guilt and regret can eat away at you."

Tom nodded. "I understand that too well." He took a deep breath. "Jill, you did it again."

"Just luck. If I hadn't had the connection with Martin Stewart because of the memorial for his son at the art center, I wouldn't have known anything about this. He's been so good at giving us money for our kids' programs, but I always sensed there was an intensity, an anger hiding under his surface. Now we know. Matthew Stewart's death was the lynchpin."

"Sure was."

We sat in silence for a few moments, each of us thinking our own thoughts.

Chapter Thirty-Seven

Word had gotten around town that Andy and Lance's band was playing at Priscilla's, so by the time Sam and I walked in the door the place was jumping. A group of thirtysomethings in the corner was doing shots and shouting every time. I knew several of them from my class in high school.

Wiley was presiding over a packed bar. When he saw me come in, he waved.

"Hey, Mr.-Handsome-Husband-of-Angie, how ya doing?" I asked from behind the bodies lined up and down the bar.

"In no pain whatsoever. Angie's in the back room. Be out shortly." He waved toward the stage. "Their band brings people in by the dozens. Would you look over there?" He pointed to a table on the far side of the stage. "That's Judge Cummings and her husband. So far, she hasn't scared off any ne'er-do-wells who probably ended up in her courtroom at some point."

"That's good. Andy promised her some Johnny Cash prison music. Maybe a little 'Folsom Prison Blues.'"

Wiley laughed. "Yeah. He did a complete set of Cash music. I saw the good judge out on the dance floor with Irvin, her husband. They can cut a rug. Pretty darn good dancers."

"Now that makes me laugh," Sam said. "I can't imagine this is quite their crowd. She's a good sport, or maybe she feels sorry for what happened to Andy. We're headed over to Tom and Mary's table. See you later."

"Take these with you," he said, handing each of us a bottle of our favorite beer.

We wandered across the dance floor, avoiding collisions, and waved at Andy and Lance. I hope they had a sober way to get home. I did not want to visit my brother in jail again—either jail. Ever.

"Hi, Mary, Tom," I called out as I neared table. Tom had a bottle of Blue Moon Belgian White and Mary, the designated driver, was drinking a cola. Tom stood up, shook Sam's hand, and grabbed my hand while Mary smiled and gestured to the seats beside her. "How's the band doing?"

"Andy hasn't missed a step, despite all those weeks in the jail. They even dedicated a rendition of 'Jailhouse Rock' to the judge," Mary said. "Andy gives a pretty fair impression of Elvis' voice. It was hilarious, and everyone hollered and clapped. Especially Judge Cummings."

"Oh, man," said Sam. "Wish we hadn't missed that."

Tom smiled, leaning toward me. "It's all getting cleaned up. Jeeter's in jail without bail, Paul Darnell couldn't get bond either, and their trials will be scheduled by the middle of the year. Andy may have to testify to what he saw at Darnell's cottage at the lake, but otherwise, he's free and clear."

I looked at them, all seated around the table. "Who would have thought there were so many loose ends to our parents' accident? You weren't on the case seven years ago, Tom. That's why everything turned into such a mucked-up mess. And all that time, drug sales were going on here in Apple Grove, and I knew nothing about it. Many times, I talked with Martin Stewart, but I had no idea his sadness wasn't only from his son's death."

Tom took another swallow of his beer. "The drug task force came really close to breaking that case back in the past decade, but since Jeeter was involved, he always knew their moves ahead of time. We suspected Quinn Parsons and Finn O'Brien for the sellers but could never connect them to a supplier. Now we know why."

"Lance tells me they're planning a huge celebration at the store, kind of like a second grand reopening. It's a good start to put this all away," Sam said.

I stared at my beer, my eyes passing randomly over the name and distributor. I was happy Andy was free, but somehow the end of my conversations with Daniel Lowry in my art center made me sad.

Mary put her hand over mine on the table. "What's got you down, kid?"

I pursed my lips. "Oh, nothing. Sam and I have had a hard few weeks between Andy's incarceration, Jeeter, all the work on the art center radio play, all his hours at the hospital, and the realization that the man who killed our parents was funding our children's classes at the art center. It's been a little too much."

"Tomorrow's another day," Mary said. "We're always given a new start when the sun comes up, and you have paintings from the judge's collection to send out. Think about all the people whose happiness begins with seeing those paintings. Tom says you have a new exhibit to begin planning. Artists will send you artwork from all over the country, right here to our tiny downstate town of Apple Grove. Now that's miraculous. And," she paused, "you have a guy in your life who loves you." She looked at Sam. "I hear your hours are going to be better. Fantastic. Things are looking up for the Madison family. You have your whole lives ahead of you."

"So true." I smiled, telling myself to end this pity party. Leave it to Mary to give me so much optimism. No wonder Tom was able to stay grounded.

The music had stopped and I glanced over at the band. Andy was stepping up to the microphone. "Thanks so much, folks, for coming in to see us after a long, dry spell. As you may know, I was unavoidably detained." Everyone laughed. Andy turned around toward Lance, who nodded, smiled, and gave him a thumbs-up. Then, he turned back to us and said, "And now we'd like to play a song for my sister, Jill"—he pointed at me—"who always has my back...and my love." Everyone hooted and hollered at that one. I lifted my beer bottle toward him.

Sam laughed. "Look out. With Andy you never know what's coming next."

After a moment, the band began playing one of my favorites: "In My Daughter's Eyes" by Martina McBride, only he'd changed "daughter" to "sister." I listened to the lyrics before, but tears streamed down my face as he moved into the second stanza. What a putz I was when it came to nostalgia. I thought about all the work we'd done to prove his innocence. Mom and Dad would have been proud. Coming back home was one of the best decisions I'd ever made. And bonus—I met Sam. The song finished, and I smiled and waved at my second-older brother, who usually made me laugh. Well, these were tears of joy.

When the song was over, Angie showed up and motioned for me to follow her. I looked at Sam, and he motioned, "Sure." She had two beers in her hands, so I followed. We walked past the bar and out the front door to the parking lot. It was an unusually mild night as we sat on a bench in front of the bar.

"What's with the tears, you sentimental slob?" she asked.

I laughed. "I'm okay. It just got to me for a few minutes."

"Geesh, ever since I've known you, you've been a sentimental fool. But I guess I can understand. It's been a tough month or two." She lifted her beer to mine, and said, "To perfect friends, the kind you spend your life with."

"To best friends forever," I said, lifting my bottle and taking a long slug of beer.

"You said you had some news about Sam, but I haven't had time to catch up with you since the night Jeeter was marched off to jail, thank goodness for the law."

I told her about Sam's new contract and how excited we'd both be that he wouldn't be virtually living at the hospital anymore.

"So, you're happy, right?"

"Oh, absolutely. My guess is this is going to become a permanent relationship. Six months and counting."

"Perfect. Sam is wonderful. I know your parents would have approved, and Tom, Andy, and Lance think he's great."

"And now we'll get to know each other because he won't be married to his job."

"So, why do I detect a bit of sorrow in your expression? You can't hide from me, my best friend."

I thought about that for a moment. "Well, living in a small town is great and brings me closer to my family, but it doesn't quite have the same excitement as the city."

Angie lifted my chin, looking right into my eyes. "Don't con me, Jill. I can see the excitement wasn't about Chicago. It was having a handsome, debonair ghost in your art center. All to yourself. No one else knew. After seeing him myself, I'd have to agree—handsome. You practically told me his life story in that tone of voice you reserve for inspiring."

I sighed. "Well, yes, there is that. But when he helped me evade Jeeter's evil plan, he touched my arm, and that's when I backed away. Unlike Sam's, his touch was icy cold."

"I see. Makes sense. Best friends are supposed to help straighten out and untangle these difficult problems. So, follow my analysis. Sam: handsome. Daniel: handsome. Sam: solid, dependable. Daniel: swashbuckling, treasure finder, soldier, murderer, businessman. Sam: loves you. Daniel: a passing fling. Sam: unmarried and ready. Daniel: married and now with his wife. But the bottom line is Sam: alive. Daniel: dead. Come on, kid, you need to leave this behind. Think of it as a dream that happened, and now it's over."

"Yes. I know you're right. It was simply so much fun."

"If you have to, create a painting of him and hang it in the art center since it was his building. Sorting things out. This is what best friends are for. But, despite all this—my helpfulness in times of trial—you must promise me one thing."

I stared at her puzzled. "What?"

"You will never, ever make me wear a pink fluffy, ruffled, netted matron of honor dress for your wedding. That choice was so my younger years."

Yes, I thought, exactly the sacrifice I'd made for my friend as her maid of honor. "You got it," I said. "Thank goodness we're more grown up."

"Ah, no. Here's to never growing up!"

And with that we clinked our beers together and chugged them to the bottom.

Acknowledgements

When I first envisioned the Art Center Mysteries, I drew an arc around three subjects: family, second chances, and forgiveness. I imagined Jill Madison going through all three of these moments in her life, events often connected by her past and the loss of her parents. To create this world, I enlisted the help of many people. I'd like to thank those who helped me with this third installment in the mysteries surrounding a small town, an art center, and its young director.

First, Kristyne Gilbert, Executive Director of the Buchanan Center for the Arts in our small town of Monmouth, Illinois. I pulled her into giving me lots of free advice about the art world, and she pulled me into being on her Board of Directors. I've learned so much from Kristyne about oil painting, watercolors, provenance, art fraud, exhibits, installing artwork, and the day-in and day-out running of an art center. Oh, and her numerous whiteboards. I still haven't figured out when she sleeps. Thank you, Kristyne.

Two people helped me make sure I had all the details as accurate as they could be. Judge Andrew Doyle of the Ninth Circuit of Illinois gave me information about the court scene in the book and the way the law would handle the indictment of Andy Madison. (I pride myself in placing former students in roles that will help me with my books. Just kidding.) Thank you, Andy Doyle. Jacob Morrison, owner of Morrison Mechanics, was helpful with information about the trauma cars experience in certain kinds of accidents. Thank you so much, Jacob.

The actual production of *Death in a Ghostly Hue* involved several people to whom I owe a great deal of thanks. My agent, Dawn Dowdle of the Blue Ridge Literary Agency, passed away during the writing of this book. I will forever be grateful to her for the work she did for me and will miss her at the other end of my phone calls. She is remembered fondly by her many authors who were also her friends. I am also thankful for Shawn Reilly Simmons, my editor at Level Best Books. She not only designed my covers and dealt with my errors, but she also answered my sometimes-stupid questions with grace and mercy. My freelance editor, Lourde Venard, of Comma Sense Editing, has edited every book I've written over twelve years, and I'm proud to call her my friend.

I am so grateful for three people who began as friends and turned into beta readers. Beta readers are "first readers" who give an author their reactions to the unpublished manuscript. In my case, three of my friends have been beta readers throughout my mysteries. I am fortunate because they are each good at catching both developmental problems and line-editing errors. Because it's important to me to put out a quality product, I am thankful for this posse of experts who make that possible: Jan DeYoung, Hallie Lemon, and Eileen Owens.

Finally, thank you to my readers, many of whom have read my books for a decade now. Some live in our small town where I am reminded every day of their kindness, encouraging words, and support. Others contact me out there in the internet universe, and I am grateful.

About the Author

Susan Van Kirk is the Past President of the Guppy Chapter of Sisters in Crime and a writer of cozy mysteries. She lives at the center of the universe—the Midwest—and writes during the ridiculously cold and icy winters. Why leave the house and break something? Van Kirk taught forty-four years in high school and college and raised three children. She has eleven grandchildren who look up the hardest words they can find and dare her to use them in her books. She's a member of Sisters in Crime and Mystery Writers of America.

SOCIAL MEDIA HANDLES:
  FB: http://www.facebook.com/SusanVanKirkAuthor/
  Pinterest: http://www.pinteret.com/sivankirk/_saved/
  Goodreads: https://www.goodreads.com/author/show/586.Susan_Van kirk
  Instagram: https://www.instagram.com/susanivankirk/
  Threads: @sivankirk@threads.net

AUTHOR WEBSITE:
  https://susanvankirk.com

Also by Susan Van Kirk

The Education of a Teacher (Including Dirty Books and Pointed Looks)

Three May Keep a Secre

The Locket: From the Casebook of TJ Sweeney

Marry in Haste

Death Takes No Bribes

The Witch's Child

A Death at Tippitt Pond

Death in a Pale Hue

Death in a Bygone Hue